An Impostor in Eden

An Impostor in Eden

and Other Stories

Irving Werner

with illustrations by Stuart Yeager

Writer's Showcase presented by *Writer's Digest*
San Jose New York Lincoln Shanghai

An Impostor in Eden
and Other Stories

Published by Writer's Showcase presented by *Writer's Digest*
an imprint of iUniverse.com, Inc.

For information address:
iUniverse.com, Inc.
620 North 48th Street
Suite 201
Lincoln, NE 68504-3467
www.iuniverse.com

ISBN: 0-595-09656-5

Printed in the United States of America

Sarah and Abraham Werner

Contents

Acknowledgements

For their invaluable encouragement

Marvin Kaye

Ralph Pessah

My son Jon

An Impostor in Eden

At noon on the Friday before Christmas our supervisor, Ethel Mulvey, led the entire office down the hall to the administrative suite. A long table covered with red paper and bookended by poinsettias held sandwiches, a wheel of brie, crackers, a punch bowl, and candy canes. Mistletoe descended through festoons of red and green ribbons. The company's bosses, men with thin hair and the hard, lined faces of sea captains, stood apart, chatting with their invited ladies. The ladies, several notably younger than their escorts, wore ornate dresses cut low enough to display jewels almost to the nipple line. The bigwigs smiled frugally; their calculating eyes flicked to decorated bosoms.

Russ Maguire plucked at my shirt sleeve. "What do you want?" I said, unable to tear my eyes from those jewels.

"Follow me," he said, "and I'll show you something."

"Show me what?"

"Fuck is this, Twenty Questions?"

He was older, past twenty, handsome and natty, but jockey small, and I'd seen his overtures scoffed at by all the pretty girls. Halfway down the hall his walk turned so unsteady that he bounced against the walls. His high tenor broke into a garbled 'Melancholy Baby.' I asked if anything was wrong.

"I'm dru-u-unk," he sang. "Can't you see I'm dru-u-unk?"

We came to a door marked 'ladies.' He raised the pitch of his voice. He shoved open the door. "Wait," I said, "this ain't ours."

"What're you, an idiot?" he sneered, and stormed inside. By the time I realized I was an idiot he'd already flung open all the cubicle doors and found the place deserted.

The other ladies room on that floor was also unoccupied. We went back to the party and circulated.

Georgie Haft was so recently out of the service that he still wore his whites to the office, a seaman's cap jaunty in his tightly curled hair. I admired his easygoing poise with the girls. He threw an arm around my shoulder, smelling like he'd bathed in after-shave lotion, and steered me to a corner. He brought his face close to mine. "See Estelle over there?" He pointed his chin at the heavily lipsticked, thick-ankled blonde down the room. "I just had her on the back stairs." (But then, he was not an officer.) Estelle glanced over and caught us looking. She blushed, spun on her heels, and ducked into the crowd.

It was a time of sartorial seriousness and the dying breath of chivalry. In film noir, Mitchum and Bogart, private eyes and perps alike, wore suits and ties and doffed their hats in elevators. Men dressed spiffily even to ball games. In the subway they offered their seats to women and the elderly. Young ladies hurrying down Fifth or Madison on the way to clerk or secretary were finely turned out on their sixty a week, down to the little white gloves they'd also wear on Saturday night dates.

Mornings, those dainty secretaries and receptionists, and even mink-wrapped matrons, clogged the subway aisles, straphanging on the pitching, rolling ride to Manhattan. I'd straddle the few square inches I managed to stake out, inhaling the warring scents of Wrigley's Spearmint gum and Chanel cologne, bounced between spongy bosoms and backsides as the train lurched screeching around curving rails.

At seventeen I'd been about to enter the city college when my old man, taciturn but hard working and quietly conscientious, went out for a pack of Camels. It was several hours before my mother remembered he didn't smoke; several days before we found out he'd been lured from us by the siren song of a bosomy, peroxided opposite of his wife. My mother melted down to a sniffling, red-nosed blob. She was anyway a professional housewife, incapable of earning a living, so I switched to night school in order to get a full-time job. But how to be hired when they wanted you to be at least eighteen? Chasing down the Times 'help wanted' ads kept me crashing against the stone wall of my chronology. Until one desperate day. The Amalgamated News Company needed someone to calculate the credits for returned magazines. I lied.

The Amalgamated office was a garden ablaze with young ladies like fragrant flowers, each bloom designed by a playful Creator to tweak a young man's heart with love, longing, and lust. I was an impostor in Eden.

Every morning I'd battle my way out of the subway car at Grand Central and lope to an underground rendezvous with the lovely Laurene Lutz. I remember her best—shapely and demure and enticingly scented—in patriotic colors: red hair, blue eyes, trim blue suit, white gloves, little white bag. At the Lexington Avenue exit, face lighting when she spotted me, Laurene would hold out a white-gloved hand. Hands clasped, we'd scoot out to the street and up the three blocks while autos honked, bodies milled, newsies yelled, coffee aromas fought gasoline fumes, and Laurene's hand burned in mine.

I was intoxicated with Laurene—as with all the other girls—but it wasn't love that connected us, it was fear.

Of all the employees of Amalgamated, Laurene and I were the least successful in getting to the office before nine. For me, something always intervened: an article of my clothing that couldn't be located; a subway platform so mobbed I'd be unable to fight my way onto the train; or, once on, my train might be held back by a red light in the tunnel under the East River.

The dreaded penalty for lateness wasn't so much the docked pay— paper-thin slices off miniscule wages—but the indignation of a supervisor pelting us with threats of discharge. I was confident they wouldn't fire me, because with a knack for arithmetic and memory for names I could handle twice as much as my co-worker Murray. But Laurene, already in her twenties, was engaged to be married and needed the job to pay for her trousseau. Laurene believed that I was her shield, that facing the music together deflected the clamor of the drums and brasses my way, and left for her only the soft lament of the violins. That, only that, was my connection to the delicious girl who waited for me and grasped my hand and needed me.

After the confrontation with Ethel Mulvey, not at all an ogre but a middle-aged lady in terror of losing her own job, Laurene would toss me a little parting wave, and we'd each head for our own section.

The sections accommodated altogether maybe twenty girls, plus Russ, Georgie, two pre-meds like oak trees to handle the man-high burlap bags of discarded paper, my co-worker Murray, and Roy, a yellow-haired, clean-cut college man who sat among the girls and shared their clerical functions.

"Think you could spare a coupla minutes?" Murray might ask. "I need you to go over my test with me."

In night school Murray was studying motion picture projection. At every opportunity he would stare apprehensively into a notebook dense enough with scrawled equations to discourage a Newton or Einstein. Only a couple of years older, Murray already carried failure like a pennant, drooping beneath a soiled and misshapen felt hat and a tented coat that overmatched his thin, stooped frame. He was unable to memorize the names of our chain store customers, so that instead of combining returns, which greatly speeded up the work, he made each envelope a separate project.

"Sure, Murray. Get you later. Listen, kid, which bag're we working on?"

Murray would point to one of the sacks hanging from a rack of mail bags filled with returns. "Okay," I'd tell him, "let's get started," and grab an armful of envelopes and drop them at my feet. I'd pick one up, slice it open, and spread its contents out on my desk. All set now, ready to start, I would instead toss down my pencil. And then, then, with a little flutter in the gut, I'd raise my eyes to Irene Palamas.

Now listen. If the ancient Greeks had never laid the foundations for Western civilization…. If Plato and Aristotle and Euclid and such had produced nothing at all, had in fact never existed…. If those Greeks had accomplished nothing whatever, nothing except only to propagate the line of descent producing Irene Palamas…. That would have been enough, that alone would have eternally marked them with genius. O, silken olive skin. O, rounded arms. O, shapely legs that promised heaven. O, heart-shaped face, soft brown eyes, perfect teeth, wavy walnut hair. O, lily wrist, gilded with a dainty thin-banded watch. And O, that sweet winsome smile that made you want to beg for the privilege of killing or being killed for her. But all that's only catalogue; how can it convey the grace, fineness, femininity that made you vow to forswear all others, stay celibate forever, if you couldn't have Irene Palamas? The Platonic ideal of Woman engraved on the heavens, of which all the others, now and forever, are only inept copies?

Irene Palamas was forbidden fruit. For one thing, the half decade age differential. But that was easy, time would narrow the gap percentagewise. For another, she was already married. Nevertheless, it was rumored the union was rocky.

Feeling my gaze from across the room she'd raise her eyes to mine and I'd quickly look away, but not quickly enough, purposely not quickly enough, and sneaking a glance would find with a tingle that her eyes were still on me, and she'd give me this little smile that was like the sun rising, flirting with me, knowing I was smitten and maybe feeling sorry for my futility, and maybe, too, enjoying the adoration. And then presently I'd lower my eyes and set to work, her image burnt onto the papers before me, but at some point in the course of the day we'd find ourselves momentarily next to one another, and she'd murmur something I was too stirred up to comprehend, and put out a healing hand to touch my arm, and that was enough, that was enough. Tomorrow is another day.

I was not alone in lust and adoration. Lunch time I'd sometimes sit off in a corner with Russ, Georgie, and the burly paper handlers, and listen to them rate the girls like Derby handicappers. Between bites of brown-bagged sandwiches, the discussion would inevitably turn to Irene Palamas, and each would offer up a lovingly detailed itemization of his ambitions towards her. With shining eyes and drooling lips they'd outdo each other in describing the sacrifices they'd be willing to endure, just for the chance to do those things to her.

It pained me to sit there and listen to those louts defile her image. It was acquiescing to sacrilege. And yet I couldn't tear myself away, because their word pictures fed into my dreams, expanding the range of possibilities for how it might be when Irene and I were finally together. But most of all I stayed on to listen because their talk ignited a secret glow, knowing that their obscene dreams were futile, while we, the beautiful Irene and I, we had an understanding. Sure, she was an older woman and already married, we rarely spoke, nothing was in writing, and yet the knowing way she smiled at me, and flirted, and lightly but with sympathy and understanding touched my arm, left no room for doubt.

Sometimes the handicappers, inflamed by their fantasies about Irene Palamas, and taunted by the close presence of so much nubility, would like dieters in a candy shop give in to temptation, and then outraged yelps from tweaked and patted young ladies would splinter the air. It was astonishing, the wildly imaginative invective that spewed from such pretty little mouths.

The center of the office was commanded by a couple of massive data processing machines operated by Mr. Fitzpatrick and his assistant Greg. Mr. Fitz, white hair and impressive stomach, triangular brows above glasses like mirrors, was a coldly genial man. When late afternoon shadowed the office, the rumpled planes of his face would refract the menace of a Maltese Falcon character. With a wife and kid to support, Greg was anxious to get ahead in this promising new field. Fitz and Greg were forever shuffling and reshuffling IBM punch cards, banging stacks against the charcoal metal of the machines to even them up, feeding them to the whirring wheels which then spit them into slots, then pulling out the cards and stacking them in shallow boxes. With regularity a treacherous finger, the snag of a passing blouse, an ungainly body shift would send a box soaring. Mr. Fitz, hands on wide hips, would watch Greg skating around on his knees recovering the cards, then scratching his head trying to figure out their correct order. Outside of those two, none of us could even guess what the sophisticated machines, resembling pregnant refectory tables, accomplished.

Muriel Gurkowski was for me a study in female architecture and the anatomy of desire. A sturdy brunette with a pleasant face and manly stride, she restrained her zaftig torso with a network of bra straps, forcing the free flesh into swellings that made lumps in her tight blouses. But she always smelled sweet, and there was a freshness about her, a jauntiness and optimism, that made her stride seem like the coltish movements of a tomboy blossoming into femininity. It pleased my tired eyes to watch her cross the office.

Despite all of the commotion with the punch cards, it seemed to me that every time I glanced up from the dancing numbers to rest my eyes on Muriel Gurkowski or any of the other girls, I found myself the object of Mr. Fitz's scrutiny. From where I sat it was impossible to see his eyes past the glasses, but the faint distention of his mouth unnerved me. I was sure it was a smirk of derision, that he'd found me out. That he knew I'd have gladly worked there gratis. Knew that every one of those little beauties owned a piece of my heart. Knew that I'd broken a Commandment: coveted Irene Palamas, another man's wife.

One morning I forgot to keep an eye out for Louise, an energetic little blonde with a quick, sharp tongue that unnerved me. She wore slippers in the office, and sneaking up on shapely legs would pinch my butt and archly hiss an invitation to foreplay. Now, ambushing me once again, she ripped a piece out of my hide. My yelp of pain rang through the office. Mr. Fitz's index finger beckoned. I shuffled over, a condemned man to the gallows.

"They tell me you're a sharp young fella. How'd you like to get into data processing?" He was confident, already nailing down a sale.

In my relief images flashed across my mind. Standing in the middle of the office punching holes in cards; banging them against the machine to even them up; wiping the floor with my knees. "Could I think it over?" I said.

I would go out to the mens room as often as I could without appearing to be neglecting my work or suffering from a weak bladder. Inside, the white-tiled corridor, running past enough urinals to service a platoon of beer drinkers, ended in a ten foot window. I loved to stand at that window, one foot raised to its casement. The cigarette smoke choking the air made me feel grown up, belonging to that sophisticated world where men competed, and made careers, and complained about mill rates in Rye and Mamaroneck. And before me, the city. I would think about all the lives that had gone into its making, the guts and determination and heartbreak. I wondered how you graduated from the ranks of the city's faceless. Sometimes I would unfocus my eyes, deliberately blurring the vision, and then imagine the panorama as entrails spread out on a table, awaiting a gypsy's reading.

Like the first Adam, I was experiencing a spanking new world filled with wonders. Me, I was riding the subway with all those purposeful New Yorkers, headed for work that came easy and for which I was actually paid; surrounded by young ladies who held my hand or pinched me, and whose splendor so engorged my heart that I sometimes had to close my eyes to breathe; prized by data processing supervisors; and all while suffused with love for Irene Palamas, who flirted with me and with whom I had an understanding.

Only, unlike Adam, I was burdened with a racial memory. I already knew that joy races you, and that most of the time you can't catch it. Even in my wonder and bliss, I was oppressed by the suspicion that no matter where my life went, it would never again be as good.

Ethel Mulvey motioned me over to a far corner. "We're way too slow with the credits. The customers are complaining." There was no anger in her voice, just concern, a bit of fear, and even some pity. "Do I have to let Murray go, or is there something you can do to help him?"

I saw Murray slogging dejectedly through the streets, notebook under arm. Rain drops slid down his hat, hung from the tip of his nose, dripped onto his shapeless overcoat. "No," I said, "leave it to me. Murray and me, we'll handle it."

I showed Murray short cuts and memory tricks, but his mind was in movie projection. In the end, I worked harder myself to take up the slack.

Shyly courteous, Roy, the college man with a blond cowlick, kept to himself, and I imagined him as working there only to accumulate a stake for his medical or legal practice. His desk was two away from Irene's. I kept watch, and saw that their contacts were always brief and businesslike. Until one day their heads came close together over a sheet of paper in Roy's hand. When they looked up their glances caught and a quick smile sparked between them. Irene reached out to lightly touch Roy's arm. They separated back to their desks, unaware that they'd just punted my heart. Dented and bleeding, it writhed with jealousy. Was that touch of the arm a sign of affection, or just a benign reassurance? A come-on, or just her gentle soul's healing contact? I shuffled out to the mens room, but this time it was only to throw up.

My schoolwork began a downhill slide and our customers' returns to pile up. What rescued me was the shock of disgraceful mid-term grades, and a repeat of Ethel Mulvey's warning about replacing Murray. And my mute conversation each morning with Irene Palamas: the flirting game, the unintelligible murmur, the gentle touch.

"Like to know how these processors work?" Mr. Fitz's eyes gleamed with the magnanimity of a magician disclosing the trick of the rabbit in the hat. He took my uncaring shrug as the mute assent of the overwhelmed.

He showed me how the whirring wheels shot out little metal brushes to detect the holes in the punch cards.

He showed me how the cards were then distributed into slots according to the holes.

He showed me how the other machine then read the holes and printed out reports.

He showed me a printout listing the titles and quantities of the magazines shipped to each customer two months before, and who had returned how many of which for credit.

I said, "I still need a little more time."

Maureen had red hair, a swan-like neck left naked by an upswept hairdo, sloe eyes, and a pointed chin, so that she resembled, had I then known about such things, a Modigliani portrait. Seated at her billing machine, the Modigliani girl was in serious talk with a bow-tied young stationery salesman. Suddenly her pencil slipped out of her fingers. When she bent to retrieve it, the salesman quickly stooped to kiss the back of her naked neck. She sat up blushing, then lifted a hand to her nape. They resumed the conversation. Her sloe eyes shone.

Irene Palamas failed to return from lunch. Hearing no fuss and bother, I assumed it had been arranged beforehand. Next morning, after parting from Laurene, I hurried to my desk, rolled up my sleeves, set out some mail, threw down my pencil, and sent a glance across the room to Irene Palamas. Anticipating the lovely shock of flirtation, I instead encountered nothingness: her soft brown eyes were hidden by dark glasses.

Throughout the morning whispers grazed my ears. Assembled, they told a tale of marital dispute and abuse.

I'd once encountered the husband; he'd come to take Irene to lunch. Soft-spoken, a choir boy sort, he was fair as opposed to her olive, and they complemented each other in this way, but also in being beautiful people, and in sharing a wholesomeness and fineness and gentleness. It had given me some black days, thinking about how obviously they belonged together.

This time he'd again come to meet her, only it wasn't for lunch. At the elevator bank out in the hall, they'd carried over an argument from the previous day, as acrimonious as it can only get between two people who love each other. He accused her, the girls whispered, of infidelity. When she protested he'd hit her and marked her up.

Seeing her like this, having to hide behind dark glasses, I would gladly have killed him. And yet I felt sorry for him too, because I was sure I understood him. I guessed that he'd had the need to manufacture a dissatisfaction, like the mother who loudly insists that her beautiful baby is ugly in order to fool the jealous gods. And he'd gotten angry because he found it impossible to encompass it all, to believe his good luck. Struck out at her because he despaired of being worthy.

Which is how I would have felt.

Friday afternoons Mr. Applebaum, the comptroller, would come around holding a tray of pay envelopes chest-high, like a night club cigarette girl toting packs of Lucky Strikes. The round little man, an oversized pipe clenched in his jaws, would go from desk to desk handing out the envelopes with an indulgent smile, as if dispensing his personal wealth to needy cases.

One Friday he broke his rule of silence. "Congratulations, young fellow." His mouth sucked on the pipe but his eyes narrowed in what might have been a smile. "There's a raise in here for you."

I split the extra three dollars, one for me, two more for mom.

Once more the serpent's song. "Made up your mind yet?"

This time I was ready for him. I put on a face of immense regret. "Data processing sounds great. But I'll be matriculating soon and have to switch to day school. Full time. So it don't make sense to start on something new."

Mr. Fitz's narrow shoulders sagged. "It's the future," he pleaded, incredulous in falsetto. He held out open hands as if to display the future there. But all I could see was open hands.

After some days Irene discarded the dark glasses. In our morning flirtation her face would light up in a smile as always, quickly fade away, and then, as if reminded of her obligation to me, re-light, but only with the low wattage that was all she could muster.

At the Christmas party she hung back. I stationed myself down the room to watch. She was off in a corner, wearing a plain brown dress, as if wanting to meld with the woodwork. Fat chance. Even subdued that way, there was a radiance about her, a surrounding nimbus. I realized now that it was this, this light, and not just the beauty, that drew all that love to her. Like visiting a convalescent celebrity, the girls took turns stopping by for a chat. They'd bring offerings of crackers and cheese or half a sandwich with a glass of something. She just nibbled at the food, but drank thirstily.

The bosses and their ladies departed. The party grew more animated. Carelessly flung voices obliterated the carols rising from a phonograph attended by Greg. As if the noise was screening Irene from my sight, I advanced a bit closer. She caught the movement. She winked at me hard. Her smile was even sweeter and longer than usual, almost a grimace. Her blood, risen nearer to the surface, tinted her olive skin with rose.

I took several more steps, close enough to see that her forehead was moist, and that beads had formed on her upper lip. Some day, I thought, I will be the one to wipe that away, taste its salt on my tongue.

A sudden pain seared my hide. I swiveled around; Louise waltzed away on slippered feet.

A heavy arm landed on my shoulder. Old Spice almost cut off my breath. Georgie bellowed towards my ear, "See Maureen over there?"

"No," I yelled, and grabbed his white sleeve and flung his arm away. "No, I don't want to know."

By the time I turned back Irene was slumped in a chair. Her head spilled forward, disclosing its pale, vulnerable part. Two of the girls were fussing over her. Maureen came hurrying, me right behind. She knelt to blot her friend's brow with a lacey square. Someone said, "How do we get her home?" Heartbeats went by in silence. I could see that factors were being weighed: obligation to a friend as against quitting a party at its height. My mind indicted this betrayal; my suddenly racing blood sang with joy and daring. "I'll do it," I blurted, "I'll get her home," not bothering to think how I'd carry it off without a car, probably without enough for cab fare.

"Hey," somebody said, "that's an idea. What about Roy?"

Somebody else chimed in about what a great idea, and wouldn't Roy be glad to take her. As if I were invisible. To assert myself I demanded, "Why'd you force her to drink so much?"

"It's not like that," Madeleine said quietly.

"No?" I said. "How is it?"

Irene lifted her head. The lovely face was clammy and pale, the brown eyes not entirely focused." No, my li'l friend," she said with a wan smile, the words slurred, "not their fault."

One of the girls said, "I'll go find Roy." The other one echoed, "I'll go with you." Their backs showed relief at escaping.

"It would be no trouble at all," I told Madeleine.

"Here he comes," she said.

"Really," I pleaded, "it'd be no problem for me at all."

Irene shook her head. "Li'l friend, I wish it could be you, my li'l friend."

"Come," Roy said, concern lengthening his face. The blond cowlick lipped down to his forehead as he bent to help Irene out of the chair. On their unsteady way to the door, her arm rested on his shoulder, his arm encircled her waist. My mind embraced an image of him falling down an elevator shaft.

Behind me someone sneered something about old Roy going to have himself a helluva good time. The snickers amened.

"Why'd they have to feed her all that liquor?" I begged.

"Liquor?" the Modigliani girl glared at me. "It's not just the liquor." She shook her head impatiently. "Think you need to show a big tummy to have morning sickness?"

My eyes snagged on the image of her bending to retrieve a pencil while the salesman kissed her naked neck, and her sloe eyes shining.

"So you couldn't be the one to take her," she added.

Breath fluttering against my heart, I persisted, stammering, "But why not? I could've taken her anyway." Still caring, with whatever part of me hadn't already just died.

"No, kid. Irene wanted it should be the guy who nailed her."

I saw the room whole, frozen in timelessness.

Russ leaned across a poinsettia, his mouth flapping a hard sell at Muriel Gurkowski. Her strong teeth insolently halved a cracker; she gazed down at him with a smirk.

Soon after, my old man abandoned his chemical blonde. My mom took him back and made us whole again. He was still taciturn, but did sometimes gift us with a smile, as if thinking maybe this wasn't so bad after all. What I'd told Fitz about going to school full time came to pass. I departed the Amalgamated News Company, cast out into the wider world.

From time to time I find myself still anxious about my co-worker Murray. I hope he managed to run off a lifetime of movies before technology made him obsolete.

My thoughts return too to Mr. Fitz. Retired now, I can't help wondering if I'd have made a better career had I let him initiate me into data processing. Got in on the ground floor.

I think about Irene Palamas with a certain fondness, like cherishing the memory of a youthful injury long since overcome. The lovely Laurene Lutz again offers me her white-gloved hand. I remember with affection Muriel and Louise and the Modigliani girl, recall their glow and enchantment more distinctly than I do their fading images.

And I wonder which of the pretty mouths is already stopt with dust.

Cat in the Rain

An expensive foreign car drew in between Withers and the Cutlass. Windswept rain drops clung shivering to its sleek surface. A young lady popped out, stylish coat flapping open to a white sweater, red hair furiously framing her cheekbones. Disdaining the elements, she looked around with eyes narrowed, then gathered herself and went off fighting the wind. His gaze followed her to the promenade girdling the beach until she disappeared past the concession stands. "A rose of Sharon," he said to his windshield. "A lily of lousy weather."

The year before, when George Withers lost his Emily, he'd begun coming to this place by the sea much more frequently. It was just a small parking lot, a sheet of gravel glued like a postage stamp to the enormous envelope of a beach. Depending on the temperature and the mood of the wind, he would either sit in the aging Buick wagon reading Civil War history and peering at the blustering waves, or else get out for a walk down the beach.

The disappointment of childlessness had brought them closer, like patients sharing a hopeless diagnosis. Still, after his retirement there was the infrequent spat, due as much to sunspots or a full moon as to any real difference between them he could ever discover. But then even love, he would think, can have too much of togetherness; it can't be easy on her to have me underfoot all the time. So he would remove himself from the site of friction, driving the few miles from their cape at the edge of town to the beach.

Now he couldn't bear to hang around the empty house, the miasma of pain and sweat and drugs still oozing from its walls. In the beginning he'd open her closet and fondle the clothes he'd yet to give away. Once, he'd stepped inside and slid the door to. In the dark he held her garments to his cheek, inhaled her persisting scent. "I miss you," he whispered. And then, not knowing he would do this, he began to softly sing the lyrics of her favorite song, 'I miss your lips, the summer kisses, the sunburnt hands I used to know....' In his sightlessness he saw himself buried among her clothes; within her modest floral scent he inhaled a fetid mustiness, the odor of rotting flowers. He reached panicked for the door's edge. Days later, he became aware that he'd fallen into the habit of talking to himself. The fear of teetering at the edge of normalcy drove him from home.

His favorite time here was out-of-season, spring or fall, even early winter. In this emptiness he'd then feel kinship with all the lonely things, with gulls trailing their cries, trees lamed by the wind, the forever searching waves. Sometimes, gazing out at the sea, he'd imagine for just a beat that he was again waiting for one of their little spats to blow over before going home to Emily.

In this lot, comfortable for a dozen cars, there would then be only one or two others. The black Cutlass was inevitable. A rusting gouge in its rear fender, it would stand parallel to his Buick wagon a good part of the day. Inside, a man and woman would sit unmoving, staring out. With a pewter clump of longish wiry beard the man resembled a naif's vision of a scraggly God on the throne of heaven. Once, George saw him get out of the car and walk around to its trunk, a tall thin man, baggy trousers held up by broad red suspenders over a sweatshirt, stepping as if guided by a puppeteer's strings. On the good days, when George could climb out and start across the lot on his way to the beach, he would feel their eyes until he was out of sightline past the shuttered refreshment stands.

This morning he'd torn off the finished calendar page. The new one was headed up November, so the sudden radical change in climate was like the weather taking its cue from the calendar. Rain, accelerated out of the dismal sky by the wind, buckshotted the Buick's roof. Clouds like smoke scudded along, tossing leaves hissed, waves leapt skyward. George liked sitting within such rancor; it would be cozy inside the car, and all that roiling made him feel a spectator at an awesome event. As if all the civilizing conventions had been torn aside to disclose the real show, the raw, majestic terror of it all.

Only this time he'd not come to get away from home, nor for the elemental display, but to see if the cat might still be here.

The day before, fine for late October, he'd walked along the promenade all the way to the end of the beach, then crossed the sand to return by way of the shoreline. It was a painterly scene: the sun highlighting pastels of white sand, blue water, clean sky; colors so vivid they sang, and he imagined those tunes picked up by the breezes. He passed an assembly of gulls, motionless on matchstick legs, gazing raptly seaward as if listening to that same windsong. When he reached a clump of stalks rising bravely out of the dunes he almost kneeled to embrace them, dissuaded only by a sudden image of himself: a decaying artifact clutching an armful of grass. In sheepish mid-smile guilt clutched at his joy, shocking him into remembering Emily.

Eventually he'd come full circle back to the lot and the innocuous tableau that later came to haunt him. A man and woman were crossing the far corner leading out to the access road. The man marched

determinedly; the woman followed backpedaling, eyes on a cat that
inched along after them. George passed them by, dragging tired legs to
the Buick. From the pile of books on the passenger seat he drew out
one of the Catton volumes. Presently, mulling over what he'd just
read, he looked up. The cat was sauntering aimlessly. It crossed uncertainly to the line of stunted trees, then padded back to the trees at the
opposing boundary. Orange except for a white underside and face, it
carried its remarkably broad tail as proudly upright as a banner.

"Little cat," George said into the window, "who made you? Who
made you, little cat, and what have they done to you? Did they find you
here and quarrel about taking you home? Or did they bring you here for
dumping? And what the hell's the difference, since you lost either way,
little cat?"

Each time George looked up from his reading, the cat was sitting in
the center of the lot or else slowly circling it. Its broad tail was beginning to sag.

When after several chapters he once more raised his eyes, they were
stabbed by a shard of drooping sunlight angled off a burger sign. George
set the book down on the passenger seat, shifted his position from reading to driving, reached for the ignition key. And then couldn't turn it. The
cat's white heart-shaped face, with intelligently separated green eyes, was
as pretty as a girl's. Seated in gravel, it raised a paw and with eyes closed
slowly rubbed the side of its face, as if trying to wipe away cobwebs of
bewilderment. Or, George thought, mimicking the leisurely and private
act of a woman toweling off after her bath.

He imagined how it would be here after the sun fell: sharp-toothed
creatures stealthy through the dark, cries of savagery and death, dry-
mouthed scavenging for food and water. He looked around, searching
for a hint of the lot's hidden life, but could find only a squirrel cavorting
in a tree. It leapt branches, skittered down the trunk, then paused at a
wire wastebasket, puzzling out how to get at its goodies. George was not
persuaded by such innocence.

He reached for the door handle, but then spotted the Cutlass. A month before, he'd decided to short-cut his way to the beach by stepping over the low fence instead of going around. His foot caught in the railing, and he sprawled in the sand like an overturned turtle. He'd nonchalanted it getting up, but was sure the car people were splitting their sides laughing. So now he hesitated to perform under those godly eyes.

"Oh, c'mon, Georgie, get real. Geezers needn't give a damn anymore what others think. It's one of the benefits, like social security."

He pulled the door handle. When his feet touched the ground, the cat alertly raised her head and took a step back. Keeping the Buick between himself and the Cutlass, George sank onto his haunches. "C'mere, kitty," he coaxed. "C'mere kitty," hoping to get to scratch gently down her forehead, and from there figure out next steps. He tried varying the drip of honey into his voice, as well as the pace of his movements, finally even abandoning the Buick's cover to make a fool of himself in full view. But the cat maintained the dozen feet separating them as an inviolable barrier ; retreating an equal distance as he crept forward. Unfolding rusty joints he got back into the car, thinking how this resembled that scientific dilemma where the act of measuring destroys the thing to be measured. It struck him then that this particular dilemma might be solved with a bribe of cat food.

The drive to the grocery took him ten minutes. He grabbed a four pound bag off the shelf, but then had to wait on line behind a shopper struggling to get her plastic accepted by the gizmo. By the time he got back to the lot the cat was gone.

Through the windshield dusk veiled the sun and calmed the waves. A gull came sailing in. Its head gilded by the lowering sun, it landed in the center of the lot. George saw, or thought he saw, because his eyes were no longer entirely reliable, that part of a leg was missing. The gray bird stood upright, but sure enough, when it lowered the stump it rested at an angle. It opened its beak and its throat lengthened and swelled to accommodate the insistent caws choking their passageway. A gull soared in, hovered, circled overhead twice, cawed a message, then flew off. The crippled bird rested aslant, unmoving and silent. George was surprised that such sadness could pulse in his throat even after Emily. He tried to parse the feeling, decided that no personal tragedy, however monstrous, could numb you to the suffering of innocents. "Or maybe," he muttered, "faking sympathy for small creatures is an inexpensive way to feel sensitive and superior." By now the light was reduced to a reflection from over the horizon. George thought about tossing some cat food to the gull, wondered if that would be sensible, but then had no decision to make when the injured bird, awkwardly upright, lifted its wings, climbed the air, and glided seaward.

George got out of the car and tore the top off the bag. He circled the perimeter, sowing a trail of little mounds of food. Enlarging its opening, he set down the bag in the exact center of the lot.

His terrors that night were of crippled birds and pretty cats and Emily. Faces and bodies commingled in insane collages. Inhuman cries howled through dark forests. Claws ripped his face and gouged out his eyes. He moaned himself awake.

He dressed before dawn. The fresh calendar page told him it was November; the radio told him it was pouring and would rain on and off all day. He made instant coffee, a fried egg, burnt toast. When he finished eating he added the dishes to the pile already in the sink. He wondered fleetingly what he'd throw together for his next meal, then let the thought lie when he realized that daylight had already snuck in. He threw on a heavy jacket, drew up its hood, and hustled through the rain to the car.

On the way to the beach he stopped off at the grocery for another bag of cat food. Just in case.

He inched the Buick through the lot, but could find no trace of the food he'd salted around its perimeter. The bag, removed from where he'd placed it, lay melting in a corner, flat enough to be empty. He parked in his usual spot. When he looked out and failed to detect life, the pit of his stomach dissolved. He considered such a curious reaction to the absence of a strange cat, then saw that it wasn't the cat, it was hope once again diminished into loss. Like waiting for the doctors' decision, life or death for Emily. Another coin landing wrong side up.

"Listen, Old Pimple Brain, she might just be sheltering under a tree. Give her credit for the sense to stay out of the rain." Searching through the murk past the windshield was like peering into a dimly lighted fish tank. His eyes glazed over. Intermittently he nodded off, shook himself awake. Presently he opened his eyes and glanced at his watch to find two hours gone. The rain had slacked off, the light grown more generous.

Hunched into his collar, he trudged the lot twice through the cutting wind and the spare rain drops beating on his face. He glanced at the Cutlass. The bearded man watched with what George took to be a faint smirk. From inside the Buick George spotted movement. A squirrel, perhaps the same little scoundrel as the day before, zig-zagged around the lot, stopped, listened intently with head cocked, then skittered off to pause again beneath a tree.

When George next opened his eyes it was two-thirty, the rain had stopped, and a battered Pontiac station wagon was just pulling in alongside. It disgorged a patriarch and a young girl. A prophet's white beard and skullcap topped off a lumber jacket and jeans. The teenager, face of an angel, hair pulled tight into a single braid, wore a long tweed coat that seemed to George's untutored eye just a bit old fashioned. At the back of the wagon, the old man with the smooth untroubled face let down the tailgate. Seated on it, they reached inside to extract roller blades they then struggled into. The man fitted a metallic blue goalie's helmet over the skullcap. He shut the tailgate. They skated off heavily, their wheels firing off gravel. Once on the paved road leading away from the beach, they surged away skillfully, white beard flowing and brown braid swinging. George watched until they were lost from view. "Sit in a parking lot and see the world," he told the steering wheel.

Sitting there thinking about things, it occurred to George that he'd never had a pet. Almost simultaneously he recalled that that was wrong, he'd once owned a dog. As an adolescent intoxicated with the great ideas set before him, he'd named the retriever 'Plato'. Plato's life was cut short by a speeding car. Even half a century later, George could still feel the grief of it. He wondered now if some part of that awful feeling of loss might have had to do with the name. After all, the name you give is a measure of aspirations. Of value. Doesn't it stand to reason that an animal you troubled to give a meaningful name to would represent a bigger emotional loss than just another 'Fido' or 'Brandy'?

Which led him to consider how one would go about choosing a name for a cat. It was something you might have to live with a long time; if you were old enough, it might be forever. One thing, it should be damned plain. 'Kitty'? 'Sweet Pea?' 'Cleo'? 'Cleo,' George repeated out loud. "Now where did that come from?" and almost instantly received a cartoon image of a cat lowering a paw into a goldfish bowl, and was sure it was from the 'Pinocchio' movie he'd seen a hundred years ago. "What the hell," he said, "why not? Plain and undistinguished. Sure, 'Cleo.'"

Which was when, around three, the beautiful girl of the expensive foreign car hurried through the wind down to the beach.

Like an apparition the orange cat suddenly materialized, padding along aimlessly no more than ten feet from the hood of the Buick. It seemed to George that she was more bewildered than before, even become a touch scrawny. He carried the bag out of the car, tore off its top, then keeping his distance poured out just a bit of the food. When he retreated the cat gazed at him, inched forward, peeked at the food, looked up to measure him, then bent to her meal. He could hear her teeth crunch the dry granules. He advanced a slow soft step and she raised her head; another furtive step started her backing away. He poured a bit more in a thin line towards the Buick, then moved back. With somewhat less care this time, the cat fell again to eating. When she finished, George stooped closer with the bag, and as the cat trustingly bent her head he scooped her up. She lay docilely in his arms and he scratched her head and heard a low purr. But when he opened the Buick's door and transferred her to his hands, she writhed, clawed at him, and leapt twisting to the gravel.

George climbed back into the Buick and slammed the door. He licked the tracks bleeding along the back of his hand. "I don't need you," he shouted into the windshield. "Think I want to have to worry about one of us being left alone? I don't need you."

At three-fifteen a Jeep drew in to his right, partly obscuring the skaters' station wagon. The young man who jumped out was tall and sturdy, black hair, pretentious little beard, pea coat and work shoes. He hurried out of the lot. "Damn fool," George muttered, "running around out there in this weather."

Watching the cat tongue-wash its paws, he pondered connections within the trinity of life, love, and death. He wrapped his arms around himself for warmth. Lulled by imponderables, he soon dozed off. In his dream he was warm; he inhaled the aroma of food and the scent of a woman; he reached out to touch companionable skin.

A car door slammed. To his left the Cutlass was still stuck in place. On his other side the patriarch and the teenager, ruddy-cheeked, breaths visible, were again seated on the tailgate, this time to remove their roller blades. George's watch told him they'd been gone the better part of an hour. The old man pressing the skullcap to his head, they came around against the wind. They drove off.

The cat was gone. George rolled down his window and tossed out the open bag of food. He twisted the ignition key, then inched the Buick across the lot and onto the road leading to the town streets. "One does what one can," he told himself.

He'd gotten half way home when the nagging slowed him, another two blocks before it forced him into a U-turn. The girl! She'd been gone, What? A half hour, an hour? In raw weather, down a long, empty beach. He saw himself being questioned by police. "Yes, officer, it was about three when she first came." "See her come back?" A shake of his head. "So you left anyway, knowing she was still out there?" But he told himself it wasn't fear of criticism, it was conscience; guilt for abandoning her.

George parked in the same spot, between the Jeep and the foreign car. It was almost four o'clock. He'd give her another ten minutes, he decided. And then found he couldn't sit still, suddenly there was an urgency about it. He shoved open his door. When he stood up he felt his joints stiff and a pull on his calf, his body yanking him back to his chronology. With a flush of anger at the insult of it, he forced himself to limp on, and by the time he'd crossed the lot he was moving easier.

From where he stood he could sight down the long parallel arcs of promenade and beach. In the gray emptiness the occasional pilings upright at the water line, dark and unmoving, stood like petrified men. The desolation of it all placed him shivering at the very edge of the world. He made his way through the wind back to the Buick. He felt eyes follow him from the Cutlass.

He sat rubbing his hands for warmth, trying to think of next steps. Her car was still sitting there, there was no real place for cover, yet she was nowhere in sight. And gone far too long. "Okay, say she's your own daughter. What would you do then? Or want some stranger like me to do for her?" He closed his eyes and conjured up togetherness with a self-possessed daughter. The instant's warmth that brought was like when he'd imagine for just a heartbeat that he'd soon be going home to Emily. But the little exercise added urgency. Thinking as a father, he'd be a damned fool to sit around debating. He'd want the police. He remembered then that the park police made regular rounds. He'd flag down the next one; he hadn't seen one of those white cars for awhile now, so it was sure to be very soon.

In minutes he spots the bearded young man coming from the direction of the beach. The young man stops at the public telephone hanging on the near side of a concession stand. He picks up the receiver and dials. When he talks to his party he moves his hand expressively. An indication of earnestness, George thinks. Or working hard at persuasion. Persuasion? Mother of God, he's selling! Of course, of course! Sorry, darling, got tied up, had to put in some overtime, be home soon.

"Oh yes," George says, "oh yes, my little redheaded rose of Sharon, better to come back separately. Won't want to give any onlookers ideas, but you'll soon be along too, won't you? I'd put fifty bucks on it. Only where the hell was the deed done? There ain't a nook or cranny in ten miles of beach. Still, love will always find a way, won't it? Oh yes, yes, yes, the power of love."

The young man hangs up, comes strolling indolently past, hops into his Jeep, fires it up, drives away. George waits impatiently, his hopes battling. Should he be wanting his daughter safe, even if it wins him his fifty bucks, or pristine but still lost?

But no, he hasn't bet wrong. Sure enough, in five minutes she comes lithely striding up, haughty as a queen. Her open coat flaps in the wind; her cheeks are flushed, her eyes shine. Nearing her car she slows to peer in at him. Through the glass her eyes bore right into his. Old man, her sneer says, screw you, old man.

"'How like a serpent's tooth...' he throws the quote at the windshield, then breaks into a broad smile. He has had a daughter, even if so briefly; his daughter is safe and sound; he is even delighted that she is ungrateful. After all, isn't ungrateful how daughters are supposed to be to fathers?

The foreign car roars off. The lot is empty again except for the Buick and the Cutlass. Under the surrounding trees the fading light has brought its mystery. Again George imagines stalkers and cries of savagery and death. Then out of the stillness comes a real cry, so faint he can't be sure he's even heard it. The cry of an infant is repeated. Bewildered, he peers through his side window. The cat sits several feet from the car, gazing up at him with unmoving green eyes.

It surprises him when the door of the Cutlass swings open. The bearded man places both feet carefully on the ground. Hunched against the wind he makes his wooden way over. With some unease George rolls down his window. The man bends toward the window, but not quite low enough, and George finds himself facing a pewter beard, broad suspenders, and a liver-spotted fist clutching the collar of a checkered woolen shirt.

Listen, friend," the man says," the missus would like that little cat."

"Be my guest," George shrugs. "It's not mine to give."

"We can't catch him. We tried, me and the missus, but we're too slow, you can see it would be hard for us."

The quaver in the big man's voice, George thinks, probably can't be helped, but that whine is his own choice.

"What would you like me to do?"

"Got any more cat food? We watched you. You coulda had the cat but didn't want it. Maybe if we put out some food? You could maybe grab her for us."

"Sorry," George motions back to the inside of the wagon, "food's all gone."

The pewter beard points at the cat sitting past the corner of the car. "We'd sure like that little thing," the man whines.

What George would like is to lean over and strike his head, his own head, against the steering wheel. So this, he thinks, this is what I let myself be scared of all these months. Damn fool me!

Just then the wind begins to shoot rain drops into the open window; rivulets score the windshield. The man yelps, "Gotta get outta this weather," and hastily turns away. "Maybe you can help us," he tosses whining over his shoulder, and makes his ungainly way back to the Cutlass.

George sits thinking how ridiculous this all is. A fuss about a stray cat. If he couldn't catch it for himself, how could he possibly help them? Even if he'd wanted the damned cat. Even if he'd wanted to be saddled with the responsibility. Like taking care of a baby, or don't they realize that? Although he can sort of understand. Something to worry about besides their own aches and infirmities. Something of interest between the bored selves of a long marriage.

Dimly through the running windshield he glimpses the cat just sitting there in the rain. It occurs to him that if he could pull it off he'd be doing two birds with one stone: making the old couple happy and getting the cat a better home than this parking lot. "All right, George," he says aloud, "what say we give it one more shot?"

Without a plan he shoves the door open against the wind. "Here goes nothing." He places a foot on the ground. Before he can get the second one down the cat is right there, close to the car. Unsure of his next move, he holds the door wide open. She just stands there. "Come," he coaxes the green eyes locked on his.

The raindrops drum on the hood covering his head. He's tempted to slam the door, but tells himself he owes the dumb little thing one more shot at a decent home. He puts a soft warm lilt into "Come, little cat."

The bedraggled creature stirs. Warily she slinks forward. An orange blur arcs past him into the Buick. She crawls over his seat and scrunches into the back bench. She lies there languorously tonguing off the rain.

He shuts them in. He fires up the engine.

In the shivering rear view mirror the Cutlass steadily shrinks.

"They have each other," George tells Cleo.

Numbers

Harry Stern, sixty-two, a self-employed accountant and sometime athe-
ist, finished wrapping the phylacteries around his left hand, muttered
the prescribed praises to the Lord, and sat down in his usual place in the
middle row. At 6:30 A.M., each of the three others was still huddled over
his own dream. The electric wall clock counted the minutes with the
ratchet of an ancient mechanism. A weakening moon peered into the
dark windows like a globular spy from eternity.

In the second row, Siegel, face whitely bristled, spine drooping into a
question mark, lifted his head to utter a despairing, "Shvach," weak, his
estimate of the odds of accumulating a quorum of ten. No one
responded to this familiar lament. Each just huddled further into himself, as if weighed down by his prayer shawl.

On his way in, five chilly slippery blocks over a sheet of new snow,
the occasional barking as Stern passed a sleeping house had raised his
hackles; an instinctual reaction, he suspected, inherited from generations of harried in the shtetls of Poland. On such dark mornings he
sometimes imagined himself there, joining others hurrying bent and
shivering down the crooked street, beards flowing onto tattered coats,
fringes hanging out. Such imaginings brought him a momentary
warmth in the belly, a feeling of peace like coming home after a long
absence. But how explain this yearning to travel back to where he'd
never been, a place of dilapidated houses, muddy streets, noisy yeshiv-
ahs, and all those sad and comic God-intoxicated characters? Once, a
child, he'd slept the night in the tiny bedroom back of his grandpa
Max's candy store on Stone Avenue, immersed in the feather bedding

brought over in steerage. Was that the connection? He sometimes had to remind himself that those imagined places were anyway buried now under paved playgrounds and modern apartment buildings.

Stern ran a finger over the adjoining seat, picking up a greasy smudge. As if to preserve valuable wood, the old benches were polished Friday afternoons with some sort of oil, presumably to reduce the chances of splinters in bony rears. The acrid odor of the oil combined with the smell of old books and old men into the musty fragrance of nostalgia, carrying Stern back a half century to the little beth medrish, house of study, in the stately synagogue next to their apartment house. With its outside staircases, balcony for political and funeral orations, and massive electric candelabra, it stood formidably amid the tenements like God's laws made visible. (Years later, he'd driven back to the old neighborhood, now ceded to a successor ethnicity. The synagogue was atomized into a vacant lot.) In its basement, place of his childhood just a bit larger than this one, they'd never had to sit and wait, hoping for lost souls to wander in by accident. Otherwise it was the same, the same greased splintery benches, desiccated groaning floor boards, velvet-curtained ark on the eastern wall; same odor of furniture polish, books, wine, burnt candles and old men.

Just before sunset, one Friday the summer he was eight, his mother pointed through their kitchen window to the adjacent stained glass of the synagogue. Drawing him close, she kissed his forehead. "It's time, my little man, to go make use of your cheder lessons, no?" He dragged himself down the stairs and the few yards across the sidewalk into the strange and fearsome dusk of the basement study house. Inside, one of the older boys guided him through the pages of the service, but he stumbled over the words running right to left, his eyes unable to smoothly assimilate the letters underpinned by the dashes and dots of vowel markings. He could keep up only by skipping sentences and sometimes even entire paragraphs; even, in desperation when falling too far back, a whole page. He was at a

loss to know if God preferred that he stick it out for a whole prayer at cost
of skipping others, or would it be more acceptable to read at least a part
of every single one. It frightened him that he might be marked a sinner for
his omissions.

With practice over weeks of Friday nights and Saturdays he gradually
became better able to keep up. Eventually he could do every word of the
entire service, even had a good bit of it memorized, and he then felt him-
self enfolded into God's good graces. Still, he never lost that edge of appre-
hensiveness, the sense of hovering retribution.

The door screeched open, admitting a stab of cold air and Mr.
Monroe Epstein. This lively septuagenarian, natty in business suit and
tie, who sometimes while waiting did pushups in the aisle to burn off
excess energy, still took the subway every morning to his son's office,
checking up on the business he'd turned over after half a century.
"Boker tov. And how is everyone this lovely morning?"

Across the narrow aisle, Herman, unsteady survivor of several bypass
surgeries, roused himself for his customary response, "I woke up today,
didn't I? So what should be bad?" Monroe unzipped his blue velvet bag
and drew out his prayer shawl and phylacteries. He set about wrapping
the leather thong around the shriveling flesh of his left arm. But
Herman, his voice drooping with sadness, interrupted. "You heard
about Sadie Buxbaum?"

Epstein shrugged his shoulders. "Who?"

"Sadie Buxbaum. My Evelyn's in-law. Last night washing the dishes she
just fell down. This morning they called me. The funeral's tomorrow."

"Oh my God," Epstein slapped his forehead. "I think I know who
you're talking about. A pretty woman, no? A little on the heavy side?
Maybe sixty-five? Sure, I know who you mean. My God, I can't
believe it."

"Last year," Herman shook his head, "when I went for my operation,
they were both worried about me, they were afraid I wouldn't make it.

So first the husband, and now her. And me, I'm still here. Can you believe it, how life is funny?"

They lapsed into silence. Epstein finished tying his phylacteries. The others subsided again into private thought.

At 6:42 Stern re-tallied the company, verifying that they were five, only half way there. Then he counted again, only this time instead of by ones he did it by lumping the three on his side of the aisle with the two across it, well aware that a shrink would classify this bit of business as obsessive-compulsive. Stern was always counting. Getting dressed in the morning, he counted the number of eyelets in his shoes; evenings he counted the steps up the two flights to his apartment. In between he counted the columns on the subway platforms zipping past his train, totaled together the Runs columns for all the baseball teams in the Times box scores. Although it was now all computerized and infallible, he even totted up the columns in client ledgers, just for the satisfaction of verifying the inevitability of it. The precision in numbers he found as exhilarating as would a musician the specks on lined paper that add up to a grand Mozartean structure. But beyond exactitude was the poetry of it. Numbers, he knew, cast shadows, set off reverberations; are shorthand similes, metaphors, the stuff of which poetry is made. Like the digit two: companionship; the end to loneliness. Seven: lucky; beloved of gamblers, mystics. Ten: a minyan, quorum; preventing its violation his reason, his only reason, for coming here. Or bigger numbers. Like six million.

Mostly, Stern's preoccupation with numbers and their connotations barely broke the surface of his mind, which would continue to operate unhindered on the more conscious level. But sometimes the numbers instigated venomous thoughts. He was like a victim of Tourette's Syndrome, subject to involuntary, though in his case unvoiced, bursts of vituperation.

A month before, the eve of Yom Kippur. Upstairs in the main sanctuary, Stern, wrapped in his prayer shawl, settled into his last row seat a full half hour before the Kol Nidrei. *The sun through the stained glass cut him in two, his upper half in gold, the lower in purple, while he gnawed at his inexplicable motive for being there. If not God, in this house of unheeded pleas, he argued, maybe what is still here for me is kinship with fellow man in his need. But in the end he could only fall back on the arithmetic of it. Calculating that this would be his fifty-fourth Kol Nidrei, he decided that the answer lay solely in his reluctance to break the chain.*

When the colors through the stained glass faded, the dozen torah scrolls were removed from the open ark; encased in white silk and topped by a silver crown, each was handed into the arms of an elder to carry in procession around the congregation. After, circled back to the lectern in their outer garments of shroud linen, scrolls clasped lovingly, they stood surrounding the cantor while the ancient melody bore aloft his plea.

The synagogue was crammed full. Stern observed like a stranger in a strange land. He saw how the women were adorned in stylish and costly garments, the men also in the finest of new clothes. Packs of little children, richly dressed, skittered up and down the aisles, evidence that the congregation had taken to heart the biblical exhortation to be fruitful and multiply. Stern started to count individuals before realizing it would be much more efficient to just multiply the number of seats in a single row by the number of rows. Which was when the thought shot through the surface: How many, it spat contemptuously, how many cattle cars would it need? Not very many, it sneered, not many at all. Just two or three should take care of the lot of you. And he began the arithmetic to verify his estimate, but caught himself. He sank into his seat even while all around they still stood, facing the emptied ark.

Mid morning of the next day the cantor intoned how all of mankind was as a flock of sheep passing in judgment, how the fate of each would this day be sealed: who shall live and who shall die, who by water and who by fire. The image rising into Stern's mind was of long lines of people, in unstylish coats against the cold wind, suitcases at their feet, and up ahead an immaculately uniformed man barking instantaneous decisions: who to

the right and who to the left. So that's how it was! Stern nodded, Of course!
Just an organization man, an angel from on high shouldering the burden
of judgment day. Who shall live and who shall die. Dr. Mengele just shar-
ing the Lord's work!

Stern counted them yet again. Five. What is needed, he told himself,
is more old farts grabbing onto religion in preparation for death; more
dying, so that their sons would have to come pray for their grubby
souls. He shook his head. Opiate of the dead and dying! False hope of
the hopeless!

At 6:45, middle aged Henry Ringer and Leo Reich, business-suited
professionals of some sort, showed up together, as they did every
Tuesday, the day of the week they'd committed to. Not bothering
with phylacteries, they just threw on prayer shawls, as if come to ful-
fill an obligation but still poised to fly if summoned by worldly
affairs. They slid onto a rear bench, absorbed in the conversation
brought in with them.

Siegel pointed to the clock. He pulled himself upright and shuffled
over to the lectern. Out of a barrage of throat-clearing his voice
emerged clear and strong, weaving melody around Ashkenazic accents
formed by eight hundred years of repetition in ramshackle houses of
study. The undermanned congregation amened responsively. Stern
counted again. Still only seven. Siegel chanted the Hebrew, "For the
Lord hath chosen Jacob for himself; Israel, for his own possession. For
the Lord will not abandon his own people; his inheritance will he not
forsake." Yeah, Stern nodded. Sure.

At 6:50 number eight strolled in. Ed, tall and fit, graying at the temples and with rimless eyeglasses, former bond trader and Wall Street hot
shot, was now, in his early sixties, one of Alzheimer's victims. Every
morning he walked the route from house to synagogue, and afterwards
the same route back again. At other times he could be observed roaming the neighborhood with a puzzled expression, as if the streets were a
maze to solve, and finding his home the prize. During the service he

would tap a neighbor on the back, loudly demand, "What's the page?" and then continue to repeat the query every few minutes.

Often it was Ed who turned up as the tenth man. Lately he'd somehow gotten into the habit of sitting patiently only until the arrival of an eleventh. Then, jumping up, he would tear off phylacteries and prayer shawl and march out, shadowed by a silent chorus of lifted eyebrows and resigned shrugs. If someone tried to persuade him to stay, his response was indignant. "You don't need me," he'd sputter with impatient logic, "you have ten without me."

At 6:57 they reached the page beyond which it was impermissible to go without a minyan. Resignedly, they dropped into their seats. Herman demanded to know why no one had phoned around the night before to jog congregants into showing up. We should call up Abramowitz, maybe he could get here fast. No, someone said, Abramowitz is in Florida for the winter. The half dozen other names thrown out were similarly disposed of. They sank back glumly.

Stern, hunched over drowsily, lifted an eye to the clock, slumped into reverie. Again he drifted back half a century, easier to recall than yesterday.

His father and maiden aunt Rachel sitting at the kitchen table. Reminiscing about the old country, from which they had emigrated two decades before, in their early teens. His mother, at the sink with the dishes, smiling at their cackling laughter, tears running down their cheeks, sides held against the happy pain. They recount the foibles of a small town's memorable characters. Such an orgy of reminiscing takes place a couple of times each year, the only times Harry sees joy on the face of his dour father, otherwise embroiled in breadwinning.

"Remember?" his father says, introducing the familiar repertoire. "Remember how Der Krimer..." ('The Crooked One,' meaning only that he was a cripple. Actually, Harry had once been introduced to him, a handsome, personable man with a club foot.) "...how Der Krimer came to get stuck with Tchucheh?" (Meaning a scatterbrain; in actuality a charming and lively lady with a stutter.) "Remember her sister, Tzipporah? A

wild beauty, tall, slim, with green eyes and red hair, carried herself like a
princess, in America she'd win beauty contests, be a movie star." Lips curve
downward as they recall that Tzipporah was left behind in the old country.
But then laughter insists on having its way. "Der Krimer was crazy about
Tzipporah. Her father, 'The Ropemaker,' begged him to marry the stutter-
ing Tchucheh, offered him a bigger dowry. ('What kind of bigger dowry
could a starving ropemaker provide? More ropes?') But no, Der Krimer
was dying for love of Tzipporah. Reluctantly they gave in. Under the wed-
ding canopy at ceremony's end, before he could lift the thick veil covering
the face of his beautiful Tzipporah, came his new bride's first words: 'Is left
for me a little chicken s-s-s-soup?' At her stutter Der Krimer fell down in a
faint."

The beautiful Tzipporah never did marry. In 1943 they gave her a ride
in a cattle car and then fed her to the ovens.

At 7:00 Harry Korn stormed in. Korn, a take-charge manufacturer of
belts, was right on time, exactly fifteen minutes late. Tuesdays,
Wednesdays and Fridays, when starting time is 7:00, he arrives at 7:15.
Monday and Thursday, when the scheduled start is earlier, 6:45, to allow
for reading the torah portion, he arrives at 7:00. Stern is positive that
Korn has calculated that fifteen minutes past the appointed time is
when he is most likely to be the much appreciated tenth man. So why
show up earlier if fifteen minutes late will yield the maximum impact?
After all, isn't it the businessman who grasps every possible advantage
who is the most successful?

Pointing quivering forefingers, everyone counted everyone else,
verifying their number was nine and not, somehow, ten. Stern added
up the four on each side of the aisle plus the newcomer in the aisle
itself. Korn, the last to arrive, was indignant. "Why should it be, that
in such a large congregation it's a battle every morning to get together
ten men?" They sank a bit lower in their seats, as if guilty as charged.
Stern shrugged at the obvious, that there are just too few left who

believe in this nonsense. "And what about the rabbi? He can't come here in the mornings?" Grow up, Stern thought, it's only his job, not his belief. A Jew'll do anything to make a living, provide for his family. "The rabbi's busy," Herman said. He raised sardonic brows. "He's got other things to do."

"Where's the phone list?" Korn demanded.

Someone pointed to the little side room. On a utility table, next to a telephone, lay a list of names with phone numbers by category: those who attended daily, those who offered themselves up on specific days of the week, and those non attendees who might be available if called upon in an emergency.

Stern heard dialing. "Belle? Hi, Harry Korn here. Belle, we're short. Can Morty come down?" After a brief pause Korn repeated the response, loud enough to inform those in the other room, "'He's not feeling well.' So sorry, give him my best." He hung up. "Poor Morty. Caught him at the wrong time in his menstrual cycle."

Vexation building with each succeeding excuse, Korn broadcast the play-by-play of rejection with mounting sarcasm and slamming telephone. When the clock already showed 7:12, half way to their usual finishing time, Stern marked the cause hopeless. With Korn's noise receding in his consciousness, his thought rotated back to origins.

In the days when he was thirteen, the snow was more benevolent than now: more frequent and more generous, yet whiter, softer, not so cold. At three o'clock they'd race home from school to apartments all over the block, devour whatever could be found atop stoves or in ice boxes, and then charge downstairs to join up in the street. Dividing into sides, they'd crouch behind embankments erected by the plows at the edges of opposing sidewalks. After firing snow balls over the street, one or the other of the brigades would charge across to breach the other's fort. In the hand-to-hand fighting, pulses pounded in temples restricted by navy watch caps, bodies perspired within sweaters and pea coats, naked hands and

faces tingled with life and health. On short Friday afternoons, when the
sun began to fall early, Harry would desert from the battle to hurtle up
to their flat and grab some potato pancakes fresh from the stove, crispy
around the edges and pungent with onion. Then, with a calmer Sabbath
gait, still chewing, he would stroll back down the stairs and across the
sidewalk into the basement study house, anticipating sweet melodies and
the warmth of virtue.

That winter of his fourteenth year, the silken black hair and flushed face
of a girl in his class ignited his chemistry. On those winter Fridays in the
study house, fingers still tingling, voices around him soared in melody, the
holy scent of wine and spices and burnt candles was in his nostrils, and the
girl's face was golden within the candelabrum's flames. And he knew the
presence of God. And he loved Him.

At 7:19, Sidney, a placidly mountainous and red-faced letter carrier
strolled in, uniformed, on one of his irregular visits, like an Inspector-
General of Worship. Murmurs of relief greeted him, as did Korn's fer-
vent, "Sidney, thanks for saving our butts." The savior dropped heavily
onto a rear bench, pulled a large red handkerchief from his back pocket,
loudly blew his nose, and joined in Ringer and Reich's sotto-voiced discussion of the football playoffs. Siegel rose and shambled to the front to
finish up. The others stood up, sighing with little groans of exertion.

At 7:23 Siegel shuffled over to the ark and lifted out the scroll for the
reading. From the lectern where it was being unrolled, Herman, patriarch of their tiny assemblage, pointed at Stern and held up three fingers,
meaning that his was to be the honor of the third of the three portions
to be read. Stern nodded acknowledgment. He sat following Siegel's
sing-song of the first portion, "…that the Lord may turn from the
fierceness of his anger, and show thee mercy, and have compassion
upon thee, as He hath sworn unto thy fathers…."

The door once more creaked open and Marty Gratz blew in. Number
eleven, an embarrassment of riches. A half foot of Gratz epidermis

showed between the bottom edge of his baseball jacket and his jeans, which clung precariously beneath an overhanging stomach. Owner of an electronics chain promoted by outrageously gross TV commercials, Gratz's visits were exquisitely timed for the post-service whiskey, coffee, and danish, return on his investment in congregational dues. He slipped into place beside the mailman, while around him they played a mute concert of shrugged shoulders, raised eyebrows, furtive smiles of derision.

Henry Ringer strolled to the lectern for the second portion of the reading. Ed began tearing off his phylacteries. Behind him, Stern jumped up and began to unroll his too. Ed zipped up his velvet sack and stepped away from his seat. Stern hastily jammed his phylacteries into his own sack. He chased Ed down in back of the last row and grabbed his arm. "No," he whispered into the puzzlement rising on Ed's face, "no, you can't go now. I'm leaving, so you're the tenth man. You have to stay."

Behind the rimless glasses Ed's eyes darted around, unanchored in a sea of perplexity. "What're you talking about?"

"Listen to me." Spacing his words, Stern hissed, "When I leave, you will be the tenth man."

Ed's tentative smile blossomed. "You're kidding, right? You're just saying that because you want me to stay, right? You never leave before the end, so come on, wise guy, why're you going now?"

"Because they don't need me," he hissed. But then out of the corner of his eye he saw them watching. "They have enough without me," he finished lamely.

Through Siegel's chanting all were turned to him: Herman, Korn, Reich, even the Inspector-General and the Moocher. As if, thought Stern, they are awaiting the results of an audit. Awaiting judgment.

He shrugged impatiently. "You don't need me," he told them. "You have ten without me."

The chanting up front ceased. The clock's ratchet thickened the silence. Stern held out a beggar's hands. "Can't you see? It doesn't add up, the whole thing just doesn't add up."

They peered at him, waiting. He imagined shrugged shoulders, raised eyebrows, furtive smiles of derision. "No. No," he insisted, "you're wrong. Me, I'm number eleven, and I'm walking out."

Still they waited.

"Don't you understand?" his voice rang out. "Eleven is too much. He doesn't deserve it." And then his cry vaulted the old benches and leapt the walls. "He doesn't deserve eleven!"

But they were not as adept at numbers. By the time Stern put on his coat and opened the door, Siegel's chanting had already resumed. The other nine amened strongly.

Il Purgatorio

And now he'd stalked off and abandoned her in the Piazza Navona. The only thing different about this particular spat is its international flavor, the first time they've ever fought outside the States.

In her cream linen coat, a bit light for autumn, Madeleine shivers within the colossal shadow of the piazza's Bernini fountain. Feeling small and ineffectual before that mass of writhing men and sea creatures, she concedes to also owing some of her chill to being stranded in a strange city by a man with whom she now connects mostly in anger.

Thinking back on it, Madeleine is convinced that what had finally hooked her was Paul's promise to teach her enough of the language to be able to read Dante in the original. She knows how silly this would sound to anyone else, but it isn't happiness that leads you to dwell on origins, and in searching for first causes to blame or regret there's little comfort in clutching lies to your bosom.

Her MSW had been like the winning ticket in a lottery for happiness. Immediately upon graduation, everything had begun falling into place. She managed to snare a job in social work for the city, the impossibly demanding but rewarding career she'd been aiming for, and she relished navigating the bureaucratic shoals in aid of the homeless, needy, and hopeless. Shortly after, she met and loved and moved in with a sparkling young man well on his way into a sparkling career. But then things began to disintegrate. When that rising star was picked to establish a branch in another part of the country, he just stuffed a suitcase and with a wave and a smile danced out of her life. After him there were others as well who didn't work out. By the time thirty loomed she'd decided that romantic love was an ill-conceived and outworn concept.

Which is when Paul, interested and interesting, happened along. Very deliberately she checked off boxes. Ivy League out of Little Italy's Mulberry Street, a lively yet considerate lover, his tall crisp darkness was a perfect foil for her willowy blondeness. He was perhaps a touch too serious about things, but she saw him as someone to make her reach, as in a tennis match against a superior player. With his street smarts, fine education, and a caustic if slightly skewed outlook that fired up startling insights, she was sure he could elevate her to places she'd glimpsed and aspired to but never yet been. But still she hesitated, because a marriage made in heaven instead of the heart substitutes calculation for ardor.

"Don't worry," he told her, "you will learn to love me."

"And how is that?"

"Because I am lovable." His little boy's grin, an irresistible mix of audacity and shyness, recast the words from egotism to plea. So she checked off another box.

Still weighing, she said, only half joking, "And will you teach me to read Italian?"

"With the greatest pleasure, Signorina."

She told him about once hearing some of The Divine Comedy in a literature course, not in translation but in Dante's own words. She could almost taste those rolling strophes, and it had developed into a passion and an ambition. "'Nel mezzo del cammin di nostra vita.' I memorized that, and it's all I remember. 'In the middle of the journey of our life.'"

"I'm just a business type, an MBA in corporate greed, so am not familiar with the Dante. But I'll teach you his language and we can read him together."

Which is what decided her. It meant they'd have better than love's illusion, they'd have mutual support and nourishment. Together with the other boxes checked off it added up to a passing grade. The wedding had been small and private.

Now, after three years, Paul, expert enough in computerized banking systems to be in demand on four continents, was away from home far too much. More, she suspected, than was necessary. She'd hoped that being together in a country new to her but familiar to him, she needing guidance and he responding, might provide the warmth and interest to melt a hardening indifference. So for the week between his Athens project and starting another in Paris, she'd parceled out her case load and jetted to their rendezvous in Rome. At the arrivals gate at DaVinci they'd flung arms around each other, and for those brief seconds she had hope, but when they disengaged it was as if caring had also been let free. "Have a good trip?" he'd asked, but she could see he was no more interested in her response than if she'd been just another client.

She is surprised it has taken this long for the spat to develop. Between the three days in Florence and the two so far in Rome, they'd encountered enough disasters and irritations to fuel a dozen quarrels. In Florence she'd finally persuaded Paul that there was more to the city than churches and galleries; she'd wanted to do some shopping, insisting if not really believing that what was being traded was just as telling a cultural phenomenon as the edifices and artifacts. So in between gazing at the unmoving ribbon of the Arno, shooting the Duomo beflecked with pilgrim pigeons, and lingering tranquil moments in monastery gardens, they'd taken the grudging time to investigate jewelers' windows on the Ponte Vecchio, finally settling on a bracelet of Florentine gold. It wasn't until boarding the train for Rome that it hit Paul that getting sidetracked into shopping had caused them to entirely miss the big one, the Uffizi Galleries.

She was sure he'd have sulked all the way to Rome, if the train ride itself hadn't been such a disaster. They'd had reserved seats, but although their tickets showed seat numbers, it was impossible to tell which car they'd been assigned to. Rolling like drunken sailors, they'd stumbled from car to car, in each one finding their seat numbers occupied. Each time Paul displayed their tickets the occupants would just shrug provocative little smiles, then turn away. In desperation buttonholing the conductor, Paul spouted the language, but got back from a Mussolini in baggy uniform only a lifted brow hung on a contemptuous shrug. They arrived in Rome having, in effect, walked the whole way.

At the open end of the plaza, a cab skids to a stop, disgorging a couple of passengers. "Hey!" Madeleine waves an arm. "Wait!" She takes off over the cobbled street, grateful for her morning's prescience in opting for low heels. Its side mirror must have caught her milling arm, because the cab patiently waits. Drawing breath, she peers into the driver's open window. "Albergo Emanuel?" she asks timidly. At his unintelligible response she raises open palms in defeat, but then he nods assuredly, "Si, si," and leisurely reaches back to crack open the passenger door.

In the rear of the aged Fiat she settles in among the stubborn ghosts of fierce tobacco and a spicy cologne. The late afternoon sun leads them past already decaying modernist housing, sand-colored cubes startlingly interspersed with heroic representations from history and mythology. Strolling couples verify a natural law: the male is the more gorgeously plumed.

Although you wouldn't know that from observing that guy up there in the front seat. And just as she begins to idly speculate as to why scruffiness should represent the international standard for cab drivers, hers pulls over to the curb behind a stand of taxis. He spurts out, the folds of his elderly coat billowing behind, and with hands and shoulders expressing a desperate ignorance, throws out a plea to the assembled drivers. After an unhurried exchange studded with covert smiles at the taxi, the young man waves ciao. He sweeps back inside, twists around to show righted palms in a gesture of reassurance, then shoots them back into the stream of traffic. Madeleine regrets she is unable to communicate her appreciation of his performance, knowing that only the most serious of mental handicaps could give a cabbie difficulty in finding a hotel famed for its location right at the head of the Spanish Steps. Resigned to being taken for a ride in more ways than one, she leans back and allows herself to dwell on this thing that's been knotting her stomach.

In three years of marriage they'd never yet gotten around to the language of Dante. No big deal, she could survive without the fulfillment of such high flown aspirations. Still, it was disappointing, less for itself than as a symbol of their failure. She thinks about how the really important stuff of life is not the obvious milestones, but the apparent insignificances that sneak up or slip past without fanfare.

Like six months into the marriage, still learning each other's ways, she sat one evening pairing up Paul's socks, one of the mindless household tasks that helped palliate the anger and sadness of spending days among the exploited and unfit. Paul was in his easy chair, immersed in some technical volume, the air between them warm with ease and comfort. She got up to carry the basket to the bedroom. From their new Country French bureau she pulled open Paul's sock drawer. Laying out the paired socks, for his convenience arranging the accumulation by color, she uncovered an ordinary letter envelope. The corner of a photograph peeped out from it, a bulge in the envelope suggesting more inside. Curious, and with a twinge of guilt, she extracted the peeping photo and recognized a Loire chateau, Chambord or Chenoncaux, she couldn't remember which, it'd been years since she herself was there. Swans floated in pools set amidst sculpted shrubberies. Intrigued by the calm beauty, desiring to further taste the pleasant reminiscence, Madeleine drew out more photos. Halfway through the pile she was confronted by a slender young lady backgrounded by a castle, blue eyes in a pretty face smiling shyly into the camera. The next photograph captured those blue eyes gazing steadily at Paul, his arm around her waist, a raincoat flung over his shoulder. Hair windstrewn, he wore a jacket with patch pockets that Madeleine recognized as still hanging in his closet.

Carrying the envelope into the other room, she perched on the arm of his chair, sharing the circle of light under his reading lamp. She held up the envelope. "I loved the Loire valley. Didn't you?"

His eyes remained hooded. He nodded,"Yes, very nice."

She said, "I wonder, could we have been there at about the same time?"

"That was four years ago," he said. "Before you and I met."

"Yes," she conceded, "for me it was about five years ago." Feeling like one of those dreaded bitchily jealous wives, but caring too much to be able to refrain from being a bitchily jealous wife, she held out one of the pictures. "Hon, do I know her?"

Without looking, he shook his head. "She was before your time."

God, how she hated this! "So what was her name?"

She had to repeat the question, detesting the whine creeping into her voice. Against his book the blood left his knuckles. "Caroline," he said evenly.

Fearful it might shatter something, she still couldn't help, "So why would this Caroline be in your drawer?"

His frown was not of anger but thought. "She's not in my drawer, some old vacation pictures are in my drawer, and she just happens to be part of the scenery."

His unweighted lines were those of an actor at the first run-through of a role he hasn't yet learned to care about. He returned to his page. She nodded repeatedly, rapid short nods as if carefully weighing his response, then stood up and carried the pictures back to the bedroom. There, she flung the envelope into the open drawer, and herself onto the bed.

For the hundredth time she racked her brain to account for his apathy, for the unfairness of the role reversal. After all, it wasn't as if theirs had been a terribly unique arrangement. Who was it who wrote that always there is one who loves and one who is loved? So even if you are only drawn to marry because, among other things, he promises to teach you Dante, and for whatever else that implies, you might still find your heart unexpectedly stirred by the little things that togetherness fans into caring. But is caring subject to some sort of inviolable calculus whose product may not exceed 100%, so that if you love more he must love the less?

She decided that the only logical solution to their shifting equation was that their arrangement had not been as one-sided as she'd thought, but even up, their needs mutual. For her it had been to escape the misery of rejection and loss. But what, for Paul? Which brought up the photographs carefully in his drawer, of the pretty blue-eyed Caroline. And suddenly Madeleine believed she knew; she was positive that she now knew.

The driver's precipitous swerve into the curb tosses her sideways against the door. Again he leaps out, hesitates on the sidewalk a moment, then snags an old woman lugging a black vinyl shopping bag. She shies away, but he manages to corner her into a brief conversation built around impatient shrugs of her narrow shoulders. This time when he clambers back inside he does not even bother to signal that everything is hunky dory. They set off again down the boulevard. Hasn't her subconscious already on this ride recorded this same scene? Madeleine decides the cabbie is missing a good bet by not filming an educational video: techniques when taking a tourist for a ride.

Suddenly queasy, she rolls down a window, even while suspecting it is more than just the stubborn odors, that it has to do with arriving at the point in her recollections that always causes her to squirm with embarrassment.

When Madeleine concluded that she'd been competing against the ghost of a lost love, and recalled how she'd been beating her chest mea culpa, blaming herself for Paul's indifference, the unfairness of it all welled up, and she fell back onto the bed. She wept soundlessly, face contorted, mascara sliding down her cheeks. Until chagrin and sadness and regret coalesced, flaring into resentment. She jumped up and plucked the envelope out of the drawer. It flashed through her mind that she hadn't yet thought out what she would say, but it wouldn't be the first time she'd made a fool of herself, and to hell with it. Without pausing to wipe away the tears, she stalked into the other room. Paul was still immersed in his book. She flung the envelope at him, then froze as the projectile arced for his eyes. It knocked off his reading glasses. Too startled to react, he just looked up dazed. Her fists

unclenched. Relief bled into an anger reinforced by his lack of reaction. More of his damned indifference. In a few quick steps she was at his chair, striking at his shoulders and chest, a pummeling that barely moved him. "You owe me," she cried, "you owe me. You can love her, go on, love her, but she didn't want you. She didn't marry you, I did." Madeleine didn't know what else to say; she despaired of anything intelligible. Weeping again, she dropped down to kneel with her head on Paul's thigh, her hand reaching out to grip his arm. His other hand went to her hair, stroking it. In a little while the sobbing wound down. Paul slipped out of her grasp and, standing, raised her up. Supporting her, he led her to the bedroom. They made love fiercely, like true lovers after a long parting. After, Madeleine drifted off, holding tight to him and to the certainty the drought was ended. But ensuing days revealed the same old Paul, as if that night had never happened. As if love could show up only in anger and apathy.

Weaving through the squealing suicidal traffic around the circle, they pass the huge wedding cake monument to Victor Emanuel, and this time Madeleine is absolutely certain they'd already been by here before.

"Avanti," she says impatiently, "avanti,"presenting him with the entire range of her conversational Italian.

"Si," the driver nods placatingly, "si, si."

In short minutes they draw up to the hotel's entrance. Ending with lira, the driver's concluding pronouncement impresses her as a demand for the price of a villa on Capri. She gets out holding up an index finger, signing him for patience. "Momento," she says, surprised she knows the word, doubtful it is what she means. The doorman comes striding over, and she asks him to please assure the cabbie she'll be right back with the money.

Paul is stretched out on the bed, arms beneath his head, staring at the ceiling. He wears wing tips, pressed trousers on his long legs, a white dress shirt, a tie, and suspenders, as if on call for a consulting emergency. She says, "The cab's waiting to be paid. He's taken me to hell and back several times, and his fare seems more like a ransom demand. If you go down, you could save us millions. Assuming you would care to ransom me off."

Stone-faced, he gets off the bed, throws on his suit coat, and barges out. Waiting, she both desires and dreads his return. Presently back, he sinks into the tapestried chair. Extended arms mimic the curve along the chair sides; one leg is stretched forward and the other planted half way, the pose favored in portraits of enthroned kings and Popes. Uncertain whether the royal response will be the gift of a castle or an invitation to a beheading, Madeleine gingerly puts forth, "How'd you make out?"

"He settled for a third. Fifteen thousand." Paul permits himself a faint smile. "So I ransomed you off."

"If he'd held out would you have let him keep me?"

"If you weren't so stubborn you wouldn't have needed the damned taxi in the first place."

"Paul," she says, "you can only be stubborn for your own interests. And this was nothing I wanted for myself."

"If I want to go visit my uncle Maurizio, why is it in my interest for you to tag along?"

"If he's your family, then he's dear to me too."

"But my uncle does not desire to meet you. Much as you find that hard to believe."

Caroline. She wonders what this new one's name is. Gina, Sophia, Claudia? And what will background her shy, pretty smile. The Fontana de Trevi, the Neptune in the Barberini fountain? And which articles of his clothing in which drawer will hide her picture.

"Listen,' he says, but then she has to wait the length of a prodigious yawn, his hands reaching for the ceiling. He tears open his eyes. "Listen," he says again. "If you insist, we can continue this silly discussion over some pasta. I've arranged something special for you tonight. I'll tell you about it while we're eating. What do you say?"

They agree on this little neighborhood restaurant he favors when in town. Walking down the Via Conditti, Madeleine thinks how their only attachment is the common purpose; they don't touch, like two youngsters shy on a first date, or old marrieds bored with an all too familiar contact. She glances across the two paces between, imagining herself a passerby measuring Paul with neutral eyes. She would judge him, she decided, one of those plumed, strutting, upper echelon Romans, flitting around at his ease within a triple tier of interests: business or profession, wife and family, a mistress or two. Too aware of possibilities to allow himself to be pinned down to a single allegiance. And maybe, she thinks, that passerby's quick glance would be as accurate a diagnosis as you can get.

Overhead, from lines running serially down the streets, banners flutter, bursts of primary colors scattering the dusk. She points up at them. "What are they selling?"

Paul surprises her with a playful smile. "I was saving it for dessert. But if you insist on knowing now, there's a Vivaldi concert at the Spanish Steps. Seven-thirty. In your honor."

She can't help smiling back at him. "In my honor?"

"Well, they didn't have one until you arrived, so isn't it logical to assume it's in your honor?"

She reaches out and places her hand on his arm. "We'd better eat quickly, then."

"No hurry," he says. "Time here is no exact science, just an art subject to interpretation."

Over dinner, she refrains from again raising the subject of his uncle. It is becoming an evening she doesn't want to chance ruining. And there is the danger that anything at all she might do or say could kill his sudden inexplicable amiability.

They make the plaza below the Spanish Steps with not much time to spare. The stairs are already filling up, tourists planted unevenly along them like flowers wild in a concrete garden. Paul leads her in a breathless climb until he settles on a step half way up. They sit among silent couples holding hands and teenagers raucous in english, wearing ventilated jeans and designer sweat shirts, guitars and backpacks at their feet. In the unexpectedly warm soft air the overhanging sky darkens rapidly. Sporadically, a mute flash of lightning blanches the eastern portion. In the plaza below, a milling mass surrounds a portable band shell, like iron filings drawn to a magnet. Inside the shell, the members of a fully staffed orchestra can be seen readying their instruments, brasses glinting in the light pouring from strategic stanchions around the plaza.

"Isn't it time yet?" Madeleine asks.

"Remember, time here is subject to interpretation."

She points her chin below. "I wouldn't have expected so many Vivaldi enthusiasts."

"Oh sure. From the people who brought you Dante?"

"How many, would you say?"

"Down there and up here, all together? I'd say about three—four thousand."

Lightning flashes more frequently now, and thunder can be heard, although still faint.

Paul says, "Vivaldi's liable to be called on account of rain."

Madeleine raises her wrist to glimpse her watch face. "It's already past eight."

High-spirited teenagers, grateful for the excuse, tear the soft air with whistles and catcalls. Even the more mature begin to call out restively.

A long-haired newcomer in a business suit arrives hurriedly down at the shell, stations himself with back to the audience, then raises his arms and holds them steady for the downbeat. The orchestra freezes, the crowd grows hushed, the air trembles with expectancy, and a flash of lightning illuminates it all. The furious downbeat brings a blast of thunder, as if the conductor's baton has disturbed occult forces. Blaze of lightning, crash of thunder. But no music.

The musicians stroke, saw, and blow mightily, but no sounds come forth. The audience waits patiently, not trusting their ears. When, presently, they begin to shift around in their seats, the technicians below are already scurrying about, pulling on electric lines, twisting dials on complex equipment. Throughout, the orchestra remains energetically impotent.

"Oh God!" Paul drops his head into his hands. "Oh Lord, wherefore hast thou forsaken them?"

Madeleine places a hand anxiously on his shoulder. But when he looks up she is astonished to find him grinning. "Don't you see?" he says. "It's a portable band shell. They bring it out here and then inflate it. Damned ingenious. But the rubber and the air in it absorb the sound. That's why the sound isn't reaching us, it's being absorbed by the band shell!"

"But they must have used it before," she says, not quite convinced.

"Maybe we're privileged to be the first. You'll see, those guys fooling with the audio won't make a bit of difference. If I'm wrong I'll donate my Paris fee to a fund for unwed mothers."

Along with everybody else they sit and wait. The lightning comes faster and brighter, the thunder follows sooner and more explosively. Technicians scramble, musicians pantomime.

Sitting there, Madeleine cannot help, "If your uncle doesn't want to see me, that's his right. But could you please just tell me why? Is it anything I've done?"

Still gazing below, he says, "When the family emigrated Uncle Mairizio refused to come along. His friends are here, and his club, and his neighborhood. He didn't want to have to learn how to be a deaf mute in a new language."

"Oh Paul, you never told me."

"Sometimes a handicap forces you into extra pride just to stay even. Doing things for yourself. Accomplishing what whole people can't. But that same pride keeps you from displaying your handicap to your nephew's new wife."

"But it wouldn't matter, I'd love him even more."

"As I say, it isn't you, it's him."

She is trying to decide whether to let it go or risk another quarrel, when the world flares up and a simultaneous thunderclap announces its end.

At the instant they feel the rain they are already soaked. Around them the audience scatters with shrieks of dismay and outrage. Paul grabs her hand and through the thunder and lightning pulls her along sprinting up the steps. They dodge into the albergo's lobby. In the elevator each looks at the bedraggled other and bursts into laughter. In their room, still laughing, they tear off their clothes and cavalierly fling them to the four walls. When they've finished toweling off, Paul distorts his face, terrifying her into a corner, rekindling their laughter. With a feint he scoops her up and tosses her bouncing onto the bed. Lying there in her nakedness, she chances opening her arms to him, knowing that a display of his indifference now would kill her. He looks down at her, then crosses to the lamp and turns it off.

Through the aura of light from an opposing window he comes to her and covers her. And then they stop laughing.

After, leaning on an elbow, his index finger describing circles around her aureole, Paul smiles down. "Name a wish."

Through the window, the anger has abated. The rain is still falling, but now in soft benevolence. My wish? she thinks. I wish I could lie with you like this forever, in this strange but dear room after love on this lumpy bed, the rain falling gently past the window just like this. But she just shakes her head mutely. Paul urges, "Go on. Anything. Anything at all and it's yours."

Afraid it is the wrong thing and silly, but unable to keep it back, she says, "' Nel Mezzo del cammin di nostra vita.' 'In the middle of the journey of our life.' Learning things together. Caring. I wish it could be the way it was supposed to."

There is a softness in his gaze she's long not seen. He says, "We can sure as hell give it a try, can't we?" And makes of his arms a cradle for her.

In the morning Madeleine awakes and stretches richly and languorously. Wanting to ingest the lovely sight of the dark ungraceful furniture and threadbare rug, she gazes fondly around the room and realizes Paul is already gone.

Slowly and without thought she goes about dressing, feeling nothing. Outside, she wanders without purpose. Down a side street she stops off at a shop fragrant with bread and cheese, and forces herself to sip a cafe latte. On another street, in an unexpected opening among tired apartment buildings, she is confronted by the huge granite of a fierce rider, balled fist raised high over a wild-eyed charger. The horesman stares straight at her, and she momentarily imagines he is wanting to tell her something—disquieting or encouraging, advice or warning. She pauses, gazing into his eyes, trying to guess his message. Then she turns away and moves on.

She opens the door of their room to find Paul, consultantly uni-formed, in his kingly pose on the tapestried chair. But when she sees his smile her heart floats free.

"I was scared you'd run out on me," he says.

She drops onto the bed. "You scared me too."

"I thought I could be back before you got up. Our last full day, I want it to be a good one for you. So I went out to arrange some things."

"And what things have you arranged, my love?" The touch of irony is unwanted but insistent.

"I thought the Vatican to start with. The Sistine Chapel, especially. It's against the law to miss that one."

"Did you have to go get the Pope's permission? Is that it?"

"No," he shakes his head. "Higher than that. Uncle Maurizio's."

At her lost look he explains, triumph peeping through, "I dragged him out of bed. We played charades and scribbled things on a pad until I got him to see he's hurting someone who wants to love him. Someone I care about."

"Thank you. And so?"

"And so tonight Uncle Maurizio will have the great pleasure of meet-ing my old lady."

"And where will he meet this old lady of yours? Over dinner?"

"After dinner. At his club. He wants to show us off."

"That's why you command such high fees. You can make things happen."

"Oh, knock it off, darling. How about breakfast and then we hit the road?"

"Avanti, darling."

By the time they get back in the late afternoon, the images of all she'd seen are trampling each other: the gilded spiraling columns of St. Peter's Bernini canopy, the mighty arms stretching forth along the Sistine's ceiling, the Pieta, all the tombs in all the churches, and even the statuary and fountains along the streets. They rest awhile, make love in the shower, dress, go out to dinner. After, they stroll along the Via Veneto, pausing at irresistibly beckoning store windows, then sit down at a table outside Doney's for espressos and people watching. All are clothed in elegance and high spirits, moving through air soft with a thousand years of usage, and Paul sits close, darkly handsome and noble. It brings her to wonder how you know when you've reached the pinnacle, the best it will ever be. She decides that maybe it doesn't matter; at the least this time, this time right now, is the best it ever was, and if it never gets any better this is damned good enough.

She holds out her hand and Paul grasps it. He bends toward her in an attitude of courtliness. "We can walk it from here. I think I know the way, but if we start a bit early it'll give us some margin for error."

In fact, they do get lost for a bit. They find themselves wandering through blocks resembling an operatic stage set, the inhabitants like a chorus crowding the scenery. The air rings with laughter and arias sung out with feigned and loving anger at energetic little Giorgios, Ginas, and Albertos, names like music. Through those sounds of life Madeleine's hand lies within Paul's, and it strikes her that maybe all this is an omen, that from now on they will walk through life hand in hand. When after a few blocks Paul admits with good humor that he has lost direction, she gently suggests asking someone, but true to his gender he insists on wandering unaided. It's just as well, she tells herself, because this is one time when the journey is more pleasurable than arrival.

Then suddenly, arm in arm, they turn a corner and Paul announces sotto voce but with pride at his accomplishment, "Uncle Maurizio." He points through a moving screen of passersby to a bearded man shambling in tight circles before a lighted doorway. In the half block before they reach him, Madeleine can see he is as tall as Paul and twice as broad. He wears sandals, a wrinkled short sleeved shirt, and baggy trousers distended by a belly regularly fed a lot more than just needed to sustain life.

Uncle Maurizio's face lights up. Still, he hangs back shyly, flushed and faintly smiling, until his nephew sticks out a hand in greeting. Then Paul places an arm around Madeleine's shoulder, signifying their bond. Maurizio grins and nods, and she moves closer and gets up on her toes to kiss his soft hairy cheek. She easily sees the familial resemblance, to Paul's mother as well, although she can't pin it down to specific features, just something in the cheekbones, the hollows around the eyes, and a lively awareness within the eyes. Maurizio points to the staircase, then steps aside with a little bow, and Paul mimics him, leaving Madeleine to lead the charge. The stairs creak with the thump of their different weights, like a series of repeating three-note chords. At the top there is only a single doorway, emitting light but no sound. Hesitant, she glances back. Maurizio motions her on. She goes on through.

Bright with fluorescents, the single square room is the size of a small ballroom. It is bare, except for stark bench seats attached to and encircling the walls. From around the walls a hundred pairs of eyes are aimed at Madeleine. The force of it shoves her back until she comes up against Paul. Maurizio urges them both forward to the center of the wooden floor, then steps out front, drawing all those eyes to himself. In the intense silence he moves his hands about, not in letter signs but the motions of stories. He sticks his hands in his pockets and tears them out again as fists, index fingers pointing and thumbs upright, pistols firing in a shootout. Smiling, everyone applauds.

"Why?" Madeleine whispers.

"There's no need to whisper," Paul says dryly. "They're clapping because the pistols mean we're Americans."

"Cowboys and Indians?"

"Chicago gangsters."

"How do you know?"

"I've already been through this. And you got more applause than I did."

"What do we do now?"

"Just smile, baby, smile."

"That's it?"

"What else? You want to shake a hundred hands?"

Smiling, Paul waves to the room at large. Madeleine follows his example. Then she moves to Uncle Maurizio and rising on her toes kisses him on the cheek. He reaches for her hand and puts his lips to it. The mutes, all smiles, applaud again. Madeleine and Paul wave once more. They walk out to the sound of clapping.

In the departure lounge next morning, Paul holds her tight and promises to shoot right home after the Paris assignment. She has the impression he is somewhat distracted, but she puts this down to the new assignment already weighing on his mind. Later, over the Atlantic, Madeleine thinks about what a great trip it turned out to be. The thawing of Paul's indifference. Meeting Uncle Maurizio. All those cultural aspects of Rome and Florence. Firenze. 'Nel mezzo del cammin di nostra vita.' The statues and paintings and tombs are melded together in memory, but she is sure she'll be able to sort them out once she's had a chance to rest. Even though experience has taught her that such trips are enjoyed more in retrospect, when you have the memories but not the trouble, she already feels quite fulfilled.

Gazing out into the eerie night above time zones and continents, Madeleine imagines the blinking wing lights as the melancholy lamps of a solitary house approached in the dark. Narrowing her focus, she is taken aback to discover that her image framed in the small window is contorted with weeping. Deflating back into her seat, clawing for explanation, she sets herself to rerunning the hours and even minutes of the last week. What comes up is the walk from Florence to Rome, the chill in the shadow of the Bernini fountain, lovemaking at the albergo, the applause of the mutes. But what arises with greatest persistence is Paul in the departure lounge that morning, promising to shoot home right after the Paris assignment, but on his face that distracted expression, as if his thoughts have already moved beyond her. Just as oppressive is the sound of clapping mimicked by the muffled roar of the plane's engines.

Why should she be so haunted by the applause of those deaf mutes? She tries to understand, but is unaccountably distracted by the Zen koan drumming in her mind, What is the sound of one hand clapping?

Outside, the bravely winking lights rush headlong through the cold and silent dark.

Providenza Sings Tosca

In late adolescence and early manhood Artie was a terrible disappointment to his father, wasting time in devouring novels instead of deflowering virgins. For this and other similar reasons, the baker let him know in a hundred small ways that he was a misfit, incapable of living life properly, doomed to failure. This dark prophecy seemed confirmed when the son of the neighborhood butcher headed off to medical school, while Artie barely made it into and through the municipal college where he diddled around with some courses in business.

So it was to reassure his disappointed old man (and maybe do a bit of strutting?) when, a scant six years later, at the age of twenty-eight, Artie invited him to his office at the Ritz-Forum, generally considered one of the top ten hotels in the whole world. After marveling at his offspring's prodigious staff, observed through the plate glass wall of his office, and his extravagant view of the Central Park duck pond, the baker followed him down the single flight to the lobby, for lunch in the Elizabethan Room.

Within the jewel like tinkle of crystal and silverware, Artie's regular waiter greeted them effusively, eagerly and gratefully recorded their desire for the finnan haddie, and then with admiration at the astuteness of their selection bowed himself out.

Clearly dazzled by the ornate walnut paneling, the worshipful hush, the fawning of the waiter, his father asked in a voice respectfully raised an octave, "You eat here every day?" but even before the answering nod stage-whispered, "You see who sits at that table? That movie star, what-is-his-name."

"Cary Grant. And over there, that's Burt Lancaster. But our policy," Artie cautioned him, "is to pretend we don't notice. We want them to feel comfortable, so they'll come back again."

"And you're responsible for all the money, the whole shootin' match?" His father's brows rose a couple of notches. "With your not-so-hot marks in school it's hard to believe."

"Pa," he said, "some are good in school and some of us are better after school."

Already, he could tell, his old man was revising downward the odds of his failure.

After Bavarian creams and espressos Artie saw the baker off in a cab, then jogged back up the front stairs. Through the gilt, crystal and marble of the lobby he waded across the quicksand of carpet, then at the rear climbed the oval stairwell one flight to his office.

From the open bay window the spring breezes flowed softly across his desk. The pond was a jewel embedded in green velvet. A ballet of ducks floated by, heads immersed and rear ends pointing skyward.

He pushed a button on the intercom and through the glass wall watched his office manager give her usual little start at the buzz.

Anxious to display an alertness and efficiency unimpaired by long service, Mary Donato sent him a smart, "Yes, boss?"

"Could you send in Provy, please?" and watched Mary call down the department, Provy's brows lift from behind her PC, Mary's chin jerk toward his office, Provy's eyes roll heavenward as she rose heavily to set off on her unhurried journey.

Waiting, Artie too recalculated his odds, but still came out on the short end. Because he couldn't forget that he'd gotten to this place only through a fluke. Just two years before, fired from yet another job, he was living his days in bed, behind in the rent, unwashed and unshaven, gorging on sweets, novels, and recorded arias grieving the death of tormented sopranos. It was the music's sweet anguish that held him, but what squeezed his heart to tears with each high C was its triumph: the aria as achievement of its creator's difficult vision, its singer's arduous feat. Quitting his bed only for quick forays to the corner grocery to replenish his stock of ice cream and Oreos, Artie was fulfillment of his father's prophecy.

Then, miracle of miracles, a close buddy was hired as VP-Finance at the Ritz-Forum and prevailed on Artie, a non threat, to come aboard as his assistant. The two worked hard in tandem, and in a matter of months, exactly as they'd planned, the brilliantly competent friend was promoted to the chain's head office, and Artie's timid hand uneasily grasped the Ritz-Forum's baton.

To the outsider, it must have seemed a really classy position. It would not be unusual for Artie to sit toe to toe with a popularly adored entertainer, tea and petit fors on the desk between them, negotiating the terms of an engagemement in the Zebra Room; or confer with a UN ambassador dropping by to discuss financial arrangements for his delegation's upcoming function in the Grand Ballroom; or lunch at an Elizabethan Room table close by a currently favorite subject of gossip columns, who'd while inhaling the soup be covertly scanning for signs of adulation.

But to admiring acquaintances Artie was quick to volunteer, mainly as a defensive measure to cushion his inevitable and no doubt imminent downfall, that it would be easier and much more pleasant to dig ditches.

"You have to understand," he would tell them, "that basically you're dealing with losers. You know what that's like? Depending on people who can't hack it or don't really give a damn? "Now, who are my night auditors? Out-of-work actors needing the daytime for auditioning. And my food checkers working for peanuts down in the kitchen? Retirees with stingy pensions. And my bookkeeping staff? Women who either missed out on marriage or failed at it. Third world generals and dentists struggling with the language.

"So that's what we're working with. And you know the scariest part? That it could rub off."

Well aware that his job depended on getting their cooperation, Artie made it a point to treat each of those misfits as if they were as normal and mainstream as anyone else. So when Provy finally opened the door and just stood there leaning insolently against it, he forced himself to ask in a tone suitable for the Queen's Lady-in-Waiting, "Won't you please come in?"

He watched her cross the room, a pudgy bad-complexioned girl of twenty-five, her shapeless dress imprinted with a zillion tiny flowers shrieking its amplitude. Like one of the larger mammals trying for daintiness, Provy lowered herself carefully into the chair by the side of his desk.

It bothered him that he found her so irritating, one of those people you resent for no apparent reason. He suspected that in a shameful corner of his mind he faulted her for being unattractive. Knowing it unfair, he always bent over backwards to be especially courteous.

Now, unable to see Provy's eyes past the glint on her glasses, he fixed his gaze instead on a flowering pustule in the center of her forehead. He said, hoping his reasonableness was coming across, "I really don't mean to be a pest. But we owe three and a half million, and creditors are threatening to throw us into bankruptcy. I've got to do some tight planning, and I really need your analysis of payables."

Patiently, as if to a mentally disadvantaged child, she explained, "If you're not paying bills, can't you just imagine the calls? After lying or crying to each one of them, how much time do you think I have left for your schedules?"

Past the window the ducks had their heads out of the water now; they seemed all accounted for. Not knowing how else to plead his urgency, Artie said, "Please."

Her face tilted toward the ceiling, imploring divine witness. "Didn't I say I'd do it as soon as I can?"

He picked up the letter opener, ran his thumb along the edge of the blade. "Could you maybe use some help? If I get Eddie to take some of the calls would it make things easier? Save you time?"

She shrugged meaty shoulders. "If that's all it needs to make you happy, be my guest. You want Eddie to take my calls? Fine, let little old Eddie take the calls."

He thanked her for her understanding and cooperation. Grimacing with the pain of patience sorely tried, Provy hoisted herself out of the chair and sauntered regally out of his office.

Artie kicked the gray metal file cabinet. He pressed the intercom. Mary leaped half a foot. He told her to send in Eddie, then in afterthought asked her to first give him five minutes.

Past his secretary at the typewriter, painting the financials with correct-o-type, he walked out on the landing, to the men's room. More and more, lately, he was feeling the need to get away from his desk. As if, he told himself crossing the small hallway, to a haven of sanity, a refuge from care. Inside, he sponged his face to cool it down a bit; arranged his hair around the beginnings of a male pattern baldness he blamed on stress; fiddled with a tie that didn't really need adjusting. He washed his hands, then pulled at the linen roller towel, trying to get it to white. It was immovably caught on filthy gray, so he drew out his handkerchief to wipe the moisture from his face and hands. Restored, he opened the door.

A cry like a wail deep out of the Inferno stopped his heart.

"What was that?" he yelped at Provy standing at the head of the landing.

"What was what?" she asked coolly.

His scalp prickled. "That scream."

She left off gazing down the spiral staircase and pushed herself away from the balustrade. "What scream?" Shrugging, she turned and strolled through the grilled door of the accounting department.

He walked back to his office shaking his head, fearing himself delusional, but then told himself it was just the squeal of a door he'd heard. Inside, Eddie already waited. The skinny redhead's eyes, not quite anchored, darted around among confidential reports littering Artie's desk.

"Find anything good there?" Artie dropped into his chair.

A chummily cavalier shrug. "Nothing I didn't already know."

"Listen. We need to get Provy off the phones. Would you be willing to take her calls?"

"Me fight with creditors? So she can go scream in the hall half a dozen times a day? For my crummy pay? I don't recall that in my job description."

Artie aimed for sympathetic sincerity. "If anyone deserves more money, you do." He held out empty palms. "But there just ain't any."

"So then why should I take on more?"

Artie shuffled papers. With the calm of true despair he said, "The job I'm offering you gets a special title," while his mind clawed through an array of military, corporate, and governmental nomenclature. "I'm thinking of calling it…," he said slowly and dramatically, "…I'm thinking of calling it…'Director of Payables Coordination!'"

Eddie rolled this around his tongue a bit. Then he shook his head regretfully. "I don't think so."

"With the title goes a name plate. Everybody will be able to see who holds the real power around here."

Eyes narrowing, Eddie computed the value of this special dividend.

"Brass," Artie prompted. "Brass shining like gold."

Unmoored, the redhead's eyes gleamed. Nonchalantly he asked, "Could I think it over?"

"Of course." But watching the prey depart, Artie felt his stomach growl, fearing shadowy things that sneak around in the night to release sprung traps. He sat back, took a couple of deep breaths, envied the ducks sliding placidly along an eternity of calm. He pressed the intercom again, watched Mary flinch, asked her to come in.

Provy, he thought. Short for what? Providenza, probably. Providenza, Providence. Provy was Providence's punishment laid on him for undefined sins. Providence screaming through hallways, wasting her time, for whatever lunatic reason, out on the landing. Forcing him to run around designing brass titles for misfits. He desperate for her information, his job with one foot in the grave and the other on a banana peel, and she making a fool of him.

Mary Donato swaggered in, chunkily mature in a black frock with a rhinestone pin at the neck. She sat down beside his desk, hands tightly clasped atop it, eyes eager. "Yes, boss?" she snapped in a mezzo cured in alcohol and tobacco.

"Provy," he said crisply, hoping it the voice of executive decisiveness. "What's this about so much time out in the hall? Half a dozen times a day?"

Mouth crimping, she held out just long enough to show a distaste for playing informer, then nodded. "I don't know if it's six times a day, but yes, she does go out there once in a while."

"Why?"

Surprise snapped her erect. "To be heard, of course. By one of those big shots passing by right down there in the lobby."

"To be heard?" Open-mouthed he thought, My job depends on the inmates of the asylum.

She tilted her head to bring him into sharper focus. "I guess you really don't know, do you? That Provy sings?"

"Sings?"

Lips pursed in disdain. "That heavy stuff? In foreign languages?"

He cast about until, incredulous, it struck him. "Opera? You mean opera?"

Elevated hands, shoulders and eyes conveyed distaste, disinterest. He thanked her for her help. Smiling cordially, Mary swaggered out. Providence, he moaned, why have you selected me for your special attention?

Gliding single file across the water, six ducklings trailed their mother, looking as if they knew exactly where they were going.

The rap on his door came simultaneous with its opening. "Okay, boss, you got it. Anything to help the organization."

"So I can go ahead and order the name plate?"

"What's the title again?"

"Director of Payables Coordination."

"In brass, right? You want me to start tomorrow?"

"If you wouldn't mind."

"You got it, boss." Draped in his new mantle of dignity Eddie closed the door softly on his way out.

Maybe, Artie thought, maybe what we have here is people with multiple lives. Not only waiting between lives, but also living imaginary, dream lives.

The phone buzzed, his secretary announcing her coffee break. Take your time, he told her, don't come back for a half hour. Anything wrong? she wanted to know. No, he said, it's on me. To make up for the gift I forgot Secretary's Day.

At the click of her door, Artie punched the button on his intercom. Requesting Provy's presence, he paid for it by enduring their Marcel Marceau routine. Two ducks raised up part way, quacking hysterically, wings beating the water.

Provy leaned her bulk against the door sill. He went to the window and shut it. Stepping around her, he pulled shut the door too. All orifices plugged, he dropped back into his chair. Above the desk he spread his hands palms up, as if to say, Okay, it's all yours. Surprised by the asperity in the single syllable, he ordered, "Sing."

From against the door she asked, almost cordially, and as naturally as if this had all been agreed upon beforehand, "What would you like to hear?"

He worried his lip with his incisors while recalling some of the more difficult arias. He culled out those he loved most, to make it that much easier to afterwards be indignant. "A bit of Puccini? Maybe 'Vissi d'Arte,' would that be all right? And, say, 'Babbino Caro?'"

"You know about such music then?"

Artie folded his arms across his chest. "Just enough to hate hearing it done badly."

"Not to worry." Provy moved her feet around, shifting her weight under the zillion-flowered dress like a wrestler trying for a perfectly distributed stance. She settled into position, hands grasped beneath her stomach's abundance as if to support it. Her eyes focused on a point two feet above his head. Gathering herself, she inhaled mightily, mottled complexion suffusing with the effort. Her mouth opened into a perfect oval.

Hearing his music sung like this, Puccini himself would have wept for joy. As Artie now wept. His eyes filled because true beauty makes you cry; because he pitied all other sopranos; because he always cried at stories about how they laughed when the boob sat down to play; because he'd forgotten that the misshapen apples are the sweetest. And he wept at her pain. My God, lugging that terrible golden burden and nobody to share it with!

Head bowed, eyes closed, he held on to Babbino Caro's last note, let its dying fall linger reverberating inside him, hunched over it like a chilled man his hot rum. It whisked him back to those bad old days in bed, lying enthralled with the outpourings of reigning prima donnas, and he sneered now at that old callow self, dismayed that he'd let himself be so moved by those clearly inferior efforts. He swiped the back of his hand across his eyes. He got up and walked over to Provy leaning against the door, catching her breath. Discarding an urge to kneel, he instead grasped her round fingers and reverently brought each hand in turn to his lips. "Why are you here?" he begged the sullen, dumpy, beautiful girl. "What the hell are you doing here?"

She plucked a handkerchief out of her sleeve and wiped her forehead. "Their ears won't listen to what their eyes don't care to see."

"Please don't give me such foolishness," he said. "What can I do to help? I would do anything. Tell me what to do."

She pulled open the door. "I've got your schedules to work up." She sauntered out.

He needed to cool his face, wipe away the needles prickling the back of his neck. Outside, he passed through the landing, treading its small white tiles. In the men's room he performed the usual ritual with his face, hair and tie. Gazing at himself in the wall-wide mirror, he thought how strange it was that he couldn't tell what he was feeling, not even whether he was closer to exaltation or to mourning. As if waiting for his being to land heads or tails.

This time when Artie opened the door, the hallway was deserted. He heard only the empty clack of his heels on the tiles. Even right up to the mouth of the staircase he didn't know he would do it. But then, gripping the polished brass balustrade, he inclined his head down the stairwell. The shout escaped from some pressured place within him, "Listen, down there! Listen, you fat, rich slobs!"

He was startled by the echo of his voice ricocheting around the marbled well; alarmed that his thoughts had been made tangible. There was more he'd meant to say, but he couldn't think now what that might be. He heard himself shout, but with faltering conviction," Come up here, why don't you, and listen to beauty."

By the time it got to 'beauty' his voice petered out. He heard the insistent slap and slide, slap and slide of footsteps rapidly ascending the stairs. Silently, he scampered into his office.

The pond's surface, more placid than the water in his trembly glass, was deserted. Not until he located the ducks plashing away in a far corner did his panic begin to subside.

Pastorale

I

Homing in on a break in the door screen, the bat zoomed into the common dining room during an informal Saturday night get-together, terrifying all the women, who knew for a fact that once a bat gets tangled in your hair you can never get it out again. Raven-haired Mrs. Gold, seated at an oilcloth-covered table near the center of the room, was if anything even more frightened than the others. Desperately scrabbling about for some way to defend her most glorious feature, she solved the problem quickly and ingeniously: simply ripped off her halter and swathed her head in it. Then, safe and feeling rather clever, she sat back, calm through the squealing at surrounding tables. It wasn't until some moments later, when she just happened to glance down, that it hit her that the shrieks were not of terror but hilarity and derision. When with a little moan she scuttled out, the halter slid off her head and she went through the door in full panic, one hand atop her head and the other futilely spanning her chest. Eventually, the incident, complete with simile comparing the unwitting display to two fried eggs sunny side up, was gleefully accreted to the lore of Bleier & Sussman's, recounted in malicious detail at least once each summer from then on, as well as during social visits out of season.

It came back to me last July. On my way to a seminar at one of those Catskill resorts dedicated to the goddess of conspicuous consumption, I suddenly realized I was driving through the section of the mountains where we'd spent the long ago summers of my childhood. As if on its own, the car exited the highway, and I soon found myself on a narrow road of decaying asphalt. I immediately felt that every tree and stone was familiar to me. The nostalgia was aching, and so powerful that it instantly wiped away all of the intervening decades.

And then, rounding a curve, I felt my foot tamp the brake. The car crept forward into ghostly sights and sounds of recollection. It stopped dead in the center of the seldom traveled road. I sat and drank in the sight through eyes and memory simultaneously.

I took inventory, checking off sight against memory, unable to tell if the pangs of regret were sharper for the structures existing now only in memory, or for the spent stream of time itself, that had washed, unheeded, past whatever still remained. Before me now was an orderly colony of generously separated, cleanly white cottages embedded in green velvet. The big farm house that had stood disheveled behind a trampled lawn was gone. The lake, down an incline dropping off from the other side of the road, was there yet, but this raging sea of my nightmares, much of which I'd guzzled in a near drowning, was now reduced to a somnolent little pond napping in the bushes. Immune to time and weather, the "casino" I'd watched them build almost a half century before remained pristine. The tin-walled shower house, sporting an exhaust pipe at a rakish angle, still floated Chagallian atop the highest point on the dozen acres, reminder that cleanliness is next to godliness.

I felt kinship to the remaining structures, whose walls had mutely absorbed our lives; resentment that they should outlast us. Gone were the Rabelaisian characters, those people of large emotions who had brought to this country, in the last great wave of immigration, a love of life and a gratitude for the privilege of living it here. Healed was the wounded earth, trodden grass and denuded soil strewn with gum wrappers and squashed Dixie cups, testimony to seasonal overpopulation and unbridled vitality. Gone were the overflowing garbage cans; Tommy Dorsey on the casino phonograph; the lakeshore bonfire parties; the acrimony, sometimes even fist fights, between the pugnacious lessee of the little on-premises grocery and any tenant foolhardy enough to shop elsewhere. Gone, the voices on soft evenings blended in song lamenting lost love, the country of childhood, and the brevity of time. Gone, then, were the sounds of life.

I steered the car some yards around a curve and pulled over onto the shoulder. I got out and sat down on the stone wall that seemed to have grown lower over the years. It was where my father would come on sunny afternoons to patiently rock my sister Rebecca, struggling against sleep before finally succumbing to the chirp of the carriage springs. I pulled out a cigarette, but then threw it away unlighted, remembering that a three-pack habit of Camels had eventually killed my father. Remembering how they were all, all gone now. I sat there and listened to the trees whisper tales of long ago.

II

The betting around was that Artie's old man would beat up his mom, even kill her, or maybe settle for just a quick divorce.

That last summer, Bleier & Sussman's was seized by a craze for card playing, as if the well of creativity, from which the inhabitants could always in the past draw new and interesting ways to amuse themselves, had suddenly run dry.

When school shut down at the end of June, the tenants, together with laundry sacks stuffed with bedding, jangling cartons of dishes and utensils, and streamer trunks heavy enough to be holding dead bodies, all strapped to the roof or somehow clinging to the sides and back of the Buick limo, were plucked from all corners of the city and delivered to Bleier & Sussman's by John the Hackie at five bucks a head. The hundred miles took six hours door to door, including the torturous struggle up the ninety degree grade of the Wurtsboro Hills, past exhausted vehicles littering the roadside, water boiling out of every orifice, hoods gaping like mouths sucking air.

Artie Lavin and half a dozen buddies rendezvoused that first day on the shadowed porch of the Big House. Somebody pulled out a card deck, and from right then until the very end of the summer they experienced the sun only when its glare pained eyes lifted briefly to rest while the cards were shuffled.

It was as if card playing was genetically ordained at age twelve; as if they'd become too sophisticated for the same old kid stuff: softball in the tall-grassed rock-strewn pasture, reconnoitering in the barb-wired dark and mysterious forest across the road, fishing in the private lake down the road, its wealth of perch guarded by long and thick bullhead snakes. As if they'd forgotten the few cows still housed in the white-washed barn, leftovers from when Sussman first threw open his farm to summer renters. Forgotten the easy-smiling man milking the cows in the cool of early morning, kids lined up, mouths open, to catch from deftly aimed rudders a stream of warm unpasteurized unhomogenized milk that they'd never forget the rich taste of. Forgotten, too, the rides on the back ledge of the ice cream wagon, on Sussman's daily rounds of the neighboring colonies, vending chocolate-covered pops and dixie cups with Buck Jones and other Stetson-hatted Bucks on the lids. On the ten mile round trip the assignment was to lean against the ice chest to prevent it spilling. In mid afternoon, the clop of the horse's hooves was the only sound in a world napping under the sun, only man, boy, and horse awake, and the breeze, the fragrance rising from the grass, and the chirping sparrows. Past eyes glued to the road under hanging feet, the gravel shoots by at a dizzying speed even while the hooves strike at just a lazy trot. But forgotten now were the wagon rides, and the barn's living smell, and in the cold morning the smoking stream of milk straight into thirsty mouths, and the kindly smiling man.

They were like the woman who drags her sable along the floor to show there's plenty more where that came from. When you're twelve, and summers are lined up before you into eternity, what's one summer more or less? So what, if you throw one away? And it was maybe where they belonged that summer of their development, that last summer before girls would become meaningful.

The plague quickly spread. It passed over the singles searching for connections, or the lightly marrieds on the lookout for a bit of diversity, or the children in their cradles. Otherwise, the shuffling and slamming of cards and the sliding of coins across oilcloth-covered tables could be heard at all hours throughout Bleier & Sussman's.

Artie's parents were among the few who didn't join in. His old man's knowledge of poker was primitive, barely gleaned from casting a casual eye at the games played Saturday mornings at the office of Local 226 of the Poultry Workers and Meat Cutters Union. Besides, Jack Lavin was a lover, not a gambler. Proportioned to appear taller than his medium height, with knowing brown eyes behind long lashes, a deeply creased chin, and a nose with just enough bump to give his face character, Jack's particular game was working up expressions of interest from the opposite sex. He just needed to know that he could if he would. It was his way of monitoring the slide down the slippery slope.

His mom referred to the players as gamblers and bums, perhaps unaware that on the porch her own Artie also played for stakes, except it was wooden matches instead of money. (If you got wiped out, you could always get an infusion of capital from the match boxes in the open kitchens, extracting just a few from each, so that contributors were not only anonymous but also unaware.) Although still in her early thirties, she was contentedly matronly, interested in dealing recipes, not cards. Her slavic comeliness—high cheek bones, almond eyes, hair of black silk—sometimes enticed one of the singles or roving marrieds into futile overtures. His father, mindful of his own games-playing, jealously guarded the castle, and would accuse his entirely oblivious spouse of inviting the advances, accusation invariably followed by quarrel, quarrel mellowing into tearful reconciliation. But Artie knew very well how Jack loved his Shirley, and she him. After all, they all lived together in that one tiny room.

That summer the leaves hung as if painted on canvas; the grass browned and died; the road's liquefying tar smelled sour. Artie's little band sat smug in the shade of the porch.

The string of hundred degree days was into its second week. No one moved about out there. Nothing and no one moved, except Jenny Bleier. But the Bleier's daughter didn't really count, and the guys on the porch didn't take serious note of her. She was an older woman—at least eighteen, maybe even twenty—and scuttlebutt had it she'd been driven off her rocker by an unhappy love affair. Day or night, no matter what was going on, she'd never wear anything but a one piece bathing suit, as if to emphasize her separateness. She was tallish and well shaped, with wavy brown hair framing regular features, which together with the freckles gave you an impression of warmth and wholesomeness. And then you were surprised by the large-pupiled gray eyes, as discordant as was her bathing suit at one of the Saturday night dress-up parties. Those unexpected eyes never seemed to quite focus on you, or on anything else for that matter, but always looked inward, as if observing her pain.

Jenny rarely spoke, but drifted around soundlessly, and you might start at suddenly discovering her next to you. Some were made nervous by her presence, though Artie knew her as gentle, palling around with the kids and treating them with importance. But there were also those who felt pity, who thought that skirting the periphery, observing, was just her way of keeping in touch with normalcy. These were longer-term renters, who remembered the bouncy girl of summers past, the girl before that summer her father took off.

Unlike his partners, Old Man Sussman's inheritors, who just enjoyed things like any of the tenants, Sam Bleier played at landed gentry, puttering around in ragged clothes with plumbing and carpentry repairs, haunting the junk yards for fixtures. Having married the unbeautiful Sadie for her money, he refused to expend his affection on her, but lavished it instead on the property bought with his soul's currency.

One noon a couple of years before, in that terrible summer of her sixteenth year, a sobbing Jenny ran out of their bungalow begging help. Those hurrying inside had been hearing the screaming and breakage all morning. They found Sam Bleier standing over his wife bleeding on the floor. They shunted him aside. "No," Sadie Bleier stopped them. "No. Leave him alone. I just fell, that's all." There was a cut over one eye and blood from a scalp wound ran down her face, staining features that might have been whittled out of a block of wood. Putting out a scraped and bloodied hand she steadied herself getting up. Sam Bleier, fire in his eyes and spewing obscenities, started for Sadie again, but Jenny threw her arms around his waist.

He shoved her aside and stalked out, slamming the door. They heard the roar of a car engine and the shriek of tires.

Sadie Bleier replaced her absent husband. Trousered, unkempt, tools clenched in thick, reddened hands, she pursued real or imagined imperfections like some androgynous avenger of damages. She repaired plumbing, raked the lawn, badgered for past due rents, always with one watchful eye peeled for Jenny. Jenny spent a lot of time down at the lake, swimming some, but mostly just sitting alone on the shore, hugging her knees, staring into the water. Sadie Bleier was always after her to come away from there. "Jenny, come darling, come, I have a delicious lunch waiting for you." There was an edge of desperation to her urging, as if sitting alone at the lake left Jenny vulnerable to danger. Mostly, though, Sadie would have to give up, and napkin over arm like an unkempt waiter would carry down a covered dish, returning later to pick it up, usually still untouched.

Mid morning on Monday of that second broiling week, the coolness of dawn already evaporated from the porch shadows, Jenny materialized at the foot of the stairs. "Hey!" She held up a pink Spaulding. "Any of you guys interested in some handball?" Someone muttered, without looking up, "Only a crazy would ask on such a day."

Artie threw down a card on the bench they used as a table, and with time to kill until his next turn sat back to rest his eyes. They focused indifferently on Jenny; they might just as easily have fixed on a tree or a bird. This time her swim suit was of some white, lustrous material. Against her thigh she slapped an ivory bathing cap in a gesture of impatience or excitement. The thin black band of a delicate lady's watch encircled her wrist.

Her slight swayback, little swell of tummy and curve of thigh he suddenly found unaccountably provocative; infinitely lovely the small movements of shapely arm and supple wrist in that slapping motion, repeatedly measuring out arcs of grace. For the first time his heart and mind comprehended the meaning of "female;" for the first time encountered an other, an opposite, that wasn't to be derided but cherished: mysterious, awesome, dear.

Somebody whined, "You sleeping or playing?" He threw down a card while his retina held fast to the image of Jenny's round arm, gilded with fine coppery hairs glistening in the sunlight.

"Well, guys," she persisted, "what do you say? Anybody?" and Artie wondered how a voice could come so cheerful from behind such sad eyes and mouth.

"Afraid to lose to a girl?" she taunted.

He took the four steps in a single leap, chased by cries of outrage from jilted gamblers. At the bottom she wrapped his arm around hers. "C'mon, little boyfriend, let's go play."

Across the dead lawn and over the cindered path her arm stayed entwined in his, while the silken skin of her side rubbed against his bony arm and the softness of her hip collided with his sharper one. A dozen feet up the gray mortised wall the faded letters could just be made out, "Sussman & Bleier's." At the edge of the court she untangled her arm to swat his butt, then tossed the ball onto the cement. Stationing herself midway on the court, she looked back once to make sure he was ready, then smacked the spaldeen against the gray boards. He slapped it back with a palm grown soft with card playing.

Artie took it easy with her. It was more than just chivalry, there was pity in it, and maybe a bit of infatuation too. (How could he yet know the difference?) He just couldn't bear to see that delicate femininity disordered, tormented in pursuit of a ball in a silly game. So he fed her soft reachable lobs. Until her returns, hard and cleverly placed, began to run him ragged. Defending his manliness, he played harder, and then as hard as he could, but she matched him point for point.

Even chasing over the court, he couldn't get enough of his new way of seeing her. She carried her head slightly forward, round-shouldered, and walked pigeon-toed; the deliberately ungainly movements of a budding girl (older woman, to him) startled by her own loveliness and trying to conceal her awareness of it. He was charmed by the way she had of clearing her hair from her eyes with sudden sharp tossings of her head. And his knees were liquefied by the womanly back blooming out of the narrow girlish waist; the waist flowing slimly out of firm and tumescent backside; the entire structure shifting continually, rippling with each leap toward the oncoming ball, each cocking of the hand, each swing.

In an hour the sun came beating down from directly overhead. For half that time he'd already been feeling hot and tired, choking back a queasiness that threatened to cut short his time with Jenny. Now he was sick to his stomach.

But she just played on, and Artie stayed with her. He didn't want her to think him a quitter. And he couldn't tear himself away from that closeness, from being the only inhabitant of her universe for so long as they played. He staggered around the court, sneaker soles catching in the prickly whorls of its roughly finished cement. The regular double thwack of the ball—first the sharper one of naked palm and then the booming one of wooden wall—was a systole and diastole hammering in his chest; the sun was held flaming in a giant fist just above his head.

On such a day intentions melt in the sun. With each return of the ball his legs grew more rubbery. He felt his body become loose, about to slip off, and his consciousness oscillate, so that for slices of time he was no longer lucid.

He said weakly, "We better stop," but Jenny just continued her serve. He swung and barely reached the wall. "Please," he begged, the nausea rising to his throat, "it's too hot." Only she wouldn't stop, and he thought they must be right, those people who called her crazy; maybe crazies just couldn't feel things the way normal people did.

He swiped at the ball and missed, and it rolled off the court. He walked down after it, legs wobbly as he carefully placed one foot in front of the other. He came to the ball lying on the grass, then kept going.

Behind him, it soon thudded again as if she meant to send it through the wall.

He dragged past the guys still playing on the porch, through the dimly cool dining room, into the narrow kitchen they shared with the Golds. He opened the ice box, rummaging through the leftover chicken and assorted cheeses and pickled salmon, but neither his family's two shelves nor the two belonging to the Golds held anything to slake his thirst. He wandered back out into the dining room. Mrs. Gold, coming through the screen door, abandoned her smile. "Why's your face so red?"

"It's nothing," he said. "I was just playing some handball."

"In such a heat? Who'd you play with in such a heat?"

He had no control over his tongue. "Jenny," he admitted truculently.

She threw up her hands. "That crazy? No wonder. Don't you know enough to stay away from her? Where's your mother?"

When he shrugged she dragged him back into their kitchen and sat him down. "You could get a sunstroke, you know that?" She brought him a glass of water from the sink, then reached up to the cupboard and took down a bottle of witch hazel. She poured some onto a clean cloth and rubbed his face and wrists. Then she placed the wet cloth against his forehead. "Here," she said. "Hold it." Satisfied he held the cloth properly, she asked, "You feeling a little better yet?"

When he nodded, she drawled, "Yeah. Sure. With that red face? Sit here and don't move, I'll go find your mother."

He sat until the cloth turned warm from the heat of his forehead. He got up and poured more witch hazel on the cloth, then dropped back in the chair. Presently he felt cooler and less shaky. He decided it would be better for him if his mom saw him recovered before learning he'd worked himself into a sun stroke.

He walked up the cindered path to the shower house to see if she was maybe washing laundry at the tubs there. He tried the grocery. He knocked on unresponsive doors. He looked around for someone to ask, but there were only the little kids playing cowboy near the barn, and his buddies gambling on the porch, and he was sure none of these would know.

Artie stopped still. Cottages deserted, no bird singing, trees and clouds unmoving, he was surrounded by the ordinary suddenly become strange. Foreboding settled on his shoulders, a feeling of loss and being lost. In the ringing silence he heard—thought he could hear—whispers, giggles, mutterings.

Clawing for explanations, possibilities, he suddenly remembered the casino in the far corner. Surrounded by high grasses poking through the bones of 'twenties autos, it was where he'd sometimes spend an hour alone, fooling with the ivory knobs and chrome levers reeking still with the romantic fumes of gasoline and motor oil. He loped over there now, chased by the wheeze of his breath and the slap of his sneakers.

Almost upon the casino, he could hear only a ringing silence. Right up to the open doorway there was only the forlorn quiet of an empty building. But when he burst through it was into an altogether different silence. The sunlight through the windows illuminated spectators ringing a table, unmoving. Two or three glanced up briefly at his footfalls on the bare floorboards, but the dozen others, including Mrs. Gold, stood as if captured by some Dutch master of dark and light. Only the dust motes moved, softly climbing sunbeam ladders. The half dozen other tables seemed to have been abandoned in haste, cards and coins lying scattered over each.

His mother, in the second tier of bystanders, wore a print smock, as if just summoned from her kitchen. Her usually smiling face was sullen beneath the tan. Gasps and titters rippled through the crowd, followed by the rasp of cards skillfully shuffled.

Peering through a chink in the wall of kibitzers, Artie discovered his father seated at the table. Sweat coursed down the hit-and-run flirt's fixed smile. Artie saw that the others seated around the table were the colony's card sharps: Mrs. Gold's sister Betty, Betty's bookie husband

Ernie, Mrs. Gold's other brother-in-law, Harry, and Mr. Jacobs—respectfully addressed as "mister" because a thick, expensive looking cigar always stuck out of his face and he enunciated english as if native born. In such distinguished company, his father as card player had the same chance at luck as a paraplegic playing center field for the Yankees.

Release of breath, swish of coins across oilcloth, shuffle of cards, absolute silence. Twice more the cycle was repeated. And then the reverent hush was pierced by a shout shrill with a woman's rage. "Why don't you pick on somebody your own size? Gamblers! Crooks! Ain't you supposed to be his friends?" There was no audible response, just facial expressions alive with dismay, and it was only when the echoes blasted off the plywood walls that he recognized the voice as his mother's.

His stomach knotted. How could it be that the gentle housewife was standing at a card game, yelling at the top of her lungs? My mother, making a fool of herself and of my father? Calling attention to our family?

"Why?" she shouted again, this time at his father. "Why do you let them make a sucker out of you like this? Did somebody steal your brains?"

A buzz of disbelief circled the ring of spectators, which shattered to disgorge Jack Lavin in knee length shorts, black lisle socks and cordovan wing tips. Jaws clenched, eyes narrowed and focused straight ahead, heels clacking, he double-timed out the door. Artie's mom hesitated, then chased close behind. The buzz thickened into snickering and chatter. He heard someone say, "By God, it shouldn't happen to me, what'll happen to her." Someone else said, "He'll surely kill her, and I wouldn't blame him." Mr. Schnall, from the next kitchen, a big-bellied tailor, parodied a croupier with, "Okay, folks, place your bets. Place your bets, folks. You get three to one on a beating, five to one on divorce, ten to one on murder."

Artie ran after them. Just past the door he had to pull up short, heaving until deep breaths calmed some of the nausea wracking him.

By the time he got down to the road they were already in the distance, his father walking briskly, his mother trailing after, like ranks in disarray retreating from a site of defeat. Then a sharp curve cut them off from view.

He sank down onto a boulder by the side of the road. He leaned his arms across his knees and laid his forehead on this bridge. He shut his eyes, but the blank screen was striated by blood-red pulses, each beat matching a stab of ache in his head, and his naked ears caught sarcasm and slander. He felt sick, wounded, alone.

Swordpoints of grass sprang up to prick his thigh. Fingers slid softly up and down his arm, and Jenny's voice was soft in his ear. "Everything will be fine. You'll see."

A buddy had once held a piece of ice to the back of his neck and called it a hot iron, and Artie had actually felt the ice burn him. Now Jenny's touch and this thing with his parents were together fire and ice all over again. Her arm was laid across his shoulder. He opened his eyes, and in one glance memorized forever the perfect line of her jaw and the golden down on her tanned cheek, and her gray eyes smiling reassurance while all around they prophesied doom.

In minutes a cloud slipped across the sun. Other, darker clouds trailed after, and soon the rains came, sputtering on the grass. The spectators, giggling and good naturedly swearing, rushed in a jumbled mass for the shelter of the casino. Abandoned on the path like a broken promise, a child's white sandal lay lonely in its singularity. They sat on, Jenny's arm on Artie's shoulder, faces upturned to the healing rain. The rain was like a curtain, separating the bad part of the day from how it was now, the strange terrible thing with his parents from Jenny with her arm around him.

"Some day, little boy friend," Jenny said softly, "you will be touched by love. Part of the time it will feel half way to heaven, and the rest like swallowing live coals."

"Yes," he said, "I know."

She turned her wet face to his. "You know?" She smiled at him, playfully astonished. "Dare I ask who the lucky lady is?"

He of course shook his head. Her hair was limp and a drop of water shivered at the tip of her nose. Her suit, wet and clinging, hung twisted. He thought how strange it was that looking a mess that way and so vulnerable should make her even more appealing.

She said, "Even with the pain, love is a miracle. When it comes you won't easily let anything chase it away. Do you understand?"

He wanted only to bury his head in her shoulder, but she gently insisted, "Do you understand?"

He shook his head.

"See, those vultures were picking his bones, but he couldn't get up and leave because grown men have such foolish pride. So your mother sacrificed herself just to give him his excuse. I promise you they're down the road hugging, laughing their heads off."

Eventually, the rain stopped. The sun glinted invitation through the windows. They came back out again, a few at first, like insects venturing feelers, then the rest. Under a palette of thinning clouds Artie heard again the taunting comments—snide, sarcastic, frightening.

"Don't mind those fools," Jenny cupped a hand against his ear. It was like a sea shell held there, only instead of the roar of the sea he heard the flow of his quickening blood.

She took his hand. "Come," she said, standing up. "'Let us arise and go now, and go to Innisfree.'" He didn't know what the strange phrase meant, only that like Jenny it was beyond his reach. She pulled him to his feet "Come. Let us arise and go now, and get the heck out of here."

He followed her across the road and down the shallow incline to the shore of the lake. They sat cross-legged facing the water. "At least here," she said, "you won't have to listen." She pointed above and behind them. "But we can still see the road, and we'll know when they come back."

The sun was exchanging glitter for color; you could stare at it without pain and already feel the air cooler in the shade. The lake's still surface was stippling with the bites of perch and sunnies. Across the lake, where water flowed out over the wooden boards of the makeshift dam, a lone eight year old intently watched the bit of twig that was his floater, attached to a rope, attached to the branch that was his fishing pole.

"Ever go fishing, little boy friend?"

Artie nodded towards the boy. "Only once, when I was just a kid. With a bent safety pin. I didn't even know you needed bait. I caught a fish anyway, a little tiny minnow. When I pulled it out of the water it was hooked through the eye."

Jenny squeezed his hand. She said, "I need to go fishing too. There's something of mine at the bottom of the lake."

"What is it?" he asked gently. "What's in there, Jenny?"

Her crooked smile was shadowed. She shook her head.

"Is that why you're always so sad?"

Just then he felt the older of the two. He turned and looked at her, openly and without timidity. For the first time he noticed the slight depression in her temple, just shy of the hairline, in the shape of a sickle. He didn't know it then as the sign of a forceps delivery, could only think it God's deliberate mark, a touch of imperfection to point up the loveliness. His eyes traced the shapely curve of the leg she hugged, leading into a sharp and strongly boned ankle, and he marveled at how she was made like this, of opposites, solid yet soft, strong yet so graceful. He felt his heart forcing its way up through his throat, the pressure moistening his eyes. He didn't even know it when his hand reached out to stroke her arm, the flesh soft and firm, golden down glistening.

Again that sad crooked smile. Like a prayer, a song without melody, she recited:

> "'The sea has its pearls,
> The heaven its stars,
> But my heart, my heart,
> My heart has its love.'"

He still caressed her arm. "What makes you so sad?"

"In this world," she said, "the choices are two. Sad or crazy. They think I'm crazy, and I would choose it every time, choose crazy because it's less painful. But so far I am only permitted sad."

She placed a hand on the back of his neck, playing with the longer hairs, pulling gently on them. She said, "All that's left of my love is out there at the bottom of the lake."

He saw a man floating beneath the surface, gazing sunward with empty eye sockets. "What do you mean?" he asked, afraid she would say.

But she only shook her head. And tried to smile, but her face contorted and tears glittered. She twisted his hair. He almost yelped with the ache of it, yet took it only as the measure of her own pain. And pitied her. Out of pity, scarcely conscious of it, he leaned over and for the barest instant touched his lips softly to hers, wanting only to suck out the hurt, transfer the pain. He couldn't know how it would be, breath of flowers, lips hot as the sun. Feelings of daring, fear, pity.

He thought her unaware of their touching; her move a bit away from him instinctual, like evading a pesky fly. She said, to no one in particular, as much to the tall weeds at the water's edge as to the swallow just then disturbing a nearby branch, "Just a little change of heart, and no longer am I his heart's love." She opened wide those surprising eyes. "Yes," she hissed, "yes, I know. Ophelia and me. Looney as bedbugs." Then a little wink and a pale smile wiped away madness. "Understand, little boy friend, please understand, we are not delusional here. Oh no, there really and truly was an engagement. Secret, of course. There was even a ring. With a diamond, if you please. Also secret. Everything secret. Easier to get out of it that way, you know."

She let herself fall back on an elbow. She closed her eyes. "It happens, change of heart can happen to anyone. But real pain is when you find out it's no change of heart at all, just part of a clever plan. Clever tricks to fool a trusting little girl. Stupid trusting girl."

Tears slid out from under shuttered eyelids. He wanted to ease her torment, pull her back from the edge. Longed to enfold her, kiss away the tears. Learn her body's secrets so as to unlock the mystery of her mind. He reached out haltingly, as if toward a fire. Lightly he touched the clothed breast of the unheeding girl, melted at its yielding. He pulled back instantly, in awe of unfathomable emotions.

Jenny's eyes flew open and she bolted upright. His heart skipped, anticipating outrage and retribution, but she only held up a forefinger to order silence, and froze into listening. He heard it too, then, a muttering swelling into a buzz, buzz exploding into exclamations. Jenny pointed towards the road atop the incline. He saw there only some of the tongue-cluckers. But then his mom and dad waltzed into view. Arms encircled waists, confounding all those disbelievers in the mystical power of love.

Jenny's gray eyes smiled, triumphant. "See? That was no quarrel about a silly card game. That, little boy friend, was an act of love." She smacked his rump. "Go on, go on." But he, dutiful son but also companion and confidant to a half-mad older woman, hesitated, pausing to weigh needs, allegiances, affections. "Go," she urged again with a little smile and a persuading nod. This time he obeyed. Half way up the incline he turned to look back at Jenny, saw her encouraging wave, went on. Up on the road he proudly marched behind his mom and dad, while before them the prophets of doom slunk away in search of other entertainments.

Once, Artie looked back over his shoulder. Jenny sat with chin resting on a drawn-up knee, staring at the lake. Regret tugged, but it was not out of generosity, and he felt no qualms about abandonment. Because how could it possibly matter to her? It was only that he missed that new feeling, that pitying, anxious, sweet feeling.

Artie couldn't find her again the whole remaining month of that season. Sadie Bleier still ran around repairing damage and prospecting in junk yards, but she carried no food down to the lake because Jenny was never there anymore. Once, only once, did he find Jenny, actually came face to face, but she walked right past him, her gaze fixed inwardly, and he couldn't tell if it was deliberate or if she truly did not see him. Nor would he call out, because by now he was too shy: after the closeness that one day, anything else could only seem estrangement.

By the following summer the recession had come. The Lavins didn't go away to the mountains, nor any summers after that.

III

In later years I sometimes thought about the tormented girl, and of how in that otherwise wasted summer she made of me a prodigy in the pain of love. When I did think about her, it always brought back that awful moment during a wintertime visit to the Gold's, a couple of years after that last season. Exclamation over Dora Gold's raven hair, shorn in sacrifice to the gods of style; exchange of gossip during the smoked whitefish salad and cheese cake; hearty laugh at the incident with the bat. Casual reference to Jenny's death. My parents expressed shock.

"You didn't know?" Dora said. "Drowned. They say she was looking for a ring she herself threw in. Maybe it was a cramp from being in the water so long. But who knows? A girl like that, who knows what she could do to herself?" I saw Jenny locked in weightless embrace with the man floating eyeless beneath the surface of the lake.

But by then I was fifteen, and survivor of the sweet torment of several infatuations. Survivor, too, of stark headlines about battlefield slaughter, of Movietone News images of young Americans dying in the snows of Asia. So I could look back at the thing with Jenny from a numbing distance, one small tragedy against a globe-full of disaster. A stab of regret for the poor girl, and then I was able to ease past the memory.

But now, decades later, overhanging the stone wall along that seldom-traveled road, the trees whispered like accusing ghosts. No, they hissed, it was nothing Jenny needed do herself, there were too many others around to do the job for her. Including a selfish, unthinking boy, troubling for no more than a single glance backward; persuaded by a wave of her hand into yet another abandonment of a soft-headed unloved older woman.

IV

My sister Rebecca, body by now slipping into betrayal, can accurately recall telephone numbers she hasn't used in forty years. I've told her that she must have scooped up all the cleverness in our gene pool, leaving me brain-disadvantaged. Proof is, my recollection of forty years ago is no better than of my forgotten yesterday, defying the conventional wisdom about memory's aging perversity.

From time to time she phones me from middle class heaven deep out on the Island. Mostly, the conversation winging over the miles of cable is devoted to an exchange of medical symptoms. Sometimes, though, we turn to bittersweet reminiscence, and when this happens Rebecca becomes a source book for my life.

"Do you remember Jenny Bleier?" I asked her the other day.

"Why shouldn't I?" she says sharply, miffed that I could doubt the persistence of her memory.

"And her mother?"

"A beautiful woman," she says.

"Beautiful? I remember her as gawky and raw boned. Features whittled out of a block of wood."

"No, Sadie had a tall slender figure, dark eyes, and she wore her hair in braids that coiled around her head."

"Jenny? I do remember clearly she was a very pretty girl."

"Pretty? Not bad, actually. Somewhat heavy around the thighs. And her eyes were a bit too close together. Maybe the boy friend found somebody prettier."

Are we both talking about the same people? "She threw the engagement ring into the lake, right?"

"Who knows if there even was a ring. They dredged out the lake, you know, but they could never find it."

I look to salvage a smidgen of confidence in my memory. "Jenny did kill herself, didn't she?"

"Oh yes," she says. "She killed herself all right."

"But how can anyone be sure? Maybe it was accidental."

"Since when is hanging accidental?"

"Hanging?"

"In the bathroom. Tied her neck to a steam pipe and then threw herself forward."

My mouth shifts into automatic pilot. "So how's your blood pressure? That new medicine helping any?"

I don't hear her response. I am thinking about how much our lives are steered by faulty memory; or maybe not faulty memory, but stories deliberately concocted to feed our needs, ease us past the dark ghost-ridden corners.

"What does your doctor say?" I ask. "Is he hopeful?"

I wonder what stories one of us will make up about the other.

Meditation from Thais

I was dying to learn enough violin to play a half decent Meditation from Thais, only my old man had me peddling chickens to cutthroat house-wives instead.

Deprivation was nothing new at our house. As far back as memory, a wet-eyed plea from me or my sister Gloria for anything beyond bare sustenance would get a thumbs down from my father and a canned speech, "Food you got? Clothes you got? A roof over your head I give you? What else do I owe you? Toys? Toys ain't in the contract."

Early on a Sunday morning, on the way back from an errand to the dairy store for the stuff of breakfast, paper bag of pumpernickel, lox, and cream cheese held against my chest and the change clinking in my pocket, I run into a couple of the guys already hanging around outside Cheap Izzy's. My friend Shelly lifts his face out of a Sunday News borrowed off the display rack, slides scorning eyes over me, then reinters his nose, rooting for news of Koufax and the Dodgers. Impetuously I snatch a News off the rack, fish a dime out of a jingling pocket, and toss it on the counter. Not me, I don't have to use Izzy's as a public library. A few steps on, doubt begins to degrade the impulse, but I reassure myself the family will enjoy a newspaper with their breakfast. Upstairs, though, my father shoves under my nose the early edition of the Sunday News he'd already bought the night before. "Go get back the money," he says. "Two copies we can't afford." The walk back feels like a ten days' forced march. Izzy hears out my explanation with a sneer. He tosses a dime on the counter. Luckily, Shelly is already gone.

We lived under a socialist constitution but a dictator's thumb. Friday nights, bringing home the smell of cigarettes and murdered cows, his clothes pin-cushioned with feathers, a bloody bandage around a finger or two, my father would tear open his pay envelope at the kitchen table. (Made anxious by nightmares about carelessly swung choppers, I'd glance nervously at his work-thickened fingers, fearing a stump.) He'd wet a thumb, count out some bills to cover subway fare and cigarettes for the next week, then hand the rest to my mother, who'd walk it across to the utility table. So we always knew where the money was, there in the unlocked drawer, and it was understood that anyone at all was free to make a withdrawal. To each according to his needs. Only no one ever took, except my mother for household expenses. Because we'd be spending sweat and blood.

In our living room, no larger than a generous closet, an oriental-style cabinet stood high-chested on tall thin legs, a Ming Dynasty emperor amid a lowly, listing tapestry sofa and two worn velvet chairs. I sometimes imagined the piece had been smuggled out of the east like a ruby scooped from an idol's eye socket. A coiled and menacing dragon carved into the ebony guarded each of its doors. Your hands itching with fear of the imminent dragons, you pulled on two ornate pendulous rings to open the doors and reveal a mysterious face formed by a tiny dial above two knobs, topped by a fan-shaped gap covered with green cloth.

One Sabbath evening, when the sun was already down but no one had yet stirred to switch on a light, my father got up from the sofa, pulled open the doors of the oriental radio, and clicked a knob. The dial gleamed like a malevolent eye in the night while we waited for the vacuum tubes to warm up. A sudden cry came from the hidden mouth. It transposed instantly into an ardent melody, an almost human voice singing of love and hope and longing, and of strange sweet and melancholy emotions I'd never yet experienced. Open-mouthed, I traced these undulations as gorgeous colors streaming across the dark, exploding in a palette of otherworldly sound. "You've been listening," the announcer stated importantly, "to the Meditation from the opera Thais by Jules Massenet, as performed by Jascha Heifetz."

I'd heard the name Heifetz before—who among us hadn't?—but knew of it only that it was spoken in reverence. In our house, music was tuned into only rarely, but affinity and respect for the violin was carried in the genes of all eastern Europeans, not just Heifetz and those other Odessans of enormous talent. I thought how marvelous it must be to construct such beauty, communicate such feeling, and be famous for it too. And how marvelous, too, if some day they'd turn on the oriental radio and it would be me playing the fiddle, and there'd be no more need for bloody fingers and stumps to be nervous about. Still believing in dreams and choices, I resolved then and there to forge myself into another Heifetz, unaware that at fourteen that most remote of possibilities had already, long ago, passed me by.

In those days, butchers were well paid, so it wasn't as if the pinched pennies rescued us from having to sleep with somebody's doorstep for a pillow. But such a fine wage, hundred and a quarter a week, wasn't for just carving meat and smiling at the customers. No, you earned your pay—hung on to the job—by creating extra profits for the boss. And none of that thumb-on-the-scale nonsense either. The true artist worked with a scalpel, not an axe. All it took was his own quick mind and a calculating skill unmatched until the microchip. Not even bothering to scrawl the reckoning on a paper bag, the artist would toss the meat or chicken on the scale, showily remove his hands, (look ma, no thumbs), and in a flash sweep off the merchandise and announce the weight in sixteenths (inflated), price per pound, and total cost (inflated even further).

Easy? Try it sometime: juggle eighths and sixteenths while the pointer still shivers and then tack on another eighth or two and multiply all that by the price, and splice in a few more cents for good measure, and almost instantaneously call out the total with authority, so that the befuddled housewife can't do anything but pay up and stumble out.

When I begged money for the violin I got THE SPEECH and the advice to get a job. Which I would have done gladly, only where's a job after school? The only taker was Roff, the neighborhood druggist, willing for me to sweep up, lug cartons up from the cellar, and deliver prescriptions on foot within a twenty block radius for a buck a night plus tips, but I'd already tried that a couple of years before, and in those tenements it was hard enough to pay for the medicine, let alone a tip.

"Who don't know Maxie Lavin?" my father the artist would say, as if referring to a third party. "What boss wouldn't fire his workingman just to make room for Maxie Lavin?"

The subject of quitting his job would invariably arise after a rare evening out with the boss and his missus. My mother dreaded the company of Phil and Sadie Becker at, say, a formal gathering of bosses and their employees to honor the President of Local 227 of the Meat Cutters and Poultry Workers Union for thirty years of high living off the members' dues. Phil Becker, who resembled one of the Three Stooges, the one with a bald spot between flying tufts, was a horse player who dressed for even formal gatherings as if he'd just hopped off the last freight from Milwaukee. Tie divorced from collar, trouser cuffs underfoot, he'd quickly guzzle enough Wild Roses to pickle consciousness, then sit all evening with a loopy little smile, staring glassy-eyed at the carnations in the centerpiece. Sadie, who could impersonate a tackle for the Packers, would uphold the family honor by nattering enough for both of them. Her repartee with the table's half dozen tuxedos and flounced gowns would be studded with superlatives for my father, most of them packed in references to him as "Phil's worker" or "our workingman." As in, "Our Maxie here, such an artist with the scale, he could take off the customer's panties and she wouldn't even know. Just ask Phil." Phil would be smiling at the centerpiece, most likely dreaming it the nosegay on his 80–1 bet that just won the Derby. "Phil, ain't Maxie the best man we ever had?" This public declaration that our family owed its living to a drunk and a loudmouth would drive my mother to the edge of tears.

My mother's dream was for my father to be his own boss, so she wouldn't any longer have to hear Sadie Becker giving herself airs.

And my father's dream? His own shop, so the artistry would be for himself, not the horse player.

Sometimes, among buddies at a comedy or musical at the movie palace on Saturday night, I'd feel my throat tighten in awareness that back in the apartment my parents were leaning motionless on sills facing the dark street, prisoners of self-imposed economic restraint. Saving up for their dreams.

And what about Shelly, what is his dream?

My friend Shelly was built in miniature, five-five or so, and he walked chest out, stomach in, neck stretched as high as his spine would allow. He had black wavy hair, a chiseled profile, and a toothpaste smile, and his horn rimmed glasses gave him intelligence. He was always fiddling with some part of himself—running a comb through his hair, polishing his glasses, inspecting his fingernails, blowing his nose and then examining the hankie—a superior being ever on the alert for sneaking imperfections.

But he was hardly special. Like mine, his parents weren't that long out of the old country: trouble with the language, menial jobs, pinching pennies to accumulate a stake. His father wore thick glasses, sat all day in a dry cleaner's window sewing alterations. Shelly made fun of him, and of his battleship of a mother, his fat-ankled sister, his little brother whose thick lips sprayed when he talked. Generosity of spirit? Forget it. If one of our gang of social misfits managed to negotiate a group blind date, Shelly would refuse to join in if it wasn't dutch. Not even a cup of coffee would he buy a girl unless it came with a guarantee she'd put out.

Still, Shelly too was an artist and dreamer. Only, as with my father, it wasn't art for art's sake; Shelly's art and dreams had to do with proving he, Sheldon Saperstein, was a cut above. He'd even already picked out his future name for when he became famous: Ian Shelburne. Question was, what could he become famous for?

Just as I got into college, a butcher shop—a pretty good one, 3,000 pounds a week—came on the market. Even with all that penny pinching my father had only half of the $3,500 needed, but he'd found someone willing to come in as a partner. Our debate was torturous. All of us, including even my sister Gloria, two years younger, weighed pros and cons, balancing risk and reward, dream fulfillment against the chance of going broke and having to start all over again. It was the thought of Phil and Sadie Becker that finally tipped the scales. My father took on the partner and became half a boss.

Shelly, whose grades weren't too hot anyway, decided to bypass college in favor of the quick buck. In vocational school he studied court stenography. He showed the guys the steno machine standing in a corner of his bedroom. Sleek and black and supported by a thin pole, it resembled a beheaded robot, with white keys its teeth, and a lolling paper tongue. But that was for days. Nights were for his art and dreams. Tuesdays he took oil painting at the local high school. The other nights he shut himself in his room, daubing away, watched over by the steno machine smiling away in the corner. So Shelly studied steno and painting, while I studied French, modern European history, and selling chickens.

Each weekday after the last class I'd lug my books to the subway and ride the train to Brighton Beach. In the shop under the el I'd mostly spend the three hours doing homework, leaning Modern European History on a chopping block and trying to disregard the customers, the roar of the train overhead, and the racket of the shoppers milling out-side in the shadow-striped street.

I couldn't understood why I was there. Fractions threw me, and I loathed the dealing in slaughtered animals. My role was supposedly backup: when the crush of customers became too much for the part-ners I could take cash at the register, sweep out, even sell a chicken or two. Only the crush never developed.

Still, I did get an assignment once in a while. "It's almost time," my father might say late on Friday. "I'll go start cleaning up. If a customer comes in, you take care of her."

After five, one of the scavengers sails in. I lift a feathered carcass out of the open casework. My father's eyes are fixed on me while he brooms sawdust. Amid a pile of feathers just inside the plate glass window, the seated chicken plucker, an apron across her tattered coat, also watches, anxious to earn another quarter. Avoiding the skeptical eyes of the elderly shopper, I mimic my father's usual patter with an enthusiasm that rings false to both buyer and seller. "Look at that breast!" and displace the gray feathers of a bird stiff with rigor mortis, smelling of spilled life, its neck dangling like a piece of rope. "Look at that color, like sweet cream. Only fifteen minutes ago this little beauty was still running around clucking."

With a sneer, "How much?"

"Twenty-two cents a pound."

An indignant jerk of the black vinyl shopping bag hanging from her forearm. "Seventeen you'll also take."

"What!? For this little beauty? See that color?"

"Yeah. Sure. So what it died from, TB?"

A glance at my father. This late on Friday, the only shoppers will be such cutthroats, counting on this hour of his desperation; but then, unsold merchandise will anyway lose value stored in the freezer over the weekend. I get a nod.

"All right, so take it already for twenty."

"Seventeen. Not a penny more."

"You want me to lose money on the deal yet? "

"You wanna eat it yourself?"

With a sigh, "All right already. Here, go ahead, take it, seventeen."

I lift the dead bird to the scale, its head lolling over the side, my hands trembling with complicity in its murder. When the needle stops I call out the weight, watching her for approval. She whines in disbelief, "How much?"

I repeat, "Six pounds and six sixteenths."

She studies the scale. Then her arm droops in defeat.

I put pencil to a paper bag and set out to multiply 6 6/16 by .17. My tongue sticks out the corner of my mouth, anxious to help. After crossings out and restartings I tell her, with little confidence, a dollar nineteen.

"That can't be right," she sneers. "Call over your father."

My father drops the broom and strolls over. "What is it, little mother?" he smiles. "He didn't charge you enough?"

Like other customers, she too, the old lady, is captivated by his dark good looks, his act: Maurice Chevalier in an apron, cap instead of straw hat. Her old eyes spark. "A dollar nineteen?" she wheedles flirtatiously. "That can't be right."

My father takes the pencil from my hand, scribbles on the paper bag, then looks up. "A dollar nineteen," he says conclusively. "Is that what my little genius said?" She and I both nod, suddenly allies. "Sure," he says, "a college boy already, he should make a mistake?"

She pays up and walks out with her prize. There is pride in my father's smile. "Good. You did good, my college boy. You used to be not such a hot figurer, but two months college, already an Einstein."

At this applause my heart sinks. "A dollar nineteen ain't right?"

"Right? Better than right." He reaches back to untie his apron. But then he suddenly gets it. "Oh. So it was only a mistake?" Sorrow shakes his head. "Still you don't know how to figure? What do they learn you there in college? How to shtup girls? And don't look at me like that. What's the matter, it's a terrible thing I should get back a little? You think from seventeen cents a pound I can make a living ?"

One night we followed Shelly up to his apartment, invited to the unveiling of a masterpiece.

The three of us filed past his father, bifocals at the end of his nose, basting a pants cuff at the kitchen table, and his older sister Lena, exposed legs haphazardly strewn, trimming her toe nails on the horsehair sofa in the tiny living room. We preceded Shelly across the threshold of his bedroom while he delicately blew his nose, clearing his passages for the big moment. At the foot of his bed, facing away from us, an easel shouldered a framed canvas.

Davey said, "It's at least a nood, I hope?"

Herbie smacked him on the side of the head, their Bowery Boys routine. "C'mon, respect the artist here. Okay, Rembrandt, what d'ya got?"

Shelly picked off the canvas and held it focused to catch the light from the ceiling fixture. Under glass we saw what looked like a cross with arms doubled. A white sliver sat in one of the dark blue spaces between the arms. We said nothing, not knowing what to say. Shelly said, "It's a study of the moon through that window."

"You coulda fooled me," Marty sneered, " I thought it was a rat caught in a trap."

Refusing to waste emotion on insensitive perverts, Shelly willed himself calm. Patiently he explained, "You gotta look at the composition, color sense, all those things." And he pointed out how the beige of the wood complemented the blue of the sky; how the placement of the moon right there in that one corner was damn genius, in the freakin' perfect spot to balance out the whole rest of the picture.

Just as Shelly's glasses gave him intelligence, the wooden frame and glass covering gave the picture professionalism. But even an ignoramus like me could tell it was a strictly no-talent affair. It was signed in flowing script, 'Ian Shelburne', a work of ambition, not art.

Near to closing time, Meyer Schneider, the partner and designated outside man, arrives. Rolling in on bandy legs inside a medic's white trousers, the little man wears the constant smile of a lover of humanity or a simpleton. The inside man winks at me, then darts fainting eyes to heaven, making clear his opinion.

"So, Max? We got anything left over?"

"Listen," my father says. "Even if every yenta in Brighton Beach took three chickens, we would still have plenty left over. How come you bought so much, Meyer?"

"Not so much," the outside man shrugs. "Remember last Friday? We sold out everything, we didn't even have enough. And such a good buy I got this morning. Thirteen cents a pound."

"Sure," the inside man says, "thirteen cents is good. But how much, Meyer, how much did you buy?"

Meyer shrugs. "Only six hundred pounds. Just a hundred more than last Friday."

"So you know how much is left over, Meyer?" My father raises his arms and then brings them down to thwack against his sides, a Jimmy Durante routine sans the humor. "Is left a hundred pounds!"

Meyer abruptly turns to me, closing off the cross examination. "So, college boy," he says, "you sold a lot of chickens today? Your father learns you the business good, huh? Listen to your father, he knows the business inside out."

"Okay, Mr. Schneider."

As if I want to be there.

We weren't invited to any more exhibits. Neither did Shelly lock himself in his room, nights; he had more time to hang around now.

He spent his free hours researching the windows of the men's shops away over on the Avenue, shirts, ties, jackets pinned to fancy displays like collections of butterflies. He of course didn't have the money, especially at those prices, but when he'd somehow get his old man to part with a few bucks his buying decision was as deliberate as some other guy's marriage decision. The adornment of his body was substituting for the adornment of his name, and the work of art was himself.

This period of reassessment ended about six months later. Shelly knocked on our door one night and waved some sheets of paper at me. "Here," he said. "What do you think of my story?" It was like volunteering homework that hadn't been assigned, and I was impressed by such initiative. But the smirk on his face told of having pulled off what was too difficult for the rest of us slobs, and it made me want him to fail. I was determined to lie if it was any good.

When he left I dropped onto the living room sofa. On lined paper torn from a notebook, the words were scrawled with a blunt pencil. I'd devoured enough of the contents of the Stone Avenue public library to judge that what I read now was totally inept. What you write before you have anything to say. "The Chess Players" was about some old men who meet regularly in the park, and one day a couple of them get into a fight. It was plotless and had fake dialogue. I did not have to lie.

Shelly made only one more attempt, a few years later, and this time it wasn't for fame or even to establish superiority. We were both just finished with school, he working at his steno, I on my first job as an ad agency copywriter, and both still lived at home because beginners' paychecks in those days weren't intended to provide for both food and rent. One winter evening he knocked on our door. In his pea coat, collar up, and carrying a violin case, he resembled a miniaturized Mafioso out on a contract job.

In the living room he tore off his coat, opened the case, and pulled out a violin so desiccated it might have lain out in the weather for a half century. Still, it did have four strings. From the case he drew out the sheet music for Schubert's Serenade, a square of resin for the bow strings, and a pitch pipe on which he blew an "A," then adjusted the "A" string to more or less match it. All set, he tucked the violin under his chin, crossed it with the bow in his right hand, and sawed out shrieks only sporadically interspersed with detectable notes.

"So what do you think?" he said. "I'm only playing a month."

I said, "Not bad, especially for only a month."

I had never actually held a violin. I took it from his hand. Cradling it in my arm I looked at the scroll work, the convoluted carvings in the bridge, the stem curled up at its end. I sensed music anxious to escape. There must have been something in my face because Shelly silently offered me the bow. I drew it gingerly across the strings, producing the shrieks of an animal in pain. But the fit of the violin was like a lost love returned to my arms. Reluctantly I handed it back. "You gonna become another Heifetz?"

He shook his head. "This ain't for Heifetz. This is for me." He looked at me straight, and for the first time ever I saw his face naked of rivalry. "I need to be good at something." He examined the floor, and I was sure he blushed. "It sings to me."

The twenty buck violin came from a pawn shop downtown, and the music lessons from the Sutter Avenue Music School. We agreed he would go with me to the pawn shop for a violin, and I would join him in the music school for lessons.

For once we'd be heading in the same direction.

The music school was in a loft over a Chinese restaurant. The principal, a big-bellied pipe smoker, asked four weeks' tuition in advance, four dollars. He wrote out a receipt in careful script, made a notation in a composition book, and scheduled me for the seven-thirty session on Wednesdays with Mr. Spielfogel. This was convenient, because Shelly's session every Wednesday was for the half hour directly preceding, also with Mr. Spielfogel who, as it turned out, was the only violin teacher on the faculty.

My first session was of course introductory. I'd been sitting in the waiting room, listening through the thin classroom door to Shelly's lesson, a series of agonized screams from the violin interspersed with little cries of pain from the teacher. At seven-thirty Shelly stumbled out with a sheepish smile, sweat beaded on his forehead. Mr. Spielfogel waved me in. I walked past him into a room furnished with a baby grand, a piano bench, a bentwood chair, and smoke-filled air as tangible as the furniture. Mr. Spielfogel motioned me into the chair and lighted up a cigarette, inhaling deeply. He was maybe forty, short and thin to emaciation; his popping eyes, glancing everywhere at once, yet dulled as in death, seemed to be recollecting horrors. Holding the cigarette between his second and third fingers, he posed questions about my prior experience with the instrument, was I going to school or working, was Shelly my friend, did I have a family.

He tapped the cigarette towards the jelly glass on the piano lid but missed, and the long ash accreted itself to the mound already surrounding the glass. Mr. Spielfogel's quid pro quo for the irrelevancies he'd drawn from me was to relate a summary autobiography. A refugee from the concentration camps, he'd formerly been a member of one of the great European orchestras. Now he was hoping for an orchestra post, but in the meantime earned his living as a teacher.

He dropped his cigarette butt into the jelly jar, and taking my bow briefly demonstrated how to hold it, thumb inside and the other fingers out. He barely waited for me to jot down the titles of exercise books he snapped out impatiently.

He opened the case resting on the piano lid. The violin he lifted out of purple velvet sparkled; compared to our twenty buck jobs it looked magical, as if playing it would be like pulling the sword out of the stone. Setting his stance, he tucked the violin under his chin and shut his eyes.

The skimming bow coaxed angels into singing of promises and possibilities; my heart brimmed with beauty and awe. Finished, he lovingly reset the violin in velvet. My half hour was up. With what seemed a certain disdain, he pointed to the door.

Some Friday nights, now, there were fewer dollars to slip into the utility drawer than when my father had worked for the horse player. Shoulders drooping, mouth turned down in embarrassment and defeat, he'd tell my mother they couldn't go on much longer, he'd picked a partner with no judgment whatsoever. Meyer Schneider, the outside man, was ruining the business with his ridiculous buying—wrong quantities, bad prices.

He's such a nice man, always smiling, my mother would say, and my father would nod, sure, idiots always smile, but he's killing us. They'd discuss switching my father to the outside, have him do the buying, but then conceded Schneider couldn't sell bread to a starving man, let alone chickens to cutthroats.

Sometimes, practicing, I'd feel sorry for Heifetz. I'd be sawing away, producing industrial noises, and suddenly out of this caterwauling would rise one brief clear sweet note. Even Heifetz himself couldn't ever again experience the thrill and promise of that first unexpected note, could he? And maybe prodigies are too immediately competent to have the chance for it anyway. Later, when the good notes came more frequently and finally joined together in a tentative but discernible melody, it was like ecstatic release after years of foreplay begun with that first Meditation on the oriental radio.

In no time at all, just a few months, I could play pizzicato, legato, staccato, sixty-fourths, and all sorts of fancy stuff, including a recognizable Brahms' Hungarian Dance, and I was ready to forge ahead to the other seven positions of the violin. I fantasized about what I might have become if I'd started early enough, to say nothing of having sufficient practice, because I was putting in so much overtime at the agency. But being a realist I settled for a more reasonable goal: to just learn that Heifetz piece that got me into it in the first place. Just a half decent Meditation, and I'd be satisfied.

Mr. Spielfogel would sit listening to me perform the homework exercise, cigarette smoke curling around his head, eyes focused on a corner of the ceiling, plainly wanting to be far away from this idiocy. Puffing away, eyes distant, he would disinterestedly bark out, "Legato, legato!" or "Pizzicato!" "Allright, good," was his signal that the exercise was over. He would motion me to sit down. "So tell me, Mr. Er—Er, how was your week?" I would assure him it went fine.

"Good," he would nod approvingly, "good." Having patiently observed the obsequies, like in a Japanese tea ceremony, it was now proper to conduct his business. This consisted of the recitation of various anxieties from his new and unaccustomed life. Mostly, his angst was provoked by an unending series of failures with the opposite sex. He was outraged by the ungrateful women of America, who would refuse to do certain little things for a man even after he'd bought them dinner. He'd conclude this portion of the lesson with a tortured little smile, "Better to stay home and use the fingers, no?"

Four o'clock one morning, Meyer Schneider leaves his house for the daily buying expedition to the meat market. The meat and poultry business being all cash, he carries four hundred dollars in his pocket. In the dark street a young man pops out of nowhere and asks him for a light. When Schneider reaches into his pocket the young man stuns him with a blow to the head, probably a lead pipe wrapped in cloth. Schneider isn't badly hurt, but a good portion of the partners' capital is now gone. After, relating the experience, he still smiles.

Our careers weren't going too well. Shelly was bored with his steno. The violin had become an obsession, devouring his time. Periodically he'd ask me up to audit him, and his playing was becoming more dexterous and assured, the pieces recognizable. I suspected that dissatisfaction with his steno was proportionate to his success with the violin: although really very modest, it was proof that he could aim higher.

As for me, it was tough going at the agency. Each word was clawed out of rock with bleeding fingers, and I was pretty well convinced that I lacked the imagination to be a good copywriter. I suspected that my old dream was more practical than I'd realized, that I should have been a musician after all, playing works created by people with imagination.

For me, then, and probably for Shelly too, the violin bridged our season of discontent and the better times hopefully to follow.

Six months into the lessons, Mr. Spielfogel listened to my homework exercise, smoke curling about his head. After, he motioned me to the chair, impatiently ran through the tea ceremony, and then set off on the recitation of his most recent woes with the fair sex. He had decided that rather than retrenchment, as he'd been threatening, the road to success lay in profligacy. So he'd taken this woman to a classy place, Luchow's on Fourteenth Street, and they'd ordered a full menu, even pastry and liqueurs. Afterwards, back at her house, she thanked him for a lovely evening, but refused to oblige.

"Can you imagine," he bleated, "she would not even suck me off a little."

I shook my head in sympathy. He sadly nodded the usual coda, "Better to stay home with the fingers, no?"

This was ordinarily my signal to get up and scratch away at some new exercise. But this time he motioned me back into the chair, dropped his cigarette stub into the jelly glass, and from its case lifted his gleaming violin. He tucked it under his chin, closed his eyes, and spun the glorious slow movement from the Mendelssohn concerto. (Recognizable to me because he'd assigned a simplified version of the opening melody.) I could tell no difference between Spielfogel and Heifetz.

Finished, he lifted off the bow but kept his eyes closed for a long moment, reluctant to return. Then he slowly opened his eyes and fixed them on me. He said, "Your friend—what is his name?"

"Shelly," I said.

"Yes, Shelly," he repeated. "You are good friends with Shelly, no?"

I shrugged. "Sure."

"You like the violin, no?"

I smiled, because the answer was so obvious. "Sure."

"And your friend, he also likes the violin, no?"

"Yes," I said. "Sure."

He fixed me with a bulging eye. "Two nice boys together," he nodded a little smile of scorn, tolerance, pity. "With violins yet. Is better than girls, no?"

I told Shelly I quit the lessons because work at the agency left me with too little time to practice. As for him, some cutie soon ensnared him, and he had no more worry about a career: her father wanted him in the wholesale egg business. The violin stopped singing to him, struck dumb by such unexpected good fortune.

They were forced to close the shop. They just couldn't make a profit; they were too incompatible, a partner who was so intense and one who was always smiling.

There was no more boasting about anybody firing their man for the chance to hire Maxie Lavin. My father went back to practicing his artistry for a boss, although not Phil Becker. He often talked of how he'd surely have been a success, if only he'd had a good outside man.

It could be said that of all of us, only Shelly succeeded in his artistic ambition. Not until much later—years later—did I realize the extent to which he had left his mark on me. The things of interest to my life, that matter beyond the mundanities of existence—music, painting, and the writing of bad stories—had all come to me out of his strivings within our rivalry. So in that sense I am truly his creation, and he had every right to inscribe his 'Ian Shelburne' on my forehead. Even if, or especially because, I am as imperfectly realized as any of his other creations.

I never did learn a decent Meditation.

Goodbye Mr. Hogan

Audrey Hepburn and Winston Churchill, Mr. Hogan counted out. Einstein, Clark Gable. My father, my beautiful mother; Aunt Catherine. FDR. Even now, a half dozen years retired, he still thought of himself as 'Mister Hogan,' the way he'd been addressed by forty generations of his prep school classes. Mr. Hogan, as in 'Goodbye, Mr. Chips.'

Gustav Mahler, Lenny Bernstein. My cousin Rosie, who owned my heart at twelve.

On this first really great morning of spring, Sunday in Washington Square Park, the small creatures came venturing out of winter to celebrate the universe and its Creator. Around his bench, squirrels skittered in fits and starts, zigs and zags, then bounded up the trees to leap about the greening choir lofts. As for the birds, Mr. Hogan hoped they weren't herniating themselves, yodeling hallelujahs that way at the top of their tiny lungs.

On a bench across the path, a boy in t-shirt and jeans sat combing the hair of an identically dressed girl lying pillowed in his lap. Mr. Hogan guessed them university students recovering from a night of debauchery. For at least the half hour he'd been watching, and presumably even before that, the boy had been running a comb through the long and burnished auburn hair with his right hand, while his alternating left stroked the cascade lovingly. Intermittently, he gathered its ends and held the bunch tenderly, like a small animal with sleek pelt glinting in the sunlight. Any utilitarian purpose of the combing had already long been accomplished, and Mr. Hogan knew that in its persistence was the solicitude of love. In proof, a young Asian couple, classified by him as tourists, the woman palely beautiful, sidled over to the bench nearest the boy and girl, as if to observe a rite indigenous only to the Borough of Manhattan, south of 14th Street. They sat transfixed by this personification of a rare and transcendent ideal.

But for Mr. Hogan the sight was a reminder of how he'd been readying himself to die.

George and Ira Gershwin. William Faulkner. Bogart. Sigmund Freud.

Not that he was thinking of sucking on a shotgun a la Hemingway, although increasingly such an exit seemed a most timely and emphatic statement. Damned fitting, to throw his life back into the face of its unheedful Creator. "Here! Take it, do me no favors with this ridiculous existence in Your absurd world." But he could only sneer at this notion of self destruction, because he'd already hung on too long for that. As an act of defiance now it would just be ludicrous, throwing back such a decrepit, wrinkled, liver-spotted carcass.

Fred and Ginger. Benny Goodman. Picasso.

Mr. Hogan was getting tired of sitting on the bench. It's starting to hurt my bony ass, was the way he put it to himself. He got a small charge out of expressing himself inelegantly, so at variance was it with the persona he'd built up over the years. Tall and spare, ramrod straight, he'd peer down contemptuously past his patrician nose at his adolescents. Amazing, how effective this stance had been in driving english literature into otherwise oblivious skulls. Like a rigidly false smile, that habit of a stern aloofness persisted, and so even now, easeful Sunday in the park, his hair whitely crowned a navy blazer, cream shirt, rep tie, knife-creased gray trousers, and gleaming black shoes.

He was about to rise when the girl suddenly lifted her head from the boy's lap. The two stood up. The sight shocked Mr. Hogan's eyes, much as his ears might have been insulted by a false note in a lovely little string quartet.

They were pudgies! Within a shaft of sunlight they embraced heavily, rigid as death, tight as a merging of souls. Mr. Hogan saw their movements as hardly more agile than a couple of baby hippos. Theirs was a comic image of love; he blushed to think how they'd fooled him. But then the girl stepped back a bit. She grasped the thick hair curtaining one eye and, aided by a toss of her head, swept it flowing over her shoulder. That single fluid motion struck Mr. Hogan as the distillation of all the world's feminine grace, and he saw that his first impression had been right, that this dance of the pudgies was, after all, the true stuff of poetry. Behold thou art fair, my love; behold, thou art fair; Thine eyes are as doves behind thy veil. But then his hand swung out in a disdainful arc, dismissing that silly constriction of his throat.

He shook his head pityingly. The foolish little ones thought they were engaged in foreplay to lifelong ecstasy; they didn't yet realize that opening up to love leaves you more vulnerable to pain and sorrow.

Mr. Hogan sometimes saw himself as a neutral country surrounded by a world at war, because he'd succeeded in fencing out all intrusive emotions. It was early tragedy that had so cordoned him off. In adolescence, his lovely younger brother Gerald, dazzlingly bright, at fourteen already seriously preoccupied with the great problems of metaphysics, waited one morning for the elevator in their hi-rise. The door slid open prematurely. Gerald, no doubt immersed in thought, stepped forward into nothingness.

The sight of each other become only a reminder of the ridiculous, unbearable loss, Alfred's parents ran off on their separate ways, abandoning him to a grandmother. And all this, while millions were dying in war and pestilence. Lost and frightened, his view of self as the target of malevolence, the studious boy searched libraries for answers but got back only his own questions prettily disguised. Until he met up with a Roman emperor. From across the centuries, Marcus Aurelius Antoninus agreed that our stay is all too brief and without significance. In a few tight pages adorned only with his modesty, the emperor convinced young Alfred Hogan that happiness consists in accepting what is, in heeding logic rather than emotion and, above all, in the avoidance of pain.

"Wipe out imagination," Marcus Aurelius advised. "Check desire. Extinguish appetite." Mr. Hogan was persuaded that love and caring could only be an invitation to unhappiness, and his contacts with women were sporadic and brief, at rare but urgent times just a hasty business transaction. And so this life Mr. Hogan could now no longer bear had on the whole been little troubled by either pain or joy.

It was enough for him: the newsprint smell of his morning Times, crosstown strolls through the succession of villages making up the city, season tickets to a seat near the ceiling of the opera, weekly dinner at the neighborhood Italian restaurant.

Only in the last couple of years had things begun to unravel. Mr. Hogan found himself beset by a series of afflictions that seemed intended to degrade each body part in its turn. Aching joints, liver spots, and memory lapses once experienced became permanent. He was sure that the auto manufacturers had lifted the concept of planned obsolescence from the example of the Creator's flimsy engineering of man. If this body were an auto, Mr. Hogan told himself, I'd now be at the crossover point, where it is more sensible to scrap the machine than maintain it.

So he prepared for the crossover. With the help of a lawyer plucked from the Yellow Pages, he bequeathed his modest estate to the aid of little fools who'd chosen emotion over common sense: a nearby home for unwed mothers. The will provided as well for cremation, with the ashes to be tossed into any convenient wind.

Rubenstein, Mitropoulos, Heifetz, he would count out, concentrating this time on musicians. Richter, Oistrakh, Casals. The planet hoards its treasures by burying them. All the finest and most talented, who fed our very souls, are dead. And all the saints and sages. My beautiful little brother Gerald. Chagall, Cezanne, Matisse (going on to artists). All of them members of a club I should feel privileged to join.

Spring morning in Washington Square. Sun dappling through soft air, birds singing, couples solicitous and embracing. Mr. Hogan sank into a moment of such tranquility that he counted it as a validation of the road taken.

It startles him when behind his drooping lids a soldier and his girl suddenly rise into life. The image is as fresh and real as if it hadn't been languishing decades in a musty corner of his memory:

He'd be maybe eleven or twelve. World at war. Miles from home in another park, huge and named for a grafting mayor. In the winesap air of autumn their gang, four or five truants, racing, shouting, leaping. Eventually, the sun beginning to sink, breath coming harder, the pace through the park slows as they start the weary journey homeward.

Alfred Hogan is the straggler. A chance twist of his head, and his eyes are caught by that other sight. On the canvas of memory it lies flat now, like a primitive painting. In its upper left quadrant the sun sinking duskward, in its upper right the military cemetery, flag writhing mournfully above row upon neat row of those killed for country. In the foreground, a couple seated on a bench. Soldier in olive uniform, bill of his cap askew enough to reveal dark curly hair; girl dressed for an important date: black coat with little fur collar, black pumps shining, hair carefully groomed. They sit pressed together, her hand in his resting on her thigh, his other arm encircling her waist loosely, as if not daring more. Her mouth reaches for his. Her throat, her terrifyingly lovely naked throat, stretched so taut as to reveal its delicate bone structure, swallows as if drinking his soul. Giving herself to him fully clothed, on a bench overlooking the clean white markers of those who might too have sat here like this, in youth and love and despair.

Within the Sunday peace of Washington Square, Mr. Hogan felt the punch of an extra heartbeat, then a flood of emotions like a fifth of 90 proof poured down his throat, setting his heart afire, choking him to tears.

The beautiful pudgies sat down again holding hands; the Asian couple were reflected in each other's smiles; squirrels cavorted, dogs tugged exuberantly on their leashes. Mr. Hogan jumped up and hurried stiffly out of the park.

Experience had taught Mr. Hogan that unwanted emotions could be drowned in music like kittens in water. So now, crossing the small neat living room, two walls of thronged book shelves, he made straight for the stereo system hiding much of the farthest wall. When the changer tray slid open his eyes grazed the Beethoven Pastoral, which he admired, but was there for his insomnia; the Mozart Mass in C, for a taste of the devotion felt by those who could still believe; Puccini's arias for when the blood called. Needing its dispassionate truth, its singular voice of unadorned intellect, he depressed the button for the Bach Sonatas and Partitas.

Milstein's fiddle pierced the air. Mr. Hogan shucked off his blazer and slipped off his tie. A couple of steps into the kitchen he stooped to the refrigerator to extract an emerald bottle. Back in the living room, he swaddled himself with the easy chair to sip the ale.

Although music filled in the little emptinesses, it sometimes threatened to move him to unwanted places. But Bach was all right, Bach was safe. Sipping with eyes closed, the base of his skull pleasantly anesthetizing, he watched the baroque master's mathematically determined notes leap about, intent on randomly touching every point on a large and complex graph.

But then suddenly Mr. Hogan tore open his eyes, set down the bottle, and jumping up strode out of the room. In his bedroom, furnishings of a monk's cell, he pulled open the door of the walk-in closet. Shadowed by clothes hanging in orderly rows, the far half of its floor was covered with a jumble of luggage, bulging paper bags, and packages wrapped in twine. Stooping, Mr. Hogan scrabbled through the mass with the zeal and ferocity of a dog excavating for a cherished bone. He snatched up bags, peered an instant into each, identified it as holding bank statements or paid bills or tax returns, then discarded it; tore the twine off each package for a quick scan, hasty retying, and tossing onto the pile.

When only the two pieces of luggage remained, he stood up, arched his back to relieve the strain of bending, hiked up his trousers to unburden its creases, then knelt again. He drew one valise closer, unfastened its snaps, and lifted the cover. It was empty. Of course, he sneered impatiently, it couldn't ever be the first one, that would be against the law. He dragged over the remaining suitcase. The lid flew up to reveal two large manila envelopes. The first disgorged some photos, cancelled passports, a birth certificate, a death certificate, and his father's eyeglasses. Mr. Hogan hesitated, then raised the horn-rimmed glasses toward the light. He drew out his handkerchief, carefully wiped the glasses clear, and slipped them back into the envelope. He lifted the flap of the second envelope. Letters spilled out in a pale blue fall. He gathered them up and carried them back to the living room.

Mr. Hogan dropped into the easy chair to sort the letters into chronological order. It was a shock of dismay to find that the earliest postmark was already so far into the past, a barely legible April 14, 1968.

Is it presumptuous to write you like this? I would not have the courage if I did not sense that you are so unhappy. We are only co-workers, but your unhappiness weighs on me. I so admire the way you put a brave face on it. Is there anything I can do to help? Perhaps just sharing it would mean something.

He still remembered the outrage with which he'd read this fatuous note from a young lady with whom he'd exchanged nothing but indifferent smiles in the corridors between classes. Unhappy? Would she have expected him to go dancing down the street, *then*? Victoria Ellman taught biology, and he was tempted to tell her that yes, that note damned well was presumptuous, and she should stick to dissecting lobsters and piglets instead of perfectly content teachers of literature.

He'd recalled then the cautionary words of Marcus Aurelius: "…I shall meet with the busybody, the ungrateful, arrogant, deceitful, envious, unsocial…." But since they are all kin to me, the emperor reasoned, how then shall I be angry with my own kin? So conceding maybe he expected too much of others, Mr. Hogan had pardoned the intrusion, only to then abruptly drop the philosophical stance when he was struck by one of those notions that at the time seem clever and opportune and *right*. If the little fool is so drawn to unhappiness, it went, why not give her her own personal share of it?

It was no tough assignment, because Victoria was a most attractive young lady. Naive, perhaps, and made a bit silly by infatuation, but by no means an airhead. Just needful. So needful that it would be a pushover.

Yes, he wrote back, yes, it was true he was unhappy, how perceptive of her to be able to see through him like that! And yes, it might indeed help to have someone share his burden. Might they meet somewhere, perhaps over dinner, to discuss it further?

In short weeks the biology teacher steered them over a swift course from dinner companions to confidants and then to lovers. Spoon-cradling her, his arms tight around in the way she insisted on, her cool smoothness melting in his hands, he would lie staring contemptuously at the fragrant mass of black hair ornamenting her misguided mind, drowning the pillow.

Eventually, his injurious intent left him guilt-ridden. Only he dithered too long over ways and means to end the unfortunate game, and Victoria struck first. "Marriage?" he found himself stammering. "I thought we had an understanding. That it would be a bad mistake." He could hardly disclose the truth, which was that a permanent attachment, no matter how immediately tempting, could only be ruinous to an orderly life. So he ransacked his brain for a credible excuse, but his hasty, desperate inventions were feeble: He was unworthy of her; he was set in habits that would be too tough to live with; his was a solitary soul not meant for cohabiting; he had inherited an incurable disease that he refused to pass on to offspring; and God knows what else. Mr. Hogan no longer remembered which one he finally tossed at her, only how she withered, shrank into herself, while the blood deserted her face to settle in her pert little nose, as if she'd been struck there. So he'd won the game, given her the share of unhappiness he'd intended. Except that after it all he'd rather have been pierced by a bullet.

I've finally gotten settled in, here in Willa Cather country. The Wingate Academy is supposedly a cut above the public schools, but the only thing superior is the price of the cars these rich kids drive.
I was right, it is a bit easier being away from you.
Please write.

He'd been glad to be rid of her, of the peaks and valleys of emotion he couldn't always control; back to the sweet comfort of his books and music. So then why had he, defying instinct and principle, mooned about so, dwelling on nothing but the silly blue-eyed, strapping girl?

I never gave you credit for such a sense of humor. Your letter kept me grinning all day. The descriptions of stuffy Mr. Sawyer and Miss Dempsey at the school theatrical were priceless. I hope you haven't kept any carbons. If they got hold of them you'd be out pounding the pavement, to say nothing of being sued for libel.

Don't forget to write.

They came to exchange letters at least weekly. He tried hard to make his interesting, as if he were submitting them for grading. He'd feel anxious if hers were a bit late.

My apartment mate is four months pregnant. Her friend is handsome and quite charming. And diligently unemployed. Gunther is always around, taking care of Mary. He accepts full responsibility, or so he tells me. Not enough, though, to go out and get a job. I sometimes hear them quarreling. The word 'abortion' often comes through these thin walls. *I should know soon if I'll be having the whole place to myself, or will it be a* menage a trois.

Stay tuned for reports of love's progress.
Write.

That one had started him worrying about her, responsible as he was for her being in a strange town, in what must have been an uncomfortable situation.

What do I do with my time, you ask? There's a pretty decent library here. Two movie theaters show the latest action films. Gunther and Mary have noisy quarrels, followed by noisier bedsprings. A man whose wife doesn't understand him quotes me poetry over dinner.

And what do you do with yours?

Oh yes, he remembered that one well. Even now he could feel the jealousy cutting through him. He couldn't understand it, since he'd been the one to send her away. Jealousy and yet pity, mixed in with other unknowns. But why this need to hurt her?

In his response he hinted at numerous romances, all fabricated.

Seems it takes an awful lot of young ladies to anesthetize against the pain of missing me. Surprised so many are so anxious to comfort such a sourpuss. Maybe they too have found the secret, which is that for one minute each evening your tight-fisted soul opens like a beautiful flower, and that is worth all the other guff. Wanting you was with the hope that lovely minute might be stretched into days.

Mary has decided to have and keep the baby. Guess Gunther will be on our hands for a while yet.

Write. If you can tear yourself away from all those comforters.

He'd been awakened before dawn, driven out of the house by a feeling that was too enormous to be contained within walls. He wandered the streets, led by Victoria's image illuminating the dark, projected onto shadowed building walls. He watched the indifferent blue eyes and obstinate chin thaw in that sudden warm smile, a special treat he never tired of. The sight of that body, big-boned yet gracefully feminine, slender, yielding, tore open a hunger in his belly. Eventually he trudged homeward, weighed down with the terrible longing. Why, he demanded of himself, this sudden unbearable surge? He decided it was her letters, with their instigation of jealousy, with her smart-alecking, with the persistence of her caring that flattered but also rekindled something within him.

By the time he got back to bed he regretted the self-betrayal: letting himself get so worked up over what was only a temporary weakness.

Nothing much has changed since my last letter.

The movie theaters have switched from action to horror.

Gunther is very attentive, between quarrels.

The misunderstood man is increasing the pressure. He now favors poems about how time is short so we'd better make the most of it. "'The moving finger writes….'" Did you both attend the same school? How many credits for Seduction 101?

In spite of that, I miss you.

Exactly who, he'd wondered, was Gunther attentive to? And why all this reporting about the misunderstood man? And why did it hurt as much as a physical pain?

I've thought a lot about what it was that might have come between us. I never really understood your reasons, so I could only blame myself. It must be that I have some distasteful physical blemish. Or that I am a poor lover. Or I can't go around quoting poetry. I make kids cut up little dead animals. I am unkind. Discourteous. Cold. Whatever.

I do miss you, but I'm just starting to get over it, and I don't want to be hurt again. As they say, fool me once and it's your fault; fool me twice, it's mine.

So no, I do not think it's a good idea for you to come out here.

There's little to see or do in this town, and it's much too hot in summer anyway. Why waste your vacation time here? Try Paris.

Please, just write.

He'd insisted, although she tried to dissuade him even while he was already phoning to let her know when his plane would land. Still, she was waiting at Arrivals with a smile that poured forth welcome. His arms flew out to enfold her. They embraced tightly, as if to renew the memory of each other's configuration of flesh and bone. To Hogan it was one of those silent moments that say everything, a rare segment of eternity never thereafter forgotten.

On the drive to her apartment the talk was of the small sort that passes between the shy or newly met, or those who have already exchanged all their larger thoughts. They climbed two flights in a multi-family building, its aluminum siding striated with an outside staircase. On a couch embedded in a jumble of furniture and mounds of clothes, Gunther sat with his arm around the pregnant girl's shoulder. After introductions to the contentedly self-absorbed couple, Victoria explained that the apartment was being rearranged to accommodate the coming baby. "We can go into the garden to talk."

Two flights down she opened a door to the outside back. They stepped into an overgrown, weed-strewn lot.

She pointed to a far corner. "How about the gazebo?"

He was surprised to see there really was one, half hidden among the weeds and tall grasses. They worked their way single file through the tangled growth. Hogan, dying to overtake and embrace her, or even just hold that cool hand, was restrained by something about the set of her back. They stepped into the desiccating, tilted structure. Hogan sat down; Victoria very deliberately walked across the creaking floor to a seat on the opposite bench.

The air smelled of grass and rotting wood. A shaft of sunlight reached the tip of her shoe. She addressed the aged floorboards. "Tell me why you are here."

"Because I couldn't keep myself from being here." He gorged on the sight of her careless part, broad smooth placid forehead.

"Have you had a change of heart then?"

"It's my mind that's been the problem, never the heart."

She looked up. "And what is the present state of your mind?"

He couldn't get himself to say it to the steady blue eyes awaiting judgment. She stared at him insistently. Dropping his gaze, he shook his head dolefully.

She waited for more, but when it didn't come stood up. "So be it."

She stepped down into the grass, and he followed. "I've reserved a nice room for you downtown," she threw over her shoulder. "I'll call you a taxi."

"When will we meet again?"

"It would be too hard tonight. We've got to get the apartment reorganized."

"Tomorrow?"

"I've got classes. But why don't you explore the town, and I'll call you in the evening."

He knew then.

"Please," he tried. "Can't we just enjoy each other for as long as it lasts?"

"I don't have enough fooling-around time left to me."

He hung on a full week, but it was no good. She remained indifferent, barely courteous, and invented transparent excuses for keeping away.

When he finally gave it up as hopeless, Victoria drove him to the airport. At the boarding gate she threw her arms around him. Two flight officers watched impatiently as, eyes glistening, she kissed him hard. Still embracing him she said, "I'm sorry for being such a bitch. But we could have been so good together, and I was furious that you refused to let it happen."

He clung to her.

She pulled away.

That was the last time.

Traveling back over the decades had given Mr. Hogan a queer feeling, triumph filigreed with regret. He considered it, how regret, if it is not over terribly important things, can be bittersweet, even delicious, as evidence of principles held fast, of hard choices made. Of life lived. A sigh of fulfillment heaved his chest. He leaned back in his soft chair.

It was only at the whisper of sliding paper that he realized that his lap unaccountably held one more of the pale blue envelopes. He peered at its faded postmark. It bore the most advanced date of all, a full three months after the last one he'd read. He hesitated, fearing it one of those poscripts that cancel out all that's gone before. Reluctantly, he unfolded the letter.

As you can imagine, I've been thinking a lot about us. I'm sure now that I was right, that marrying would have been a mistake. We have different goals and our interests are different. What they mean by 'incompatible.' It was good while it lasted, but it's time now to go our separate ways.
I wish you all the best.

Mr. Hogan felt as if he'd been swallowing bites of a sweet, juice-dripping peach, and then a half-eaten worm had crawled out of his mouth. No, he insisted through the sick feeling, no, it is not possible. No way could I have been thinking about it wrong for these thirty years. It wasn't her, it was me. *I was the one.* And then, because he needed it so badly, the memory came trickling back.

That time so long ago, the first time he'd read the letter, it hadn't made him sick, just outraged. He'd begun drafting a scathing response, in pencil on lined paper angrily ripped out of a notebook, laboring to get the message just right, murderously right. Until Oscar Wilde came buzzing into his head, Each man kills the thing he loves. No, Hogan objected, not me, and sank back deflated. Not me. Not if she needs this victory so badly. And he'd balled up his angry sheet, and with an arcing shot sank it in the wastebasket.

Mr. Hogan hoped that the years had been kind to her.

He slid this last letter back into its envelope. He stared a long moment at the pale blue rectangle, then tore it into strips, and the strips into bits. He got up and carried these into the kitchen. He dropped them into a dish in the sink, then found a match in the cupboard and set the bits ablaze. When the paper curled into ash, he returned to the living room. He gathered up all the preceding letters and stuffed them into the manila envelope.

Jack Dempsey, Sugar Ray Robinson, he enumerated on his way to the bedroom, this time concentrating on sports figures. Mickey Mantle.

Still holding the manila envelope, he pulled open the door to the walk-in closet. He stood contemplating its dusky interior. Then, having made his choice, Mr. Hogan carefully set down the envelope in an unobstructed corner, where they wouldn't fail to find it.

The Kimono

It was like making love with a Ming Dynasty empress. She was tall and willowy, and through the dusk even more darkly beautiful than I'd recalled, and she'd chosen to wear a kimono, cream embossed with gold, and all evening long we'd talked softly while her lips curved in a secret little smile and her black eyes glittered in the moonlight pouring through the glass wall. Later, in the blind hallway, our lips chastely touching in goodbye, her kimono slithered to the floor. Silken skin shocked my finger tips. She drew me down onto the gold-flecked fabric.

This hadn't been my intention nor expectation, nor to revive what was dead. We'd had a thing going a while back, but it had expired for good reason, and we hadn't seen each other in a couple of years. Julia Cheng was inviting me over, she'd said on the phone, just to renew old acquaintances. When I told her I didn't think that was a good idea, she'd begun to sob, her ultimate weapon. "I miss you so much, I just want to see you and talk to you." If you refused her she had a way of making you feel guilty of some heinous crime. But even aware of her ruses and deceit, I couldn't help wanting to look at her again.

"Let's go upstairs." Julia whispers even though it is her own house and no one else is present. She hasn't lost her flair for the dramatic. Nor has her voice lost its lilt, although she'd come here as a kid and is by now a dozen years past a grad degree in nursing. Nor has she changed her way of addressing me, which was to not call me anything at all. We'd of course long outgrown 'Doctor,' but a modesty that showed up in no other way still kept her from addressing me by my first name.

We used to cause accidents all up and down I-95. She was a nurse anesthetist employed by our group, not a physician, yet I saw to it that together we attended every meeting or seminar between Greenwich and Boston touching on the practice of medicine, no matter how remotely. Anything and everything, from the ethics of euthanasia to maximizing income. Once out of New Haven and onto the highway, she'd hike up or remove whatever garments necessary to ease access to her sweet spots.

I learned how to steer with just the unaccustomed left hand. Her breasts were small but assertive, nipples like the rosebuds poets worship. We would drive deliberately slow, in the center lane. High-seated cross-country haulers would crane their necks sticking to us, weaving dangerously in the right lane, sometimes even in the illegal left. Cars with angry horns took crazy chances trying to pass this motorcade.

Sometimes we'd pull into one of the commuter parking lots, relieve the unbearable tension, then get back on the road and start all over again.

Climbing the stairs, I recall things about her house. Even though large and expensive, it was sparsely furnished. I couldn't remember ever seeing pictures of Chinese homes, so I imagined hers as in the Japanese style: cleanly spare, utilitarian. All the usual furniture, actually, sofas and chairs and carpets, but no garish accessories. In the living room, next to the glass wall facing the garden, an earthenware flower pot half as high as a man held a plant growing a single broad white flower. I never knew its name. Each year the bloom lives for just twenty-four hours. Once, in a year we were close, we were sitting in the darkened room when the blossom suddenly flared fullblown into the moonlight. Julia leaped up and gently coaxed it from the branch. She held it to her face and breathed it in, then offered it for me to smell. In the kitchen she boiled the blossom in water and made me drink it for my health.

She'd said to me once, early on, "I saw you in the cafeteria today with a woman and a child. Somebody say the woman is your wife."

'Yes," I said, "the woman is my wife. And the child is my son Matthew."

"Your wife is quite beautiful. I walk all around her. I look for her defect, everyone has defect. But no, her profile is perfect.'

"Yes, she is beautiful and perfect."

"I watch when you hold your son. Your eyes show great love."

"Is it possible not to love a young son?"

She said, "It would be easy to fall for a man whose eyes can show such love. Your wife should be careful."

Julia carries the cream kimono over one shoulder. As we climb she reaches back to take my hand. My other hand rests on her undulant hip. "How is Henry?" I ask. "Is he doing well?"

Henry is Julia's husband. A Ph.D. in chemical engineering, he's a recognized authority in some esoteric field beyond my comprehension. Henry Cheng has big ambitions in the money making line. Mostly he's in Taiwan, starting up and abandoning business ventures. He comes home to Julia two or three times a year for just a couple of weeks or so. He has yet to hit it big. Except, according to Julia, he does hit it big with her, big enough to sometimes send her battered to an emergency room. She of course wouldn't come to our own hospital, so I never really knew whether this was another of her exaggerations. I'd seen her tears flow too readily and generously when grieving imaginary injustices.

Before me, her legs flex gracefully in climbing, fluid and shapely as a runway model's. "He was here last month," she says with that lilt. "He want to stay longer but I tell him to go. I say to him I want a divorce, but he refuses. He thinks I will love him when he gets rich. As if I will forget the beatings."

"There is always Shah," I remind her. Shah is an Indian doctor on the staff of a neighboring hospital who's been in love with her for a long time. A very decent fellow I'd once met.

"Yes," she says, "if not you then Shah," and turns to send me an exaggeratedly provocative smile.

The reason Julia is able to kid about marrying me is because I am no longer married. The reason I am no longer married is Julia. I always blame her for breaking up my home. Until I stop lying to myself and admit it was my own damned fault.

Between cases on a slow day the two of us sat sipping stale coffee in the OR lounge. The next one scheduled was uncomplicated, a wrist reconstruction, and as usual I would be starting the anesthesia and then leaving the rest to her. She appeared impersonal, almost inhuman, as I'm sure I did too, in androgynous greens, head capped, mask dangling over chin, shoes wrapped in nonconductive cloth. I'd often thought that this costume encouraged indiscreet disclosures, as if the speaker was confident of going unrecognized. That OR lounge had seen the gestation of some ridiculous but surprisingly poisonous feuds.

We'd worked together long enough by then, and fought through enough ambushes, that we could be comfortable chatting about things outside the professional. For some reason, the subject of origins came up. She talked about how her father had been high up in the government, then forced out by a scandal, so they'd taken off for the States. She'd met Henry at UConn, and it had been an on-again, off-again courtship, the uncertainty and hostility fostered by his interfering mother.

The OR supervisor stuck her head in. "Anybody seen Rothberg?" I shook my head. She said, "Any nurses missing? He got one in the broom closet again?" and ducked out. Rothberg was the orthopod on the case, which left us plenty of time yet to talk.

Julia said, "Want to hear more?" I nodded, because it would cut the boredom, but also because I liked to watch her dark eyes refract with each thought.

With a brave little smile she laid out a story of incredible abuse, of beatings by her husband, sometimes by his mother, of concussions and the loss of a baby and hospital stays and months of recuperation. The reasons? Anything from a poorly cooked meal to accusations of infidelity. The beautiful eyes glistened and her perfectly formed lips trembled, even while she held that little smile. I told myself it was shallow to feel greater pity for an attractive than a plainer woman, but still couldn't help thinking of the evil it took to inflict such pain on someone who looked like that. And I couldn't help wanting to comfort her. I walked over and sat down next to her on the sofa and put my arm around her shoulder. She leaned into me and raised her head. Her lips came so close that kissing them was just the seamless extension of a moment of sympathy.

We reach the top of the stairs. I follow Julia down the uncarpeted hallway to the master bedroom. She hangs the cream kimono on the bedpost, then spreads herself out on top of the covers, arms beneath her head. The rosebuds point at the ceiling. I sit down on the side of the bed and begin to undress. At the second shoe I freeze, holding it suspended, paralyzed by remembrance.

One day she threw out the challenge. "By the way, Dr. Dolan, I will be in Manhattan tomorrow morning at ten o'clock in front of the Carlyle Hotel. I do not think you will have the courage to meet me. I will wait until half past."

Her facial expression was indecipherable. I was positive the dare was just another of her little teases. I couldn't believe she meant it. As if fooling around on I-95 was perfectly within the bounds of morality, and it was only truancy and taking off for the big city that marked things seriously illicit.

I told her, "You will have to wait there till the cows come home. If you are unfamiliar with this idiomatic expression, it just means no."

But in the morning I arranged for an associate to handle my cases, then hopped aboard Amtrak. A cab from Grand Central dropped me off at the Carlyle. There was no one out front except the doorman. I paced up and down, back and forth, another poor slob made a fool of by a woman. Betrayal and embarrassment itched for a hand around her throat. Presently, just for the hell of it, I wandered into the lobby. Fatuously chortling at the barbs she lobbed at them, admiring bellmen and assorted other staff encircled the moment's celebrity. When she spotted me, Julia flipped them a goodbye and broke through the ring. Outside, she slipped on dark glasses. She took my hand as we crossed the street heading west.

"What did you have in mind?" I asked.

She shook her head. "Today I belong to you. Do with me as you wish."

The face around her dark glasses was impassive. Carefully I said, "Should we try for tickets to a matinee?"

"Your ambition is quite small."

"There's a motor hotel on West 57th."

"Fine," she said.

We walked crosstown holding hands. The breeze was still fresh with morning. The sun wasn't overhead yet; ascending, it bounced off the windows of the tall buildings. We didn't say a word, just held on to each other. Conscience flashed an image of my son Matthew in the arms of his mother, but I shut it down. Some defiant moments are beyond civilizing conventions like morality and duty, beyond allegiance, beyond even love; they are what this our life was made for. Carpe diem.

The desk clerk saw me with no luggage and an oriental babe wearing dark glasses, and stuck me for double the going rate. Fool! I'd have given him a second mortgage on my house.

When we got upstairs she admitted to feeling a bit shaky. Room service delivered a glass of milk. It gave her a white moustache, so I reached across and wiped the milk off her lip with my thumb. With fierce little teeth she bit down on it. In revenge I picked her up and tossed her onto the bed. Through hours of exploration and ravishment, the image outlasting all others was of Julia's eyes smiling down at me. There was something in that smile beyond pleasure and fulfillment; I imagined them the eyes of a lepidopterist with net poised above a butterfly.

Not until three could we tear ourselves away. In the elevator she snickered, "Don't forget to cut the nail on your left little toe. Much too long." In Grand Central I let her go first, then took a later train.

In a hospital, if you lock yourself all alone in a small dark room, let's say a linen closet, and whisper something under your breath, by the time you step out thirty seconds later your secret words will be circulating through every department. So how long could it take for our little assignation to become known? The divorce was, as they say, messy. They took everything from me, including my son Matthew.

Julia switched to another hospital; I moved to another town. When not in OR greens, I sat in my apartment on rented furniture staring at the walls. Unless I wanted some real excitement, in which case I could monitor the traffic speeding by under my window. There was too much time for thinking and regretting. At first I told myself that what I'd done wasn't really that bad: at my fortyish time of life, half the medical staffs exchange the cellulite thighs who'd put them through med school for svelte little nurses or therapists. Compared to those guys, I decided, mine was a petty sin. Still, it wasn't too long before I had to concede arrogance, irresponsibility, and just plain stupidity.

It took longer to solve Julia. You know how sometimes your eyes see things you don't register, but they do get stored in memory, and you're able to pull them out later? Well, I thought about her, at first with grudging pleasure and much longing, but then recalled measuring glances out of the corner of her eye, inflections in her voice, even certain incidents. And it burst upon me what I should have known all along, that for her it wasn't love or even desire. What it was, it was rage. Rage and vengeance.

In summer, a touring orchestra stopped off at a nearby city for a concert at the waterfront. I drove down there to get away from the apartment. Walking along the grass, looking for some unoccupied inches on which to place my rump, I heard my name called. I searched for a familiar face and within the mob spotted Julia, whom I'd not seen since the divorce. "Come sit with me," she called. "Plenty of room." Instinct urged me to get away, but I told myself, What the hell, anything for some good music. I stumbled over a hundred legs and made my way to her. In a stand of beach chairs sat Henry and an elderly couple, thin, gray, bespectacled, the parents he'd brought along from Taiwan for this visit. "My old boss," she introduced me. I took the chair she offered. Herself, she sank down on the grass.

Sank down on the grass at my feet! And rested her hand on the arm of my chair. The elderly couple glanced meaningfully at each other. Henry, handsome in an almost round-eyed way, gazed straight ahead at the white-jacketed musicians blowing and sawing away in the bandshell. The pale enigmatic smile could mean he was enjoying the concertized Boheme. Or maybe not. At intermission I chanced moving my chair closer to his. Our exchange about economic conditions on Taiwan was surprisingly amiable. Later on, when the soprano had coughed her last and expired, I said good night and went off alone to the car. From a distance I saw them walking in formation, Henry first, his parents next, a smirking Julia last. I prayed her ultimate stay in hell would be long and searing.

Lying there, she inserts a caressing hand under my shirt. "Hurry. I miss you." I wonder why the silken touch of her hand, even while arousing is yet irritating too. And then I turn my head and see her spread out at ease. It is a position that only a woman of great confidence would dare. Arrogance is the opposite of love, which is humble.

I drop the shoe and rid myself of my clothes. I lie down next to Julia. Her eyes smile with anticipation, maybe even a hint of love, but most definite is triumph: she has again proved her irresistibility. Her flesh accommodates the pressure of my hand. Wherever I touch, in the dim light, the pink surge of blood under her transparent skin is tinged with gold. This time, the small breasts and the sparseness of pubic growth strike me as evidencing a lack of generosity. Twisting around, she rises up. A mirror reflects her riding me. The bed posts are dark wood, as is the sombre bureau across the room. I wonder idly whose taste this is. Which leads me to remember that this is Henry's room too. Which persuades me that this is another of her little schemes. All at once I am sure she has drawn me here to defile the conjugal bed, to mock him. To once again be her agent of vengeance.

I withdraw. She tumbles off me awkwardly, her long legs akimbo. She rights herself angrily. "What is your problem?"

"I can't," I tell her. "Not here."

She sneers, "Is the mattress too lumpy?"

"The bed is his."

"So. Wife okay, but not bed?"

I can only shrug. "That's how it is."

"We cheat on my husband, we cheat on your wife. But suddenly you have very fine ethics."

"It is not ethics," I tell her. "It is you."

"Me? How so?"

"Did he beat you again? Is that it?"

"Yes," she says. "Yes," and turns to display a welt on her upper arm.

"So now you want me to help you get even?"

"It just makes me to know how much I 'ppreciate you. That's why I call you. That's why I want to love you."

"I've had enough of your little games. Count me out."

I hop off the bed and start throwing on my clothes. Her head falls forward in a little drama of hurt and defeat. Then she snaps upright, wraps herself in the kimono, and glides out.

Dressed, I pause momentarily, already missing her bed, her room, her scent of short-lived blossoms, even while scorning them.

When I get to the bottom of the stairs I find Julia blocking the front door. I've never been as angry with her as at this moment of parting. I despise her for her scheming and manipulations. For shattering my life. Above all, for showing me myself: irresponsible, immoral, boneless.

"Are we saying goodbye forever?" she asks, little-girl-lost.

"Maybe we'll bump into each other in the A & P."

Her eyes glisten with those phony tears. "Then will you kiss me goodbye?"

I just look at her, thinking I should have kissed her goodbye a long time ago.

"One last time?"

Even tearful, she is still as regal as an empress. How dark are her eyes, how perfect those smugly curving lips! I lean forward to brush them ever so lightly. For old times' sake. And just to remember the bitch. But her lips clamp onto mine, burning them; the breath of her mouth is fragrant with spices. Her kimono slithers to the floor. Silken skin shocks my finger tips. She draws me down onto the gold-flecked fabric. Knowing it my fate, I descend blissfully into hell.

Stolen Berries

I was only twelve, but the blood thirst that rose in me was as strong as a man's. I really wanted to see them kill that toy man.

When I try to recapture those Catskill summers of childhood, it's as if memory is engraved on a wildly spinning wheel; I manage to snatch up some of it, but mostly I'm left with colors and sounds bleeding into one another. Except for some of the bad moments, which come back with the greatest clarity.

I do remember us sitting in a black Buick taxi the day after school's end, trunks and cartons and laundry sacks strapped to the roof, the hot and filthy streets pulling away, and somewhere in Jersey the scenery opens up into trees and mountains, and out of the mists of dawn the sun rises cleanly bright, and I, as new as the sun, wonder what it all means, for the endless summer, for my endless life.

And I remember, up there in the mountains, the lake at sunset, its surface stippled by the mouths of perch rising as if for the departing sun; the dark and barb-wired woods across the road we'd sneak into to explore for nothing at all, just to tread its soft carpet of pine needles, breathe its primordial scents and tickle the tadpoles wiggling at the sides of its brook, all the while in delicious fear of whatever ogre meant to fence us out; a campfire in the field beyond the last cottage, shivering with the night chill and the ghost stories, smoke hovering above roasting spuds, while periodically one of the older, more worldly, couples of fifteen or so get up and still holding on to each other lope for the moon-shadowed trees on some mysterious errand.

And I remember, very early on, several of the mothers leading a gaggle of us kids on a five mile trek, over roads at first stone-strewn then nearer to town covered with melting tar. By mid summer the tedium of primitive homemaking, of shared fly-specked kitchens and ice boxes, is no longer bearable, so the handbill trumpeting the arrival of civilization, an itinerant motion picture exhibitor, is irresistible. In the village's combination lunch counter, pool parlor, and bowling alley, torn felt on tables and tornup floor boards in alleys, a dour little man in slept-in clothes hangs up a bed sheet, collects a dime for each attendee, then runs a flickering Jimmy Durante musical through his projector.

But such excursions were rare, undertaken only out of desperation. Mostly, the women had to be content with knowing that their kids were sucking up cool fresh air, and with waiting like prisoners for weekend conjugal visits. But even then parole was unlikely, because who owned cars? So out of this immobility, business opportunities developed. A dairy truck rattled up in its whiteness every morning, its horn summoning inhabitants compensating for boredom with food. Fruits and vegetables made twice-weekly rounds, the truck's tarpaulined sides rolled up to display the primary colors of fresh produce. Less frequently, three or four times a season, a black Ford sedan would chug up, passenger space and trunk crammed with soft goods, and women and children crowding around would measure themselves against sweaters and blouses like islanders bartering copra for trinkets.

And I remember, a couple of miles down the road, acres and acres of huckleberry bushes, unfenced, unposted. Not like Juniper Lake opposite, its entering trail secured by a carefully lettered sign, red calligraphy against a white background, No Dogs or Jews. But the lore handed down from summer to summer was that the berries belonged to the same owner as the forbidden lake. We had no great desire to plunge into his sacred water, but those huckleberries in August, purple and sugar laden and bursting with juice, begged to be picked and eaten, and the threat of bullets only added urgency to our errand of mercy. Nobody else ever picked those berries, and if not for us they'd be left to rot on the ground or dry up on the bushes. Morality never entered into it; maybe the berries were considered a quid pro quo for the hate and the threat. Still, even while I joined the salvagers, conscience whispered an admonition, only I allowed its small voice to be drowned out by their enthusiasm.

Several times each August an expeditionary force would stealthily trek the two miles, half way there passing the old farmhouse atop the hill, a hundred yards beyond it the family graveyard's two dozen scaling markers recording birth and death across centuries. Each of us, women and kids alike, carried a cooking pot, its size reflecting the bearer's degree of optimism or avarice. A mile on, amid the heavy bushes, there was a quick reconnoitering, forefingers upright against compressed lips, and then the ping of berries dropping into pots. The warm sweetness rising from the grass lulled fear, and the hypnotic buzz of dragonflies, the fluttering blacks and golds of butterflies lazy in the sun. After, we'd march our berries home. By evening the fragrance of simmering berries would float sweet in the air about us.

And I remember Dora Gold, the colony's life of the party, that time leading home from berry picking two or three other women, a half dozen kids, and old Pinsky, a retired baker, jauntily manipulating a whittled tree branch to support his arthritic shamble. A quarter of the way home in the August afternoon, sun dappling through the trees, dust kicking up from the road, Dora sang out a line and someone else joined in, and soon we were into one of those folk songs brought over from the old country, a melody at once sweet, joyful, and nostalgic, and old Pinsky hobbled livelier even while he dabbed at his eyes. Then someone started on another one and we sang up the hill, now half way home nearing the old farmhouse, and then at sight of the graveyard stilling our voices out of respect for the dead, or fear of ghosts, or maybe awe of the generations living and dying right here, belonging here, truly of this land.

Once past the graveyard Mr. Pinsky, in a rusty tenor, hawked out a rhythmic verse, this one about a pretty little cousin from across the sea, and by the downslope each voice strained to contribute its share of sweetness to the swinging chorus. Little Artie Messing, carried along by the music, stooped for a twig and then marched apace drumming it against his blue marbled pot, chubbiness overflowing his drooping shorts, until someone squealed out that he'd spilled half his berries. Out of pique he dumped the remainder into a fern-covered roadside ditch, and then flung the empty pot after them. But a slap on the arm from Fanny Messing, a generously proportioned blonde, persuaded her ten year old to retrieve the pot, and with the splotch still marking his arm he sullenly rejoined the marchers.

Eyes above the singing mouths monitored the tantrum's progress, which was why we were so startled when the two young men suddenly materialized. They were clean cut young men in white shirts with sleeves rolled to the elbow and clean black trousers, and their hair, one's blond and the other's brown, was combed straight back, neat furrows deep with water. Their smiles were easy. They fell into step with us. "What a pretty song," the blond one said. The brown-haired one placed an arm around little Artie's shoulder. "Hi," he smiled at Fanny Messing. He glanced at the pot she held close, white with black scars where the enamel had chipped off. "Hey," he said admiringly, "what a nice collection of berries." His teeth showed white and even, and Fanny couldn't help the blush that rose in her fair skin. "Think I could I have some?" When she held out the pot he carefully picked a few off the top. He popped them into his mouth. "Sweet," he nodded, a bit of the purple juice running along his lower lip. "Very, very sweet. Must be Jew berries. Stolen, no?" Still smiling, he wrenched the pot out of Fanny's outstretched hand. With a small grunt he scaled it over Artie's head far into some bushes along the road. At first shocked motionless, with a little whimper Fanny recovered enough to rake at his face. He brought his hands up as cover. The blond man sprang over to pull her off. She spun to flail at him too. He ducked inside Fanny's arms and shoved at her chest. She tumbled awkwardly, striking an elbow on the road's gravel.

"Bestid!" Mr. Pinsky rasped, raising his walking stick.

"Crook!" the blond man spat out, and the other one slipped over and tore the stick from Mr. Pinsky's hand. With a single swift movement he broke it over his knee and tossed the halves into the shrubbery.

"Bestid!" Pinsky rasped again, breathing hard.

The man pointed a finger between his eyes. "You want to die, old man?"

The blond man skipped around, slapping and punching at pots held in frightened hands, scattering berries over the ground. "Crooks!" he spat at us. "Stay where you belong!"

The young men took off, trotting back up the hill. Their laughter sailed back to us. On the road Fanny sat rocking from side to side, dead leaves pasted to her legs, cuddling her elbow and weeping. A couple of the smaller kids were sniffling. Dora Gold was white-faced, and a pale Mr. Pinsky, struggling for breath, sank down to the ground.

Shaken, I still couldn't help thinking that they were right, those fellows. We were stealing, weren't we? And even if it was just arrogance, sharpies from the old country thinking we were too clever for the natives, or that the laws didn't apply to us, or maybe just ignorance of the customs of the country, they were still right to despise and hate us. Greenhorns, couldn't even speak the language yet, but already running around breaking rules set by the people who'd built and bled for this country. And the feeling that came over me, what I mostly felt, was shame.

This time, no aroma of simmering huckleberries wafted over the colony.

There were still four weeks left to the season, but no more attempt was made to pick berries. We kids played handball, explored the woods, sneaked peeks into the shower house on the hill, traded cowboy stars on dixie cup covers. The women waited for the food trucks, quarreled about leftovers stored in the shared ice boxes, gossiped about pretty Sylvie Schatz, who after her kids were put to bed one night was spotted heavily made up, tip-toeing down the road to the waiting Buick of the next colony's resident bachelor. In other words, things went on the same as always, and yet I had the impression that everybody was more sub-dued, like in a town where a foreign army has passed through and gone but they're afraid the invaders might still return.

I became an observer. I needed to learn who and what we were. How we were different. Why we were classed with dogs. And I watched the parents, and saw how, like mine, they were so concerned about their off-spring, so eager to sacrifice for them. "Finish your milk," and, "It's get-ting cold, put on your sweater," simple and ordinary parent-child communications, were wrapped in intensity and drama, as if each plea concerned life and death, and each was addressed not to just a name, but more usually to an orientally ornate endearment in an untransfer-able Yiddish idiom, roughly, "Little grandfather," (if named after the father's father), "My kaddishel," (little one who will pray for me after my death), or maybe, "My little son," (simple words oily with love). There was a theatrical excess about it that led me to wonder if those others, those belonging to Juniper Lake and the acres of berries, were also smothering and smothered, but I decided that no, they'd never be party to such extravagance, they'd be too cool and assured, too easy moving around in this their world.

And I saw how my buddies were as guilty of excess as their elders, with bodies that were either too heavy or too thin, noses too long, voices too loud, appetites too voracious, tempers too hot, play too raucous; even their Americanese was inflated, fattened with echoes of Russia, Poland and the streets of Brooklyn. And I so envied the Juniper Lake kids. I imagined them David Copperfield and Oliver Twist after having risen into respectability: precise speech, regular features, respectful, self-assured, confident, perfect. Like those clean-cut young men avenging the stolen berries. And I saw that we were an inferior race. And that they were right in deriding us, excluding us, punishing us.

And I remember a Sunday afternoon, a softball game in the cow pasture back of the cottages. Weekend fathers—butchers and bakers wide and solid as century old tree trunks—relaxing in shorts, wing tips, and lisle socks, yelled encouragement at gawky pre-adolescents. Street stickballers unaccustomed to the real bats and balls, the tall grasses on the uneven terrain masking rocks and cow flop, the sun blinding, all of us awkward and error-prone. But some infancy disease had marked me with a thin angular frame and a skeletal chest, and at twelve not yet filling out I was the very embodiment of clumsiness, so I was special, it was my blundering that stood out from all the rest. My lapses drew catcalls and sarcasms, and with each strikeout or dropped ball I could feel the fear and anger hotter in my face, legs shakier, movements even more erratic. In a late inning the shortstop, as if to make it easier for me, but really to show off my futility and his cleverness, rolled me the ball at third base instead of lobbing it. I picked it up and slung it back at him, wanting to knock his head off. The momentary hush of fright until it whooshed past his head was shattered by derisive hooting. Just then, just when I began hurrying weak-kneed off the field, catcalls stinging my ears, I heard my name called, my father calling my name. "Hoimeleh," his Austro/ Polish/ Yiddish spin on the diminutive of my anglicized name, echoed in shrill "Hey, Hoimeleh" parodies from all around the field. I stalked off, my back a shield against the hateful scene.

My father followed. "Where you running? You didn't hear me calling?"

Still aware of the others, I snarled, "Leave me alone, will ya?" concerned more with my embarrassment than his feelings.

But nothing I ever did could erase that smile of indulgence when he looked at me, his damaged offspring. "What's the matter, little father, you don't like me anymore?"

"Cripes," I said, "can't you even say my name right? When are you gonna learn some english?" Even as the insolence tightened my throat I relished the pain it must cause him.

"Yeah, Maxie," somebody yelled, "when you gonna learn to spika da yinglish?"

We walked on. My father's hand was heavy on my shoulder. I looked straight ahead, cold indifference meant to show anger, but in my mind's eye I saw his muscular forearm and work-thickened fingers and the swollen vein parting the hairs across the back of his hand. With all the fervor of a weak misshapen boy I coveted such strong arms and deep voice and dark good looks. "You're ashamed of me?" he asked, not in reproach but with little nods, as if just verifying the answer. I shook my head. I couldn't tell him that I knew his mangling of my name was out of love, and that it so embarrassed me only because everything embarrassed me, there was this terrible need to not stand out.

"Why is your face so red?" he asked. "On such a hot day you gotta play ball yet?"

I insisted on the silence of anger.

"Put on a shirt. You want you should get burned?"

Grudgingly I shook my head.

"Why don't you go cover yourself?"

"I'm already dark," I said, "I can't get burned any more."

"So you gotta walk around like that?"

'Like that?' Like what? I wondered. Which is when I looked down at my scrawniness and knew that he too was embarrassed. I was his embarrassment.

And I remember one Saturday night, the annual bonfire on the shore of the lake, branches and logs gathered over several days piled high as a small building, crackle of burning wood and sparks shooting for the stars, reflections blazing in the water, thwack of beer kegs tapped, "Dumb kid, stop swallowing the franks already, you want you should get cramps yet?" From above the din and beyond the circle of light came my father's voice, this time in an unaccustomed timbre that mocked, challenged, flirted. I heard other voices from that vicinity as well, including a woman's, and laughter too, until it became clear that there was some sort of game going on, and then I heard my father coaxing, "Go ahead, I'll follow you," and the woman's doubting, "Yeah. Sure," and his reassuring," Go ahead, don't worry, I'll come right in."

Almost immediately I saw Sylvie Schatz, eyes aglow in her pretty, made-up face, lope through the edge of firelight to the incline, shorts and a halter pocketing her breasts, and then she charged down the hill, breasts swaying, everybody pausing openmouthed to watch, and then she shattered the water's silver glaze and stroked out into the lake, and with a catch in my belly I wondered what my father could possibly have to do with this sexy lady, and was my mother seeing this. And then I heard the buzz that Maxie, my father Maxie, had dared Sylvie to join him in the cold water, and now somebody yelled, "Hey Maxie, ain't you goin' in?" and then my father's chuckled, "What am I, crazy?" I knew that it had to have been just a joke, he couldn't even swim. Then someone else jumped in, one of the younger men, and cut through, and quickly drew abreast of Sylvie treading glittering water, and the words they called softly, tones erotically modulated, and their intimate laughter, reverberated humidly to us over the water. And I saw my father, hunkered unsmiling, as a coward and a fool and yet a victim too, and I was sorry for him, and embarrassed for both of us, and for that moment despised him.

And I remember a hot midweek afternoon later that same August, cool in the darkness of the posted and barb-wired wood. We'd spotted a green creature hopping about in the ferns near the brook, and were leaping after it, arguing was it frog or toad, when the sudden tinkle of a distant bell pulled us up short. Reconnaissance disclosed an old dusty LaSalle auto across the road in the center of the colony, and next to it a boy shaking a hand-held bell. Sliding under the barbed wire, we dashed back across the road. Of all the vendors, this was the one we most looked forward to, Bernstein the toy man, and it was only his second visit that long summer. By the time we got there he'd already laid out a blanket and was drawing merchandise out of the back seat. He ducked his head out of the car momentarily. "Shimmy," he called to his son, and the boy, about ten, yarmulke on head, long curly earlocks and pretty as a girl, went around to the other side and began to pull out stuff too. We watched them cover the blanket with chess and checker sets, jacks, Monopoly, rubber balls, baseballs, bats, dolls, and one I would have killed for—a really fancy football game, a pinball kind of affair, green wooden field with chrome sides, ivory bumpers, spring levers.

Kids circled the blanket with large and gleaming eyes, while the knitting and gossiping in the beach chairs nearby became more intense, studiedly oblivious. Money for the vegetable man and the dairy man was necessity, but for Bernstein's chochkes?

I didn't even try for the football game. It wasn't just that it was so unlikely—we weren't a family that indulged in frivolities—but also that I was aware that money didn't grow on trees, that my father had to sweat and bleed sixty hour weeks in that butcher shop to keep us clothed, fed and roofed, and I could never get myself to squander that kind of money. Still, there was no harm in hearing the price; just, I suppose, to have an idea of possibilities and losses.

Bernstein stood on the other side of the blanket, nose drooping over thickish lips fixed in a smile sour with the certainty of failure. He was a little man, cleanly dressed in tan trousers wrinkled from the car, a brown short-sleeved shirt revealing clerkly arms, and a white linen cap worn, I was sure, more to hide his eyes from the blinding glory of his omnipresent Lord than his skull from the sun. His small frame was bent by the shyness that kept his eyes to the ground. He glanced up guardedly only to get a fix on the toys being passed around. He rubbed a fist into the other palm, as if from cold. For a tickled instant I imagined him a sidewalk hustler nervous about a cop sneaking up. But then it came to me that the little man was just another one of us, worried about providing for his family, scratching for a living by selling to people who couldn't afford to buy.

I pointed to the football game. "How much?" I called to Bernstein across the blanket, above the voices pricing the cheaper stuff, the pink rubber Spaldeens, the jacks, the checker games. "Feer thaler," he answered, nodding encouragement before dropping his eyes again. I nodded back thoughtfully, as if genuinely considering, silently calculating that the four bucks represented nearly a week's rent for our cottage. Then I set off on a contemplative stroll around the blanket's perimeter.

Little Herbie Schatz, who'd penetrated the circle of beach chairs, came out leading a willing Sylvie by the hand. Attractive even without makeup, long-legged in shorts and a halter that hid little, she was today playing doting mother. Maybe salving a tattered conscience, she smiled indulgently, "Remember: whatever you want, but just one." So Herbie, not a fool, pointed to the star of the display. "That one," he called shrilly to Bernstein. "Gimme the football game."

"How much is that?" she asked.

I prayed she'd find the game—my game—too expensive. Bernstein bent to pick it off the blanket. Obeying precept, he averted his eyes from the woman so as not to chance inflaming his desire. "Feer thaler," he said, looking away.

It was just then, just at the instant the game was handed off to Herbie, that it was torn from his hand. I hadn't even noticed them sneak up, those two young men who'd wrenched our berries from us. This time they wore identical white shirts open at the neck and brown short pants. It was the darker one who held the package. He made a show of reading from the back of the box. "A football game?" he said. "Ah futbol!" he repeated in a mockery of Yiddish accent. "Since ven do Chews play futbol?"

Sylvie swiped at the box, but he held it aloft, out of her reach. She clawed at his arm. "Get away from here, you bastards!" she screamed. Coming around, the blond man placed his hands against her chest and shoved—his specialty. She fell over and hit the ground. Grimacing with pain she struggled upright, then sat there swearing. "Crooks!" the dark one spat out, and sailed the football game. "Crooks!" It splatted on the road below. Shimmy ran over and punched the man's back. "No," Bernstein screamed, "no, Shimmy." The man elbowed the boy aside like a pesky fly.

The blond one fell on Sylvie. She sobbed while he straddled her, rocking back and forth to mimic copulation. He slipped his hands under the halter and grasped her breasts, pressing on them to keep her down. Screaming for help, she bucked to throw him, but he was securely on her midriff and couldn't be dislodged. The dark one stood arms akimbo, guarding his partner against the women and children. The women clucked hysterically but sat as if nailed to their beach chairs, except for Dora Gold, who skittered off towards the little on-premises grocery with its phone. When Herbie tried to tear the man from his mother, Bernstein ran over too, clutching at the blond one's shirt. The dark one easily swept him aside.

I finally got my legs to move, and ran over to scoop a bat off the blanket. The dark man couldn't see me raise the bat from behind. I wanted to drive it down on him, smash his skull open. But I couldn't. I saw it as if being done to me, and I just couldn't. The bat landed too lightly on his shoulder. He swung round. Lightning exploded in my eyes and struck my cheek, and I went down.

The blond man lifted himself off the sobbing Sylvie. He walked over to the blanket. Raising his foot high he stomped the more fragile toys, then stooped to fling the balls, jacks, bats, over the bushes into the road. "You gonna come steal more berries?" he snarled.

The darker one joined him. They stood hands on hips, two lithe young crusaders surveying the field of vanquished infidels. But it had all been too easy; they needed more. The dark one prompted, "The car, c'mon, let's get the car," and they strode unheedfully, tall and clean cut and strong, toward the LaSalle. Even through hatred and rage I couldn't help an admiration for such manfulness, confidence. One on each side of the passenger compartment, they ducked through the open doors and began to fling toys and games over their shoulders onto the grass, or else popping out to sail angry arcs thudding on the road below.

"No! Vat are you doink?" Berstein stumbled towards his car. "Yunger man, vat are you doink?" he pleaded with the blond man's back. When the blond, unheeding, continued to flip merchandise out of the car, Bernstein snatched at his shirt. "Yunger man," he begged, "please." Wordlessly the blond man shoved him aside. When Bernstein came at him again, the man swung an open hand and caught him on the face. This time the toy man fell onto his knees. The sound of the slap hung in the air. A tentative smile haunted Bernstein's face, embarrassment at the ludicrous sound thinly coating the pain. In his reddening face the eyes liquefied. "Papa," Shimmy screamed, and came running. "Gei avek," Bernstein hissed, holding out an arm, "er vet deer derhargenen," and the little boy stepped carefully away, his eyes on the blond man. Nobody else moved.

Where was Dora Gold? Where were those troopers?

The darker one came around the car to his friend's side. He glanced with disgust at Bernstein sprawled on the ground. "All done," he pronounced with satisfaction at a good day's work. "Think the kikes learned their lesson?"

"What about the car?" the blond man said.

"We already did the car."

"No, I mean the car."

Breaking into a broad smile, the dark one snapped his fingers. "Oh yeah, the car." Eyes to the ground, they moved off in expanding circles, tossing found rocks onto a heap growing next to the La Salle. The others, the beach chair ladies and the kids, Shimmy, Herbie, even Bernstein and Sylvie Schatz lying where fallen, remained frozen by the game playing out before them. The two young men left off the search and came back to the heaped stones. Stooping to pick armfuls, they backed off a dozen paces and began to fling the stones at the car. When the driver's side window exploded in shards and crystals, Bernstein stumbled to his feet with a little cry. "Vhy?" he ran to the young men. "Gentemen, *far vas tuest du dos tzu mir*?" But they continued to fire away. The clang of stone against sheet metal shot a puff of dust from a fresh dent in the side of the hood. Bernstein lurched toward the darker man. The blond man intercepted him and shoved him back toward the dark man, who returned him. They vollied him that way; the little man's head snapped back with each shove, his cap flung off tightly curled graying hair, breath gasped past the terror hideous on his face. His short legs, struggling to keep up with his tossing body, stumbled, and with a moan he fell to his hands and knees. "*Helf mir*," he cried. "*Rotevet mikh*."

"*Helf mish*," the blond man mimicked. "*Helf mish*," he screamed in a trembling falsetto, "*Helf mish*," he threw his hands at the sky, shaking them fervently. The dark man joined his laughter. I wanted to cry; I too wanted to scream out. And yet a bubble of mirth rose to my throat, because I suddenly saw it from where they stood, those two young Americans: saw the little man's incomprehensible squealing, the tears spilling out of wild eyes in the long-nosed sorrowful face, the thick-lipped gold-toothed mouth wet and trembling. Crying, begging, fawning, totally ineffectual, he was a caricature of perse-cuted helplessness, and watching this embarrassing display I saw us, saw how we did not come up to standard, were a bit less than human. Even the endless struggles back to his feet seemed an insistence on being punished for this.

And just as I thought this, the shelling of the La Salle resumed, stones clanging and pinging, dust exploding in new wounds, and the ridicu-lous little man stumbled to his feet again and again ran at them. And yet again there was the squealing and the unintelligible pleading and his scrabbling at a white shirt, and then the whap of flesh against flesh, and this time when he dropped blood spurted from his nose and down his chin and shirt and he sat there, tears streaming into the blood.

The two young men took off running just minutes before the trooper's black Chevy slid to a halt on the graveled path. The door cracked open and the trooper leisurely unfolded himself. Gray uniform shirt skin-tight over broad shoulders, thick chest, slim waist. Steady blue eyes gaz-ing down out of the sun surveyed a snuffling Bernstein and all the rest of us. Narrrowing, they assigned a failing grade. Out of a smirk came his drawled, "What seems to be the trouble here?"

Dora Gold identified herself as the caller. "Two men, two young men, all of a sudden they come and they beat up everybody. And Bernstein, they throw away his merchandise and look how his car, they smashed up the whole car."

I could see the trooper's almost-smile. "And why would they do such a thing?"

Dora shrugged and held out empty palms, but Herbie Schatz piped up, "Because we picked the huckleberries?"

The trooper nodded. "Whose?"

I looked around and tried to see what he saw: an old car, some women and kids, a huddled snuffling little Jew filthy with tears and blood. A fuss about some huckleberries.

"Whose berries?" the trooper insisted.

Herbie's voice was now shakily uncertain. "By Juniper Lake?"

The nod this time weary, shake of head exasperated. "Can't you people read signs?"

And I remember thinking, We look like dumb greenhorns. Damn toy man, made us look like fools.

"What sign?" Dora said. "We don't see no sign."

We just ain't important enough. Maybe if they'd killed him. If only they'd killed him. They should of killed that son-of-a-bitchin' toy man.

The trooper strutted back to the car. He folded himself into it. The tires shrieked. Sharp stones shot back at us.

But by then we all knew which sign he meant.

Pictures

Arthur sprawled in an orange plastic chair in the Jacksonville airport, wondering what the hell he was doing there. It drove him crazy that the bureaucrats thought it perfectly reasonable to drag in five guys from all over the country, who had to spend long hours traveling and being away from home, for a really dumb one hour conference that could easily have been handled by phone. His right lid began fluttering. He tried to decide whether it was weariness or just nerves again, then opened his eyes to rid himself of the disconcerting sensation.

On a Wednesday afternoon the terminal was less than crowded, with sizeable gaps between such groupings of families, lovers, and uniformed airline employees as might be found in any airport. Arthur wondered if airports retain interior decorators with a sharp eye for the usual, to blend the groups and position them according to a standard layout approved by the Federal Aviation Administration.

He let his eyes roam back and forth in lazy arcs over the banal vista. It was not until they had followed her for some seconds that the image registered in his mind and hoisted him by the collar.

At the far end, she strode back and forth across the entire width of the lounge, toting two pieces of luggage. Each time she reached the doorway at either side she disappeared, exiting the stage, and each time reappeared after a short interval, as if for an encore in response to Arthur's applauding gaze.

A man's gray felt hat failed to contain all of the gold spilling onto her shoulders. Arthur thought the hat, whether idiosyncracy or fad, strikingly at odds with the rest of her. Her dress, an unadorned gray, high-necked and nominally demure, was cunningly sculpted to reveal an underlying structure that could easily have provoked yet another war among the ancient Greeks.

He shut his eyes again, chasing her persistent image with lines that had served him well over the years, "If she be not fair for me, What care I how fair she be?"

He was in the midst of erecting a structure of calm around himself, with his mantra as the bricks and slow deep breaths as the mortar, when the crash brought his walls tumbling down.

His eyes sprang open. Pointing to the luggage dumped onto the chair next to his, she commanded, "Could you keep an eye on this for me?" and without waiting for a response marched away, bottom twitching, high heels clicking, hem twirling.

He was still mulling over equations to account for the long and elliptical trajectory bringing her to a halt in front of his chair, out of all those in the huge room, when she startled him with, "Okay, I'm back. Thanks."

Assuming the transaction completed, he nodded acknowledgement but said nothing. She asked impatiently, "Okay if I sit here?"

"Please." Arthur leaped up to help her transfer her luggage one seat further on.

"So," she said with a little sigh as they sat down. "Where are you headed?"

He was surprised to find her not quite so young as he had at first thought. "New York," he answered. There was a fine webbing at the corners of her eyes, adding interest to skin that was otherwise smooth and unblemished, or at least successfully made up.

"Ah yes. Spent a couple of weeks there, once," she said. "The Big Apple. God, what a time! Of course," she added, reaching back to finger the overflow of hair, "that was quite a while ago. When I was still young and attractive."

Arthur gave her his best shy smile. "How could you possibly be more attractive than you are right now?"

He liked the way she laughed at that clumsy transparency, unstinted, full-throated. With the laugh still hanging around her eyes and mouth she said, "The minute I spotted you across the room I knew you for a liar."

They grinned at each other, accomplices in the small verbal misdemeanor. But then the subject seemed exhausted. When the silence began to swell, he punctured it with, "I don't really live in New York, by the way. That's just where the plane lands. Then I still have to go on up to Connecticut.

"Say no more," she said, "the picture becomes quite clear. A four bedroom colonial. White with green shutters. Flower garden in front. Am I right? A wife, three kids, and a dog?"

"Not exactly. To begin with," Arthur corrected her, "just two kids."

"Boy and girl?"

"Alicia, ten and Jeremy, twelve." He changed his opinion of the man's hat. He now found it saucily attractive, underscoring the femininity rather than detracting from it. Perhaps, he thought, because of all that golden hair flooding out.

"I'm from Atlanta myself," she explained. "Came out here to look at some real estate. What I do is, I buy old houses, fix them up, and then resell them." In the unhurried voice with the round soft accent it sounded like a cultural activity for gentil ladies.

Actually, her hair was darker than gold. Maybe copper shot through with gold. He liked the way it peeped out of the hat in front, delicately crosshatching part of the forehead.

"What time does your plane take off?" she asked.

"Four-thirty." He glanced at his watch. "Three quarters of an hour to go."

"Why I ask is, I still have a couple of hours to hang around this God-forsaken place."

Their eyes met again, but this time bounced off. Each searched the large room, as if hunting for something remarkable. Something worth talking about.

Then she asked, "Got any pictures? Of the kids, I mean."

Arthur looked down at his hands. "I haven't had a chance to take any recently." He glanced at her. "What about you? Got any of yours?"

"Nope. No kids. No kids, no husband, no pictures." She wilted momentarily, then pulled her shoulders back. "So tell me: Are you down here on business?"

He shook his head, miming exasperation. "A totally unnecessary meeting is what I'm down here for."

"My plane doesn't take off for two hours and…," she peered down at her wrist watch, "…and ten minutes."

The loudspeaker announced the boarding of an unintelligibly numbered Delta Airlines flight to an unintelligible city. They watched an airliner taxi in slowly over the tarmac right up to their glass wall.

She crossed her legs. A finely wrought ankle swung close to his. "Actually," she said, "the reason I asked when your plane leaves is I wanted to find out if we have enough time to be friends."

Arthur, brow rising, weighed, measured, evaluated, then shrugged. "Sure," he said tentatively, "we can be friends."

"Oh no," she said. "No we can't. Not if you answer like that. Trying to decide if you're humoring a crazy lady or accepting an invitation for a roll in the hay."

"That's not at all what I was thinking."

"Yes? So then why are we blushing?"

Arthur, feeling the blood in his face, smiled a sheepish admission.

"What I mean is," she said, "everyone has something they want to get off their chest. But maybe there's no one to listen, or else it's too embarrassing. Right now, we—you and me—we have the chance to open up about the most personal things, or to say the craziest things, or anything at all. Like real good friends. And no worry, no embarrassment. Because probably, we'll never meet again."

Arthur hesitated, then permitted a grin to show. "Well, why not? But only if you go first."

"Oh, don't you worry about me. Once I get started, my mouth'll go on flapping for three days without any encouragement whatever, and no stopping to even draw breath. Hon, if I were you I'd grab this opportunity while it lasts."

"No, the idea was yours, so the honor should be yours." He had a momentary vision of his head in her lap, her coppery hair hanging down over him, tickling his face.

With a rueful smile she shook her head slowly, pityingly. "That's right, keep it buttoned down and bottled up." She reached out, then, and lightly touched the sleeve above his wrist. "Friend," she said softly, "are you aware how much pain shows? Even when you're smiling?"

Arthur, looking at her carefully, felt himself inching closer. But her calm gold-flecked irises only reflected his own image. "Sorry," he said, "I don't know what you mean."

"The hurt is flooding out right through your eyes. It's there for anyone to see who wants to. But you're married, poor fellow, so you probably don't have anyone to talk to about it."

"Wait." He raised his hand in a stop signal. "I don't remember saying I'm married."

"Aren't you?"

"Only until a year ago."

"Is that why you don't carry a picture of the kids?"

"They change too fast at this age."

She reached out and took Arthur's hand in hers. She held it in the palm of the hand resting on her thigh.

"She tells them lies," he said, not knowing he would say it, "and then they don't want to be with me."

She pressed Arthur's hand and he averted his face, shaking his head as if impatient with himself. After an interval he cleared his throat and turned back to her, smiling thinly. "How about yourself?"

She placed her free hand over his already held in her lap, making a sandwich of it. "I'll talk your ears off, if you'll let me. But perhaps we could do it somewhere else? Over a drink or a quick bite?"

He stifled a vision of the two of them entwined, weaving the tapestry of an illicit afternoon. "They'll be calling my plane in a few minutes."

She said, "Don't you agree we're getting along pretty well?"

"Oh yes," he nodded vigorously. "Very well."

"What would happen if you missed your flight? If you took a later one? Would anyone be harmed?"

Arthur's gaze dropped to his hands. He studied the fantastically complex system of tendons and delicate bones making precise movement possible. He clenched and unclenched his fists; turned his hands palm up and then palm down; bent his fingers to bring the nails under inspection. He could feel the shape of his mouth change, as if the corners were melting upward.

He lifted his head. "No," he said, brightening as if pleased at having solved a knotty problem, "no, there would be no harm." He stood up. "Let me help you with that luggage."

She smiled up at him hopefully. "You're with me?"

"Yes," he said, "I'm with you."

She sprang up. He tucked her overnight bag under the arm that held his own case. She picked up her attache case, then offered her free hand. He grasped it tightly in his.

They started down the aisle. Arthur tried to imagine what they would do when they got outside, but couldn't, and quickly gave it up as irrelevant. He was game for anything at all; this was the beginning of a new chapter. No, he corrected himself, not a new chapter, a whole new book.

Hand in hand they walked briskly across the lounge. The clack of her heels on the polished floor seemed to Arthur a drum roll, a flourish accompanying a brave explorer's departure for unknown shores. He intercepted the glances of male passersby, flashing desire at her and envy at him. And then he gave himself up to her fragrance, to the feel of her smooth cool fingers. To the idea of her.

They were through the lounge. Then they were past the ticketing area. Through the plate glass outer wall they could see the taxis lined up just beyond, waiting.

It was then that the clatter of her heels slowed. He heard them falter. She disengaged her hand.

"Is anything wrong?" he asked.

They stopped, confronting each other. "Didn't you realize you were holding me back?" she asked. "Pulling on my hand?"

"No," he said, defending himself. Even more adamantly, "No." Then, conceding somewhat, he asked, more gently, "Did I really?" And at the same moment he posed the question the answer became clear to him. His shoulders sagged and he bent to set his briefcase on the floor. Still looking down, he shook his head mournfully. "I really wanted to. But I guess I just can't do it."

"Can't do what?" she asked coolly. "Skip the plane? Have a drink with me? Talk?"

He peered up at her. "Go with you."

She grabbed for her case. Straightening up quickly, he lifted it and held it away from her. "Please don't," he said, touching her arm. "Sit down with me. Please."

Grudgingly, she allowed him to steer her to an empty seat. Almost immediately she jumped up again. "No. I'm going to leave you alone to enjoy your pain."

"Don't go," he pleaded. "I want to explain. Something I'm not sure I understand myself."

With a quick little shrug of exasperation she dropped back onto the seat. She lifted off the hat and let it fall onto her lap. Her hair, cascading, was a living thing. He seated himself facing her. He took a deep breath, and she turned her ear toward him as if to better concentrate on the disembodied voice.

He said, "There's no picture in my wallet, but there is one I carry in my mind. Alicia and Jeremy sitting at the kitchen table, doing their homework. The dog's poking her head into Jeremy's lap and he's patting her with one hand and writing with the other. Supper's cooking, and the heat from the oven fogs the windows. Alicia asks me to help her multiply fractions."

They stared at each other through a departure announcement. Arthur marveled at how quickly her features and facial expressions were becoming familiar to him: the faint quarter inch tomboy scar on her temple, the way she had of worrying her lower lip when thinking.

He said, as if mulling over the inexplicable, "Whenever something good comes along, I get scared. That it'll remove me from that picture."

She considered, then nodded slowly, comprehending. "Oh my dear," she smiled ruefully, telling a joke on herself. "I was wanting to help mend your wings, and you're still imagining you can fly."

He couldn't tell if she intended contempt or pity or regret, but he heard only caring when she softly added, "We have met too soon."

He pushed himself to his feet. "I think they've already called my flight."

"Yes," she said. "Good luck. Don't forget your briefcase."

"Good luck," he said, gazing down at her shining copper hair. Its naked center part, not quite straight, seemed touchingly vulnerable. When she glanced up at him he hesitated, then said shyly, "Goodbye, friend."

He took a dozen steps before he heard her call after him, "What's your name?"

He turned, backpedaling, still moving away from her. "Arthur," he yelled.

She stood up, as if to make herself better heard. She shouted back at him, presumably her name, but already he was too far away to hear it distinctly. Then a group of travelers came between, and he lost sight of her.

June Twenty-Second

He hurries the two blocks from his house to the beach because it is already past nine, and at ten the lifeguards will be climbing into their chairs, and the joggers and volley ballers and surfers and young lovers begin to straggle in and violate the peace and freshness.

Mounting the boardwalk he's relieved to find he's made it in time. As far as he can see from that elevation, there are yet few souls along the miles of duality—sand and sky, intersected by whitecaps. He descends three steps to the sand and starts across it. It is still damp from the night's rain and the tractors are late to comb it, so that although less slippery than when powder it has formed into deep labyrinthine furrows, and crossing it becomes a torturous minuet. He wonders will the shoreline still be nicely solid, or so saturated with rain as to suck at his heels and spoil his morning's jaunt.

For him, June 22 is only a couple of weeks into the season. Before then, even though the climate was for many weeks already mild in the streets, the beach still clung stubbornly to winter, and he stayed away from its chilly insistent winds. At his age now illness is more difficult to shake.

This June 22 he seeks a man, a dog, and a girl.

Graffiti'd walls of concrete protect the facing houses from marauding sand and water. At each intersection the wall bears the street's number, so that by glancing up from the water's edge progress along the shore can be measured. He's anyway come here often enough now, that he can locate himself by house style rather than the painted numbers.

Half way across the sand, he slows to disentangle the ear phones from around his neck and fit them to his ears, then run the dial of his Walkman across its FM band. His search ends when he encounters the sweet piquancy of a Schubert impromptu.

A figure comes into view up the beach. Even from that distance he can make out the long robe and white makeshift turban, so already knows it the Orthodox woman who comes here almost every morning. He has several times glanced at her in passing, and has seen that she is no longer young, almost surely older than even himself, and he is always impressed by her stamina, the length and brisk unflagging pace of her daily walk. Judging her level with the round-edged, glass-walled art deco house, he places her still about a half mile away.

It always bothers him to come abreast of someone here, because it is invariably a moment of incivility. Long long ago, his hand in his father's as they walked along a country road, he heard him bid good morning to a man passing by. "Do you know that man?" he'd asked. His father laughed. "When you meet someone in the morning you always say hello. Even if it's a complete stranger." But on this beach he'd discovered the mores different. That first summer he'd moved here, three years before, he would come down early, the sun still low on the horizon, and be feeling kinship with sweet nature and the few other early-rising humans. But his expansive greeting to a passing jogger or a fisherman trolling the waters or a pretty girl strolling by invariably met with indifference, sometimes even with a sneer. So he'd learned. Now he kept his eyes lowered in passing, or gazed toward the sea or in the opposite direction at one of the houses, or overhead at a plane in its takeoff arc from one of the nearby airports. Occasionally his covert glance might surprise an expression—tentative smile or slightly parted lips—that hinted at the other's desire for acknowledgment, but then he'd regretfully watch it stifled by his own mask of impassiveness. Eventually he came to realize that the seemingly callous practice was not a breach in the walls of civilization but, on the contrary, evidence of a higher freedom: tacit agreement that each one's envelope of solitariness is inviolable.

He stops at the lifeguard chair level with 127th Street. Leaning against its scaffolding of iron pipe, he removes his sneakers and athletic socks, then reaches high to place them on the seat, safe from the maws of the rapacious tractors that will gobble anything within reach of their huge teeth.

He sets off leisurely, intending the first minutes as a warmup, disdaining the elaborate contortions of the more athletically inclined soon to be littering the beach. When he reaches the shoreline he gratefully finds its footing solid enough for a decent pace. In deep breaths he sucks in air of distilled nectar, delicately flavored by the salt of the sea and the pungency of its creatures and the Schubertian piano. And then he lifts his eyes to a sky that has been scrubbed so clean, is so outrageously perfect, that its color is the very definition of blue, and a bubble of laughter escapes him.

After thirty years of childless marriage, the survivor does not need solitude within memories and longing. He'd found himself sinking into abnormality: sitting unmoving on the floor for hours, staring at an empty wall. So, frightened and lost, he'd sold their sorrowing house in a nearby state's suburbia and moved books and clothes to an attic apartment in this city's seaside enclave.

At the sea's edge the waves gently expire at the top of his ankles. The water's temperature is cold in the sun-warmed air, cutting the sense of his body in two. He picks up the pace, rhythmically swinging his arms high, getting up on the balls of his feet, kicking the shallow water into spray.

Even though isolated by etiquette, there are beach people he has come to know. He's seen them enough to have learned somewhat of their habits, and this has led him to speculate about their lives and imagine their stories. In this way he has gotten to know them better, or so it seems to him. And in a couple of instances over the three summers, he's even exchanged brief words. Because of their rarity and unexpectedness, the few words passed have become memorable, and during the winter he sometimes pulls them out for reiteration, like favorite lines of poetry.

Around nine-fifteen each morning the old man would arrive at the boardwalk behind his dog, then they would both walk down the steps and across to the water's edge. The dog would stroll along the shore plodding and pensive like a retired ambassador with hands clasped behind his back, the old man emulating her leisurely pace. She'd dunk one tentative paw in the water and stare out at the sea awhile, deciding whether to brave it, or maybe recalling the more impetuous days of her lost youth. Then they'd turn and plod back up to the boardwalk, and crossing it head for the street.

The old man, seventy-five or eighty, was always cleanly and carefully dressed, trousers and shirts knife-edged, on his head a neat fisherman's hat, and on his upper lip a trim white mustache. His ramrod back and set of face bespoke morality and rectitude, but the young eyes looked for the chance to laugh; his sluggish pace seemed only for the dog's accommodation, he himself surely vigorous enough to be one of those octogenarians who run marathons. The dog was a large poodle of some sort, wire hair perfectly white except for one flopping black ear.

Once, that first year, he'd been resting on the boardwalk after the morning's jaunt, and the old man with his dog had walked past his bench. Glancing up, he'd found the old man's eyes locking with his, a small smile on his face. He'd blurted inanely, "That's the gentlest dog I've ever seen."

"No," the old man shook his head, "just old. In dog years he's even older than me."

A couple of mornings later the old man passed by again, and they exchanged good mornings. After that time, as if recalling protocol, they averted their eyes. They never talked again.

Lowering its landing gear, a gull glides down to settle a yard in front of him, at the water line. On matchstick legs the little grayhead opens its assertive orange beak, and with all the strength in its powter chest caws a complaint at the inattentive sea. In support of its claim, another gull lands nearby. When it opens its beak to add voice, its prize drops onto the sand. Something impels him closer, and he discovers a creature the length of a finger joint overturned on its turquoise shell back, half a dozen tiny legs trying to climb the air. He picks it up gingerly and carries it to wet sand and sets it gently down. In half an instant it is already half burrowed into the sand. In the full instant it has disappeared. His spirit soars with the righteous deed; it deflates again when he thinks about a creature needing to be buried in order to live.

Several times each winter he'd find himself worrying about the old man and his dog, afraid one of them would fail to return the next spring. And each spring, within a day or two of his first visit to the beach, he'd sure enough spot the old man and his dog wandering near the water, perhaps just a tad slower than the previous summer. His heart would leap as if at sight of a lost love, because it signified a renewal of life, and he still loved life.

His eyes continually sweep the beach. Each time he turns his head he is startled, even a bit frightened, to find the vastness of sand, sea, and sky behind him as empty as Creation the day before man.

The white turban of the Orthodox woman is closing on him. Within her robe she advances insistently, with only a regal sway to betray humanity. When she is almost abreast of him he lowers his eyes to the ground, feigning a search of some sort. By the time she has passed he finds himself truly engrossed in sorting out some of the creatures and minerals cast out by the sea. As always he is confounded by what he sees there. The phrase, Death in the midst of life, leaps to mind at sight of small bleached skeletons, an empty carapace turned inside up, sluiced by the tide. He considers the uncountable deaths occurring that very moment and every other moment in the placid sea, and all around him, and everywhere. But then he spots a little stone, alabaster, soft and chewable in its perfect roundness, something for a Michelangelo to chip away at until a miniature Pieta emerges; then a sea shell, purple outside and inner surface cream, long and gracefully convoluted like a flower spun by a sea nymph. As always he finds it difficult to assign such incredible complexity and perfection to chance, yet cannot reconcile that beauty at his feet with the death next to it in the sand.

Above the sea the darkening sky has erected a bank of clouds big as apartment buildings. A shaft of sunlight cutting a window through it throws everything into relief, the darks darker, the light more golden. The sea heaves churning waves impatiently following close upon each other. It spits foam further up the sand. He remembers then the hurricane reported working its way through the upper Caribbean, heading for Hatteras, already affecting this weather.

Reaching down to the Walkman he clicks it off, then disengages the ear phones and coils them around his neck. What can music add to the majesty of such a morning?

On that day near the end of last summer, he'd found a shell he couldn't resist. There was no telling himself there'd be another along just like it; this shell was singular, infused with such art and intelligence that a debater could hold it up as proof to the cosmological argument for the existence of God. It was a brittle, yet delicately colored, striated flower—stem, pistil, stamen—stylized as if by some contemporary artist. He picked it up to carry with him the rest of the way and then home.

Her voice at his shoulder startled him. "You too?" it said. He turned to it and found a young lady he'd seen every morning that summer, although never up close. She'd stick to the higher ground, and from that distance he would observe her walking or being run by a frisky German shepherd, the rope leash so long that it sometimes obscured the connection between dog and owner. Smiling up at him, she held out a shell of a beauty and complexity to rival his.

As on every morning she wore white shorts and a flowered halter on her tightly athletic body. Up close the fine webbing around her eyes showed her somewhat older than he'd imagined from observing her vigorous strides with the dog. The face was pleasant, very pleasant, the kind you wanted to talk to.

"My God!" he said. "How beautiful yours is."

"I thought it would make a nice paper weight."

"Mine too. First one I've ever picked up."

She said, "I guess we've both been lucky."

"Yes," he said, "I guess so."

"Well," she smiled, letting herself be tugged away by the leash, "maybe this will mean a lucky day for both of us."

As it turned out, he did have some good luck that day, although soon after he couldn't remember what it was, only that it was pleasing while of no great consequence. He rehearsed how he would dramatize his luck for her. But next day and every morning thereafter he searched for her in vain, and then in a couple of weeks came the cold winds of September, and he stopped going to the beach. In thinking about her during that winter, he imagined her a school teacher who'd been just finishing up summer vacation when they'd met, and he was sure she'd be back in June when vacation came around again. Now, every morning, holding in readiness the news of his good luck, he searches the high ground for her.

The sudden roar is so tumultuous it all but shakes the globe. Directly overhead the Concorde is powering heavenward, and he looks up at its white wide flat belly, wheels folded into it. In a matter of seconds, already well on its way to Europe, the plane disappears as if into a fold in the sky. He checks his watch. Yes, he nods, nine-twenty, right on the button.

He expects that a couple of blocks on he will pass the young man who every morning tosses bits of bread to the gulls swooping and shrilly bickering around his head. Olive skin and tightly curled black hair, he will be wearing a shiny black suit, possibly an old tuxedo, buttoned to the collar, sleeves hiding his hands, trouser ends underfoot. He imagines the young man, whom he sometimes refers to as St. Francis of Assisi, as a former musical prodigy whose talent and cleverness brought him, still not much more than a youth, appointment as conductor of a midwestern orchestra at the top of the second rank.

At his debut concert, decked out in white tie and tails, already the idol of teen age girls, their mothers, and expectantly salivating local critics, he brought down the stick and almost immediately the score, Strauss's Ein Heldenleben, began to dance before his eyes. He froze. The limbs of the headless orchestra entangled each other with shrieks of pain and outrage. The audience too shrieked, but with hilarity. The young man ran out into the night and anonymity, and now, a thousand miles away, coaxes gulls' cries into avant garde compositions.

He strides past an aggregation of sandpipers, the tiny birds scurrying in tireless circles, Pinocchio noses sniffing from sand to shallow water and back again. Each is closely followed by its mirror image in the gloss of water left by receding waves. He smiles at the purposeful intensity of the little creatures busy going nowhere.

Half way between the water and the houses, closer to the shoreline than he knows was her habit, a young woman is briskly led in his direction by a dog tethered to a long leash. From a half dozen blocks away he can see white shorts and a flowered halter. Tentatively he veers a couple of steps towards heading her off. But then he holds back. It's a different dog, hers was a tan shepherd and this is a gray something, a pointer type. Still, you can't go by the dog, dogs have shorter lives than their masters.

He moves slow, wanting to make sure, until just a hundred feet away he decides to confront her. She watches him anxiously, beginning to arc away. "Wait,' he yells. "Please wait, I just want to ask you something." At this she halts, glances around to see what help might be close at hand, then reels in the dog until it heels beside her.

When he advances further a stiff palm shoots up. "Stay where you are!"

He tosses down his hand in disgust and turns to move off. "Wait," she says in a more reasonable tone, "I'm just afraid the dog might bite you."

Her age seems about right, although after all this time the face is not really familiar.

He inches closer. "Do you remember me?" he asks.

She shakes her head, plainly puzzled.

"Last September? We compared sea shells?"

She shakes her head again, this time faintly sneering. He sees now that this face is made up of rigid planes and sharp angles. Unlike the other, it does not invite confidences, would not tempt him to talk to it. Still, he could be wrong, his memory is not as sharp as it once was.

"You said that the shells might bring us both a lucky day?"

Showing exasperation, she pulls on the rope, starting to draw the dog away.

"I just wanted to tell you about the luck I had that day." But even while he says this, he already knows it a lost cause. It is not the same girl. Or she does not want to remember.

"Sorry," he says to her back. "I'm sorry, I thought you were someone else."

He starts off down the beach again, walking faster this time. Opposite the yellow house, newly renovated to gain more water views, he breaks into a jog. Everything comes at him faster now as he bobs up and down, but he is still sharply aware of the threatening sky's grandeur, the soft brown of the waterlogged sand, the tiny shells littering the ground. What a beautiful day to die, he thinks, a line he once read, now often recites to himself on the great mornings. He says this because it really is a beautiful day, because he is keenly aware of time dwindling, and because medical reports have cautioned that exertion like this would be foolhardy. He's making that little joke out of his fears, but at such moments he genuinely feels that there is no place on earth he'd rather croak, as he puts it, than right here, so inviting to lie under this water-smoothed earth, hearing the breath of the sea, the forlorn cries of the gulls.

He jogs along steadily, concentrating on the bounced levering of his legs, the soft air rushing at him; disregarding the tightness in his chest, the extra thumps of his heart compensating for misses. Defiantly, he begins to run even harder. Until after a bit more he reaches the end of breath, struggles to inflate his lungs, and is forced to a stop. He stumbles around in little circles, chest heaving, heart knocking. Eventually, able to draw some breath, he drops to the sand he's imagined lying under.

Presently, breath and strength recovering, he gets up and slowly resumes his way towards the fence at the end of the beach, still a couple of miles off. While observing the waves, the sky, he still watches futilely for the old man and his dog; by 140th Street even St. Francis in his distressed formality has not yet appeared. Still far enough away so that he cannot yet distinguish male from female, a jogger bobs up and down. In a little while, the jogger will be upon him, subjecting him to the usual sidelong glance of disdain cast at the less athletic. Somewhat to his right, on the higher beach, a young man plods along while a dog dances around him.

Alongside, the sea is angrier, driving its waves higher up on the shore. As always, thirst flares at sight of the foam topped waves, which remind him of tap beer. This small momentary want leads him to recall other desires, losses, and deprivations, not in lengthy specifics, but as instantaneous pictorial enumerations. Some symbolize good times and minor triumphs, but mostly they are of the death of a wife, childlessness, nagging illness, loneliness. He is drawn out of meditation when the jogger finally reaches him and sails on by. The disdainful young lady is graceful and smooth limbed, trailing sunlit hair.

They would refer to it between themselves as their "scientific" marriage. Already in their thirties when they'd met, they were drawn to each other by compatibilities rather than any intemperate call of the flesh. Weighing and measuring, comparing and totting up individual likes and dislikes, interests and peeves, ambitions and life philosophies, even giving weight to his ability to make her laugh, they concluded that the factors were there for a successful marriage. "Our chances have to be better, don't you think," she said with that little off center smile, "since we go into it with eyes open and reasonable expectations?" So they came together in logic rather than love. And thirty years proved their logic impeccable. On her sick bed, that last day, she'd reached for his hand. Wan eyes almost smiling, she'd said, "Our arithmetic added up correctly, didn't it, my dear?" Only after she died did their logic go awry: his mourning heart broke not with reason but love.

The young man he'd spotted a little while before on the higher ground is suddenly close. His energetic dog is a large terrier of some sort, the seamless black of its wire hair marred only by the white of one floppy ear. It occurs to him that this dog is the photographic negative of the old man's, and he smirks ruefully at this conceit. But then another one strikes him, that maybe the dog represents a mirror universe. Maybe somewhere along the beach, passing the art deco house, say, he'd crossed into uncharted territory.

Plodding across the sand on the way to the boardwalk he turns to contemplating the remainder of his day. When he gets home he will shower and breakfast, bran flakes today after the oatmeal yesterday. He will drive to the supermarket and rustle up some grub, if he can just decide what it is he'd like to eat. That's as far as it gets, except that it occurs to him that he might try to hit the beach an hour earlier tomorrow. He might like to see what it's like, an hour earlier.

Up on the boardwalk, the sun pouring through the slats of the green benches scores the boards beneath with stripes of gold. What's it mean? he wonders. What's the significance of four stripes of light beneath a bench? His brow wrinkles over this puzzle he is sure must have a solution. Until he notices that his shadow on the boarded floor insistently keeps apace, the distance between himself and this dark ghost unvary-ing. He veers abruptly to the right, then sharply back to the left, but still it clings to him as if glued. Oh, leave me alone, will you? he cries out at his shadow. Why don't you just fuck off, he silently screams, and leave me alone, leave me alone?

The Girl Who Played Beethoven

The luminous notes leapt up like fireflies aspiring to the glittering chandelier. The girl at the baby grand wore a sleeveless dress, whiter against her tan; upswept golden hair left naked a ravishing neck. Nimble fingers flowing out of supple arms coaxed the Mooonlight's adagio movement into incandescence. Love had Marty by the throat; his knees trembled, and he had to hold on to the piano.

No, this is not a love story—just a bit of remembering by an old man with too much time on his hands. You know how they say that old age finds it easier to recall half a century ago than yesterday? Well, we're talking about the late forties, when he was twenty-six.

That December, one of his assignments was the Pine Meadow Club, deep out on the Island, usually a three day job. Ever been out to a country club with the golf course buried in snow? Nobody around except for a caretaker staff: couple of ladies in the office to handle the bookkeeping and answer the phones, somebody to take care of the cleaning and maintenance, the club manager dropping in once in a while to check up on things. Ice boxes almost empty, and anyway no one there to cook anything.

Marty parked his '48 Buick in the deserted lot and trudged a hundred yards over crackling snow to the main building. At nine in the morning his breath was almost solid, and in the bright sun he heard trees snap with the frost.

Evidencing the members' progressive outlook, a new glitzy dining room, all sharp-angled glass and metal, protruded out of the art deco mansion like colored glass pasted onto expensive jewelry. Inside, it smelled of tired carpets and the locker rooms of dead athletes. Behind the dutch door of the business office, the ladies were already gabbing away a mile a minute. Spotting him, Mrs. Anderson, an Eleanor Roosevelt look-alike, gurgled hello as if Marty had fought his way to their side through blizzards and avalanches.

Hanging up his coat, he inquired about her arthritis, which she assured him was as bad as ever, and about Mrs. Williams' daughter's long-running divorce action, which turned out to have been settled satisfactorily: the ex-spouse was a now a candidate for the poorhouse.

Only then did Marty notice the figure hunched over an adding machine in a darker corner of the office. When the girl lifted her head to glance toward him, Mrs. Williams, a shorter but wider version of her co-worker, said, "Oh, Mr. Rosen, this is Christine Bishop." The older woman's smile embraced the girl. "Crissie helps out during school holidays."

Crissie tossed him a casual, "Hi," and returned to her papers.

Mrs. Anderson asked, "Where would you like to work? Do you think the card room again?"

He lugged the invoices, bank statements, and cloth-bound ledgers up one flight to the first room on the right of the staircase. Inside, he unloaded his burden onto the farthest of the half dozen round maple tables standing in coolish air on blue-green carpeting.

He walked over to the window. Three gaunt, gray-haired trees knelt in the snow; a lone lost sparrow fluttered panicky from one to another.

The door opened. The girl who was Crissie stood there, the cup shivering on the saucer in her hand. "Mrs. Anderson asked for a volunteer to bring you coffee."

Glasses removed, the nearsighted eyes through which she peered at him were violet in a heart-shaped face. Bronze hair down to her shoulders was silken and simple straight, a way he'd always found attractive; the body outlined by her fitted jumper shapely and tightly athletic. When she moved closer to set down the cup and saucer, he had an impression of strength and determination gilded with grace.

He said, "Thanks for volunteering."

She smiled coolly. "See you at lunch, Mr. Rosen."

Sensing a hesitancy in her retreat, he called out to her back, "Are you new here?" and when she faced around explained, "I haven't seen you before."

"No, I've been here," she responded amiably enough, "but sporadically. I can only come on school breaks."

"Where do you go?"

"Caltech."

"Majoring?" he asked in the shorthand of these things.

"Physics."

"Really? To do what with?"

"I want to get into the theoretical side."

So of course that launched him on his favorite topic. "I hope it's because you really want it, and not just because somebody else decided it for you. The worst thing you can do in this life is to work at something you don't enjoy."

She looked at him a longish moment—probably, he thought, estimating the extent of his lunacy and deciding it wasn't enough to form a clear and present danger. "See you at lunch," she said again, leaving.

Returning to his vexation, Marty opened a bank statement and with a red pencil marked off the paid checks against the disbursements ledger, following that up with other mindless boring tasks, like adding long columns and examining invoices for proper signatures; doing each procedure nine times, once for each bank account and once for each of the three months under review.

Periodically, as if to temporarily relieve a chronic pain, he got up and went to the window to look out over the stark white landscape. The surrounding open acres made it easy to imagine himself on the deck of a ship sailing a white sea. Between bits of the plodding work and trips to the window, he sat and stared at the opposite wall, at the framed print of a golfer wearing knickers and a beret topped with a little red woolen ball.

A remembrance flickered up out of his subliminal, a lightning flash illuminating a scene from a life: gentle yearning air of the blue hour— circle of light cast by the street lamp—teens leaning against the schoolyard's spiked fence—talk of baseball, girls, hit songs, and sometimes of less immediate concerns, like school and the future.

Fed into their calculations are principles as immutable as any of the Euclidian propositions they study in geometry class: there's no chance in hell of ever getting a job with an insurance company, bank or utility; advertising and architecture are also pretty well closed down; squeezing past engineering school quotas would be a real long shot; as for medical school, forget it unless your old man, who is making maybe a hundred a week, can scrape together the bucks to send you across the ocean to quota-free schools.

In the gentle compliant air of endless blue hours they make their plans to settle. Some will reluctantly embrace one of the promising new trades, like air conditioning and refrigeration; the rest will attend the local municipal college as business majors.

It is possible, Marty supposes now, that eventually some of the guys even enjoyed what they settled for. But he, he still had daydreams in which he doused a client's records with gasoline, dropped a match on it all, and grabbed the next boat outward bound for anywhere.

At a little past twelve the wall phone rang, Mrs. Anderson inviting him to lunch. Arranging the work into piles, he covered these with blank sheets of paper, for confidentiality as well as to protect curious innocents from death by boredom, and went downstairs.

Golf clubs and balls patterned the dining room's pillow-thick carpeting, a hundred muted spotlights shone out of hiding places in the ceiling, and at the far end a sea of snow showed through the plate glass wall. The ladies and Crissie were already seated at the table nearest the kitchen. Jumping up, Crissie dragged her chair a pace through the dense pile to give him more room. Mrs. Williams waved an invitation toward the dishes set out in the center of the table. "Help yourself."

Crissie asked, "Would you like me to make up something for you?"

"I'm not sure," he said. "Unaccustomed as I am to being served lunch by theoretical physicists."

"We have our practical side too," she said. "Now, would you prefer the stale cheese or the carcass of that poor long-dead animal? Or perhaps some of the rancid potato salad with the month old bread?"

"I think," he told her, "some of that strangely colored cheese with tomato on stale bread, and a side order of the antique potato salad."

Her movements were hesitant and angular enough so that Arthur could tell she was less used to serving than being served. It lent the action a touching intimacy—she was doing something for him she didn't have to, and going out of her natural way in order to do it.

Eating, they traded gentle ribbing, probing for feelings, reactions, attitudes—the currency of mutual assessment. "So tell me," he said, "is it your ambition to design a bigger and better atom bomb?"

"And is it yours to add up the world's longest column of numbers?"

It helped ease them past the bad lunch. And their smiles were passing grades assigned each other.

Afterwards, he went back upstairs to doodle check marks with a red pencil, look out the window, stare at the print of the ruddy-cheeked, tam-o'-shantered little golfer corkscrewed into the top of his swing.

In mid afternoon the door opened and then closed with the slow creak of a horror movie. Arthur could see no one there, but then a small sound came from behind the slender crook in the wall next the door. Bronze hair inched out, followed by violet eyes.

"I was afraid to disturb you, "she said, coming full way into the room. "I know how important your work is." At which they both snickered.

He said, "Are you answering a call for volunteers to come up and annoy me?"

"No, this is serious. Mrs. Williams would like the ledger. She needs to make some entries."

"Sorry, but I can't relinquish it just now."

She moved in closer, to better press her argument. "You're just being difficult." She pointed to the book open on the table. "You're not even using the silly ledger, you're only working with the cash books."

"She can have it in the morning."

When Crissie grabbed for the ledger Marty already had his hand on it. Her lithe arms were surprisingly stubborn. Both tugged harder, each advising the other to let go in voices needing more breath. Gradually he managed to reel in the ledger while she held on to it like a fish caught by the hook. She gave up, finally, and dropped into his lap.

Gently, he took the book from her and placed it back on the table. Her lips drawled breathlessly into his ear, "You like to play, don't you?"

The door screeched open. The maintenance man passed through, his face taking on a sneer. Crissie, jumping off Arthur's lap, said gravely and too loud, "Okay, Mr. Rosen, I'll report to Mrs. Williams that she can have her ledger in the morning."

"Yes," he said. "And thank you for working so closely with me." But despite the little flippancy he felt his heart pound and his breath labor, and he was surprised at how these symptoms could be brought on by so little exertion.

At five o'clock of the restless afternoon, he carried the books and invoices and bank statements back down the stairs. Stacking them in the safe, Mrs. Williams said, "Crissie said to tell you good night." She smiled, shaking her head in admiration. "Say, isn't our little girl really something? Would you believe she has a full scholarship? Yes, she's not only pretty, but exceedingly bright." She pushed shut the door and twirled the tumblers, then added with obvious affection and pride, "And quite a hot little number too, wouldn't you say?"

For three hours the next morning, sitting at the round maple table, Marty made red check marks in ledgers, went to the window to gaze out at the forlorn trees, came back to make more check marks.

At twelve-thirty the wall phone rang: Mrs. Anderson wanting to know where he was, they were already eating. He told her he wasn't having any lunch. She said, "She won't eat without you. The poor girl has a crush."

"I'm really not hungry," he said.

"Do you want her to get sick?"

So he went down.

Crissie shifted her chair to make more room. "I have your sandwich all ready," she said.

"What's in it?"

"Better you shouldn't know."

"No, really," he insisted. "I have to know."

"Oh, you're one of those? One of those picky eaters?"

"Yes," he said, "I'm one of those."

"It's just a cheese sandwich. Same as yesterday. You enjoyed it so much, I thought you'd like it again."

"That was clever of you," he admitted. "It's just exactly what I did want."

She shrugged modestly. "Laws of probability. Once financial types establish a pattern, they find it difficult to change: they enjoy being in a rut. So it was a very simple deduction. All in the day's work for us theoreticians."

"It's quite an honor to sit next to someone so bright."

"Yes," she nodded, "it's true we're bright. We're also kind, considerate, and very loving. That's why we make such terrific wives."

Eyes cast down, he took a bite of the sandwich. She watched him chew, then asked, "Want to discuss your audit?"

"What for?"

"To figure out why you're making so little progress."

"It happens to be going quite well, thank you."

"Oh, don't be so huffy," she said. "You're among friends here. So tell me, what seems to be the trouble? Your mind too much on a certain little cutie? Is that your problem?"

"What're you talking about?" he said, indignant, then saw the gleam in her eyes and his laugh burst out and met up with hers.

"So you really do like to play, don't you?" she said, still laughing.

In his bed that night, Marty gave up on trying to get any sleep, kept awake by that delirium described in a zillion poems and novels, and that he himself could best define as love and lust combined as intense as a fire, as holy as a religion.

He wondered if it was true about infatuation being merely propinquity, physical nearness activating chemicals in each that then want to mix with the other's. Wondered, What if the office assigned me to Perrone Aluminum instead of the Pine Meadow Club? But then he decided, To hell with the science of it, with the mathematics of probability, with second-guessing fate. Think of it as an unsolicited gift.

At nine, that morning of the third day, the ladies struck, staging a refusal to give up the books and records. Not until, they said, he listened to something they needed to tell him, and it had to be done quickly, before Crissie got in. So Marty surrendered himself in ransom for the invoices and ledgers, and followed his captors out to their usual table in the dining room.

"You probably don't know," the shorter one said, "that Crissie is engaged to be married?"

"An April wedding," the taller one added.

"To one of her professors."

"No, I didn't know," he admitted, feeling mugged.

The ladies traded conspiratorial smiles. "She's not crazy about him."

It was a matter of expedience, they explained. When a girl gets into heat, better to marry her off—quick, to someone solid and safe—than risk her going off wild and plunging into heartache. So reasoned her parents, with their old world notions. Crissie, being an obedient daughter, and greatly pressured, was simply following their wishes to marry her pursuing professor, a kind, solid, safe man, although of course somewhat older.

And yet…the girl was still a trace reluctant. So she was searching for an acceptable alternative, a sort of last fling, and maybe, the ladies suggested, maybe Marty had the inside track.

"If you like her," Mrs. Williams said, "here's your chance."

He shrugged disinterest.

Mrs. Anderson said, "Come now. We've been watching you. It's obvious that you do like her."

"Quite obvious, and quite a lot," Mrs. Williams seconded.

"Never in a million years will you do better than this," Mrs. Anderson said, with a warmth that startled him.

"Mary," Mrs. Williams cautioned, "we mustn't push too hard. Mr. Rosen is quite capable of deciding for himself. And the heart has its reasons, you know."

Mrs. Anderson regarded him through narrowing eyes. "Unless," she said carefully, "unless Mr. Rosen objects to going outside his own persuasion?"

Marty, standing up then, thanked the ladies for caring. Back in the office, they released the records to him.

In the chill of the card room he broke down the pile of books and records and redistributed them around the table. He put pencil to paper, but almost immediately his gaze lifted instead to the print on the opposite wall. He shook his head, smiling sorrowfully at the happy little golfer. Old friend, he thought, you they would welcome here with open arms, you with your ruddy Scots complexion. But us?

Burnt into his eyelids are the endless stacks of naked pipestem bodies. Sightless eyes open and mouths agape, their howls to heaven are silent, lost in the ether winds. And always attached to that image are the words, those same unbidden words in a million-voiced cry, "No, it was we, we it was who died for your sins."

This time it was't the phone that summoned him to lunch. Instead, on this third and last day, Crissie herself showed up in the card room. "Your cheese sandwich is ready and waiting," she said cheerfully.

"Thank you, but I have too much to do."

Her smile flickered, then brightened again. "Why don't I bring it up here and we can eat together?"

"Really," he said, "I don't have the time for a community lunch. Why don't you just go join your friends?"

"Too boring," she said. "They're entirely normal. With you it's much more interesting."

"Very funny," he cleverly responded.

"You've just spoiled my little surprise, you know."

When he refused to bite, she explained, "I was going to spice up your silly sandwich by playing a little concert for you."

Brilliantly clever to the bitter end, he asked, "And what is it you play? The phonograph?"

She shook her head at his boorishness. "No," she said bleakly, "the piano. Sometimes," she added, "you can say things better than with words."

"Maybe next time," aware of his churlishness like a pain, but unable to soothe it.

"Next time doesn't always come."

Yes, he thought, you're exactly right.

"Later, when you're finished?" she coaxed.

He considered. "Well, all right," he said, thinking, What the heck, maybe there is still time for one more time. "Around five."

Close to five and not yet done, Marty decided to pack it in anyway and finish up the job in the office Monday morning. He threw the papers into his briefcase and then bundled together the client's documents and ledgers.

But he sat on. He thought how he had no more choice than the tree out there kneeling in the snow, or the little man on the wall frozen into the top of his swing; told himself that, beyond minor details, we're all of us frozen into place by what's gone before.

He picked up the books and papers. Downstairs, Mrs. Anderson asked, "Anything doing?" He shook his head. "Too bad," she said.

Marty walked down the dank corridor to the ballroom. Under the glittering chandelier Crissie already sat at the baby grand. Watching him cross the windowless echoing room, she raised her hands over the keyboard. When he reached the piano her hands descended and he heard the familiar limpid opening of the Moonlight Sonata.

It went on to speak of love, happiness, and the sharing of sorrows.

An old story, but he'd never before heard it from the girl who told it now, who wore a white sleeveless dress out of which lithe arms moved gracefully and surely, whose hair, the color of precious metal, was upswept from back to front, leaving naked a neck fragrant with scent of myrtle and thyme and pomegranates, who caused images to swirl about his head, of a neck like an ivory tower, and breasts that are twins of a fawn, and little foxes, and the voice of the turtle, and comfort me with apples for I am sick of love.

He held fast to the piano while her fingers sang through the adagio movement, danced through the witty allegretto, stormed through the presto agitato.

She finished. Her hands dropped to her sides, forehead damp, wisps of hair come undone and settled back onto her neck.

He pulled out his handkerchief and stooped to gently wipe her brow. She smiled up at him. "Do I get a passing grade?"

"An A Plus. You're even better at the piano than the phonograph."

"Then we can be friends and lovers?"

"Is this a proposal," he said lightly, meaning only to continue the banter, "or a proposition?"

Her eyes turned more grave than the smile insistent on her lips. "Any way you want it."

Slowly and with concentrating precision he folded his handkerchief, then stuffed it back into his pocket. He lifted his arm to read his watch. "Got a long ride ahead of me," he said.

"Be careful," she warned. "This offer is good for a limited time only."

His feet seemed to drag as if crossing a carpet of glue, even while he heard his heels strike the naked wooden floor. She sat on amid the bare echoing walls, a girl fragrant as the Song of Songs.

Assignment Out of Town

In the snow and gloom of a late Sunday afternoon, the entire firm rendezvoused at Idlewild, not yet renamed in memory of a murdered President. Slogging through the tarmac's slush they one by one boarded the Capital Airlines DC-6.

Only weeks into his first job, this was Arthur's first flight as well. Deferentially stooped, he waited his turn to mount the platform. The twin propellers gleamed sucking in snow flakes; their engines coughed and exhaled darkly, like an old smoker with damaged lungs. He screwed up his eyes trying to put a wrinkle in time, wring a hint of the future from such subverted chronology: start of an exciting career or tragic end to a short life?

Otherwise empty, the plane took off into gray sightlessness. Under way in the turbulence it repeatedly sank into precipitous vacuums, then reluctantly regained height; linear progress seemed only incidental. The others were bunched at the front of the cabin: the partners, Weisbrod and Becker; Jeanie, the thirtyish redhead who operated a calculating machine and often relieved Becker's tensions; Jerry, who with Arthur Lavin made up the junor accounting staff; and Helen Ruskin, a regally imposing, fortyish lawyer-CPA taken on just for this project. Arthur camouflaged his terror by scratching away at a Times crossword puzzle, assisted by a pretty, fragrant and plainly nervous stewardess. The DC coughed and wheezed and bucked all the way to Cleveland.

The firm staggered off the plane and piled into two cabs. The caravan drifted through oceans of snow to Akron. In the lobby of the Longfellow Hotel, dead bulbs dimmed the crystal chandeliers, under ornate wall sculptures paint flaked into relief maps, and the air clung to memories of ingested entrees and illicit couplings.

Becker gave them forty-five minutes to freshen up and meet back in the lobby to negotiate dinner arrangements.

Arthur's room was hospital white, the ripples in the paint suggesting an infinity of layers. Above the white headboard, three white knobs under three fanned slots indicated where ancient thoughtfulness and clever engineering had built radio reception right into the wall. Each of the three stations whined that season's hit. He clicked off Patti Paige begging, "How Much Is That Doggie in the Window?"

Outside his window, the empty boulevard ran broad enough for a May Day armaments parade. The department store opposite was mysterious in the dark. He craned his neck and located light a block away. On a marquee a frame of orange bulbs flaring rapidly in sequence darted around the titles of three horror films.

He wanted so much to be back home.

In the bathroom, white tiles, claw foot tub, he sponged his face, reknotted the striped tie. Slipping on his tweed jacket, he walked out into the corridor and down balding carpet to the elevator bank. The operator, middle-age in a badly fitting scarlet jacket, pulled down on the lever and deferentially requested "Sir's" destination. Arthur marveled at how easily they could be fooled by a jacket and tie.

In the lobby Jerry's greeting was a roll of the eyes and an exasperated nod at the debating society. Becker and Weisbrod, voices straining for moderation, argued dinner. Evenly matched in mutual contempt, their disagreements were frequent and acrimonious.

Presently, Weisbrod stepped out front with a victor's smirk, and in order of rank, Becker first and Arthur last, they trailed him through the lobby to the coffee shop. Its door opened on 1960's Mediterranean: heavy dark wood, dimpled translucent partitions, chains spilling from chandeliers.

They cooled their heels, waiting for a sign of life. Presently the flustered hostess appeared, menus chest-high like a seal of office. "So sorry, we weren't expecting anyone. How many, please?"

Jerry pointed a deliberate finger at each of them. He said, "Six, I think."

She tapped a foot while her eyes skittered over the empty room, overwhelmed by all those possibilities, until finally the cogs meshed. "Please follow me." Down the aisle her body moved purposefully within the shapeless black suit, wrinkled skirt, and her flashing legs were sturdily graceful.

"Ellie" by her name tag, the hostess assured them their waitress would be along shortly. Her smile revealed white even teeth, too much of pink gums, and joy at having patrons. She dealt out menus, then hovered. Her wide brown eyes smiled, as if observing merriment, yet inside them Arthur thought he detected uncertainty and a plea. Only after the waitress filled water glasses and set down bread baskets did Ellie wander back to her station at the front of the room.

Through the wilted salad and chewy London broil Weisbrod sold the project's make-or-break importance, how this was their chance to get into the big time. Ajax Aluminum, their first client away from Manhattan's garment center, would if held on to be the firm's largest by far. Then, with confirmatory glances at Becker, he parceled out assignments. "Arthur, you'll verify the inventories. Inventory's the most valuable asset on the balance sheet. You gotta do it fast and do it right. Any questions, ask Jerry."

Over dessert the partners agreed, almost amicably, to all meet in the lobby next morning at eight. Indicting the others for laziness, Weisbrod made it known he'd probably be up half the night studying SEC regulations; Jerry headed upstairs to "phone the ball-and-chain"; Becker asked Jeanie to his room to discuss her assignment; Ruskin plopped onto a lobby sofa to await adventure and romance.

In his white room Arthur dropped onto the bed. He picked up the phone and requested a connection.

"Did you have a nice trip?" his mother asked. "Was the train ride comfortable?"

"It was fine." He hadn't told her they'd be flying, it would have made her anxious.

"Where are you staying?"

He gave her the Longfellow's phone number. "You feeling okay?"

"I'm fine," she said, then a bit touchily added, "Why shouldn't I be fine?"

"Sure, why not? Pa okay too?"

"He's fine too."

He promised to call back the next night.

He'd never before been away, college only a daily subway ride. So that was part of the grayness, the strangeness, the loneliness.

A bigger part was fear he wouldn't be able to handle his assignment. After all, school was only theory, .and much of that had eluded him. He'd not even had practice yet in adding up long columns, so what did he know about bringing a company public, about the aluminum storm door and window business, about taking inventory, about anything?

But most of all was the arithmetic of his life.

Of late he'd begun culling out the accumulated memories of his two decades. He was putting two and two together, connecting things.

Childhood had many flavors, but they'd mostly seemed sweet. Sure, he'd known that other people didn't need the government to buy them food, had neighbors who didn't vanish in the night to beat overdue rent. But you couldn't miss what you'd had no experience of. And not missing anything, he'd assumed happiness.

Until he added it up.

He'd begun to recall suicide.

The roly poly little man from across the street, with the roly poly wife and kid, would stand like him in the shadows of the opposite stoop for hours every night the winter Arthur was fifteen. Arthur wondered if the other shared his outrage at the senselessness of it all. On a night near to spring, the little man climbed to the roof and threw himself off.

And he recalled murder.

In the facing apartment across the courtyard, the skinny little man— it was rumored he worked for the gas company—with the wife twice his size. Every screaming match ended with the slap of flesh against flesh through the open windows. One summer night Arthur's cot shook when the little man splattered against the courtyard's cement floor. The widow told the police he'd wanted air to cool him, in his fever misjudging the window's opening. And who could prove otherwise?

Breakfast next morning in the Longfellow coffee shop was hasty, anxiety heightened by Becker's admonition to act as professional as poor upbringing, inferior education, and sloppy work habits would permit. They squeezed into a cab for the slippery ride to the city's outskirts.

The Ajax factory and warehouse, brick grimy and small windows barred and broken-paned, resembled a maximum security prison. The firm was conducted on a tour of the badly lit premises. After, Arthur apprehensively set off on his assignment, escorted by two clerks to the base of a mountain of inventory. Additional mountains, they assured him, awaited them on other floors. The clerks, an arthritic oldster and an unbearded rookie, crawled through bins and stacks of completed storm doors and windows, as well as angled frames, colored and raw frame sides, white panels, panes of glass, door knobs, screws, nuts and bolts, springs, extruded aluminum of various widths and lengths, tools, maintenance supplies, and other more exotic parts and supplies, calling out description and quantity for Arthur to check off with a red pencil in thick ledgers. After an hour of scrambling, the old man, sweating and breathing hard, sank onto a dolly. His continued participation was limited to mopping a brow while bellowing advice and encouragement to the junior clerk.

At noon a secretary came scurrying: the firm was hungry and awaiting Arthur at the front door. Downstairs, he trailed the expedition over snow and ice to a pizza restaurant around the corner. Within the aroma of frying peppers and mozzarella they analyzed the first morning's progress. Weisbrod accused Becker of not carrying his weight, and the ensuing acrimony poisoned everyone's food. In the biting cold they skidded back to the barred, grimy-bricked factory to reenact the morning.

After, in the free hour before dinner, Arthur settled himself on the bed, reached over his shoulder to try the radio, yet again clicked off three simultaneous renditions of "How Much Is that Doggie In the Window?" He concentrated on his dog-eared paperback clarifying Relativity for the layman. Presently he snapped shut the book and hurled Einstein across the room. He lay staring at the ceiling.

He recalled yet another suicide.

Mannie Schreiber, the janitor of the building next door, never hung around yakking with the neighbors. He would emerge only to wrestle up barrels of ashes from the cellar. Otherwise he'd sit in his ground floor window, forearms on the sill, embarrassed into exile by a ballooning slob of a wife and two sons already prodigies of the police court. His chosen way out was a tie around his neck in a dark closet.

The telephone connection to Arthur's mother yielded no more than on the previous day. He was okay, she was okay, work was fine, regards to pa, he would call again tomorrow.

He put on his jacket and rode the elevator to the lobby. A firm-wide referendum favored coffee shop dining: the food wasn't that exciting, but it would be easy to get a table and less trouble than running around searching in the cold.

Ellie's smile encompassed them all. "How many, please?" Playing the mental defective, Jerry counted with difficulty. "Six, I think." They followed her purposeful lead—same shapeless black suit, wrinkled skirt, milkmaid ankles—through the empty room. Arthur felt an appeal in such innocence, rude health, exhuberance. Jerry helped her push two center tables together. She handed around menus. "For you," she said, showing Arthur teeth and gums. Helen Ruskin waited for her to scamper away. "Arthur, my boy, I think you've made a conquest." He could only smirk his embarrassment.

They pinned their hopes this time on the Tournedos Rossini. Half way through, in a rare if ineffectual display of humor, Becker asserted dryly that if Rossini were still alive he'd sue for defamation. Not to be upstaged, Weisbrod banged spoon against water glass for attention. In the ensuing quiet he announced a change in plans. They'd all be going back to New York the next day to consult with underwriters, service accounts, do some research, etcetera. Only Ruskin would stay, to extract legal documents, and Arthur, to complete the inventory verification. They'd all be back in a week or so.

Arthur's call home that night was repetition.

As was inventory verification the following morning.

At noon he went down to the office to find Ruskin. She shoved some folders into a pile. "In the mood for some pizza again?"

"Could we maybe go back to the hotel instead?"

The husky lady's smile was arch. "Ellie waiting for you?"

"It's just that I'm used to more simple food."

"Like mother makes?"

Tables were occupied mostly with lived-in suits, ties at half mast: the uniforms of neighborhood businessmen.

Glorying in usefulness, Ellie enveloped them in a distracted but cheerful, "Good afternoon," showed them to a table, distributed menus, smiled at Arthur, abandoned them for a party of three blockaded behind the "Please wait to be seated" sign.

Helen Ruskin donned horn rims, examined the menu. "Think I'll try the scrod. How about you?"

"Sounds good to me."

"That old joke? Cab picks up passenger at Logan. Man says, 'I'm really looking forward to some of that Boston seafood. Where's a good place to get scrod?' Driver says, 'I been asked many times before, but never in that tense.'" Arthur thought about it, was a bit slow on the uptake, then blushed. He said, "How's your work going?"

"These hicks want to go public, but don't understand or care what the hell's in their legal documents. I think she's got it for you."

She saw Arthur's puzzlement. "The farmer's daughter. Didn't you see that smile she threw you?"

He shrugged it off.

"Now don't get a swelled head," she said. "She's probably just off one of those West Virginia farms and most of her romances have been with cows."

The waitress served the scrod and left. Ruskin speared some flakes. "Not bad," she nodded, chewing.

He searched the table. "See any tartar sauce?"

"Tell me," she said. "Would you know what to do with her? Don't be bashful, you want me to teach you things, just say so, we can slip into my room. Or would you prefer yours?" Her leer was exaggerated, funning, but her eyes held speculation.

The black-clad arm reaching over his shoulder set down a thimble of tartar sauce. His backward glance found Ellie smiling. She came around to sit next to Ruskin, facing him. "How's your lunch?"

"So far, so good," he said.

"I'm sure the rest of it will be just as good." Her smile held that plea again; Arthur guessed her needy—to be liked, or maybe only to be taken seriously.

Ruskin asked, "This your first job off the farm, hon?"

"My first job, yes."

"Know who this gentleman is, sitting here right across from you?

"Mr. Lavin, room 509."

"Very good. But I mean, who he is. This young man, you should know, is the foremost auditor in all of New York City. Number one, numero uno, in the whole of New York!"

"I could see right away he was special."

Blushing, Arthur waved aside Ruskin's propaganda. Rising, Ellie smiled at him. "Will you be staying a while yet?"

"A while," he said.

"See you at dinner." She hurried off to rescue a party of two from behind the sign.

"Have pity on her," Ruskin said. "This'll be like taking candy from a baby."

No, he thought, more like one baby trying to take candy from another.

With their room keys, that evening, the Longfellow's front desk handed them a scrawled telephone message. Ruskin needed for regulatory presentation. Grab first flight home.

So now Arthur was alone, imprisoned by strangeness, grayness, self-doubt.

And he wanted to be home.

He recalled funerals.

A couple of years earlier, over supper, his mother telling them, "Mrs. Kahn goes in the hospital tomorrow." She shook her head. Dread shuttered her eyes as she whispered, "Cancer." Arthur's mother was one of those people others confide in. She was barely out of her thirties and wonderfully nice to look at, with black silken hair to her shoulders and model's high cheekbones, but even the dour older women didn't resent her; they saw kindness and genuine concern behind her smiling brown eyes, and they valued her ability to keep a confidence. She couldn't walk down the street without being buttonholed for endless recitals of woe. The night she told them about Mrs. Kahn, a ground floor neighbor, she smiled adding, "The foolish woman is so sure she won't come back," but her eyes glistened. "Not come back?" she threw out indignantly. "A widow with two children that never lifted a finger in the house, they wouldn't know how to stay alive without her?"

But it was Mrs. Kahn who'd been right. Arthur remembered muted bystanders, and old Mr. Kramer, the butcher, at the curb in his black suit and hat under a black umbrella in the rain, paying his farewell. The image of Kramer stuck in his mind because soon after the old man was himself carried down the street. Always the funerals, inching their way past hand-wringing neighbors, at their head keening survivors demanding Wherefore from God.

Some weeks after Mrs. Kahn's funeral, Arthur's sister Gloria called from the front window, "Ma, c'mere quick, you gotta see this." She pointed down to a disheveled Phillie Kahn loping along the sidewalk, late again to his first job out of college. His coat hung askew, trailed by a long lisle sock flapping down his back. Gloria stopped giggling when she saw the tears form in her mother's eyes. "You mustn't laugh. God will punish you for making fun of an orphan."

That's what Arthur recalled.

And he wanted to be home.

He took breakfast and dinner at the Longfellow, and each noon rode a cab back for lunch as well. The coffee shop was now an island of familiarity, a refuge to come back to. And its personification was a farm girl, apple-cheeked, friendly, even worshipful, with a smile so broad and generous it revealed teeth and gums both.

The coffee shop was almost always deserted, so Ellie often sat opposite, watching him eat. Over breakfast they might discuss his professional plans for the day, fanciful strategies he concocted to provoke her adulation, but also because he saw it pleased her to have a share in his 'cleverness.' "What I'm going to do today, I'm going to order the president to cash in the receivables, factor the payables and finance the inventory, that way the balance sheet will look terrific. And you know what? The stock price will rocket." Encouraged by her shining eyes, he might add modestly, "I don't know why nobody ever thought of that before."

Over lunch he might get her to talk about growing up on the farm. Speech that was otherwise halting came easy when she described the birth of animals, the sounds of dawn; milking cows, steam rising from the pails; the hard work and endless responsibility for all the lives they owned. But he somehow felt that her nostalgic descriptions obscured travail and pain, indefinable longing and the need for escape.

And dinner was for the exchange of confidences. At first these were weightless little anecdotes intended to amuse and impress. Later, when they felt safer with each other, the stories took on an edge of sadness and regret, pain and blood.

Arthur told her, "They loved each other and they loved us, our house was filled with love. We'd have done anything for each other, even gladly die, I think. But we couldn't say it, and we were incapable of a kiss, even a hand on the shoulder. In the nighttime, once, my father passed by my cot and patted me on the head. I cried myself to sleep with happiness."

Her hand would reach across the table to stroke caring into his. He no longer felt as alone. As the days sagged by, he developed a tenderness for her innocence and naiveté. But her hand strong and warm on his led him to speculate about what lay beneath that rumpled black fabric, and he imagined sturdy limbs and generous roundnesses, silken skin the color of pearls and breasts that could drop into his hands like ripe pears. Such thoughts shamed him. Because Ruskin's sarcastic plea for pity, implying that boys will be boys and men are obliged to manliness, was a goad to seduction. His openness and empathy, sincere though he'd thought them, would now be put to use in taking candy from a baby.

But wasn't that how the game was supposed to be played, men as liars in seduction, women wary and distrusting?

Ellie sat across the table, watching Arthur read the dinner menu. Two shiny suits across the room were the only other diners. "How was your day?" she said.

"Fine," he said, "very fine. Say, what's finnan haddie? I've never had that, I don't think."

She said, "I'll go ask the chef."

"I don't want to put you to any trouble."

"Oh, don't be silly," and scooted off.

She was back in a minute. "Chef says it's mackerel fish with boiled eggs and potatoes, very good."

He tossed down the typewritten menu and reached for her hand. "How will I be able to order when you're not there?" He wondered which side of him was saying this.

"You're not leaving yet, are you?"

He'd once read that it's the voice that gets them, so he pitched it low and filled it with sadness. "Much as I want to, I can't just keep this thing going forever."

"How soon?" she asked, less a question than a plea for reconsideration.

He motioned towards the front of the room. She faced around, set down his hand, gathered up her menus and went forward to intercept a party of two. By the time she got back he'd finished with his food.

"How soon?" she asked again.

"Pretty soon. Couple of days, maybe."

"I'll go crazy in this place without you."

"You think I want to leave? You're somebody very special to me."

"You're special to me too," she said.

"Listen." He leaned forward into greater intimacy. "Why don't we show how special?"

She shook her head as if in pain, objecting beforehand to the response that would follow her, "How do you mean?"

"Come up to my room."

"Arthur!" like berating a little boy for mischief.

"I want to show how special you are to me. Is that wrong?"

"Yes, it's wrong," she bleated. "It's wrong if you go back to New York and I'm left alone here to bring up a baby. My father would kill me."

He twisted in his seat, recrossing his legs, as if to signal a change in subject. "What about your mother? Is she still around? You never told me."

"Yes, she's around. Why not?"

He shrugged. "Just asking, that's all. Do you love her?"

She was almost indignant. "Of course I love my mother."

"Good," he said, "good."

He reached across, smiling reassurance, and captured her hand. She shook her head. "I'll do anything for you, you know that, but don't make me go up there. Please."

"Yes," he said, "yes, you're right. You mustn't do anything you don't want to."

In a couple of days Arthur saw that most of the items in the ledgers already had his red check mark next to them. He phoned Weisbrod and got the okay to come home. He picked up a railroad schedule at the Longellow front desk.

Outside, a cold wind swept everything before it. They were alone in the coffee shop.

"What time?" she asked.

"I'll be taking the ten-fifteen."

"So this is our last dinner?"

"Our last meal. I won't be in the mood for breakfast." He pushed aside his plate. "Does food have to be our only connection?"

"I can't go to your room."

"I just want to be close to you. Nothing will happen, I swear it. I only want to hold you."

"I'll be fired, going up to a guest's room."

"You really think anybody in this joint gives a damn? I just want us to be together these last few hours. Maybe we'll meet again, but who knows." He was startled by the moisture he felt rising to his eyes. Strange, that honeyed words intended to ensnare the victim should get him too.

They went up singly. At her tentative knock he opened the door and led her in. In the too warm room the white radiator wheezed the odor of scorching paint, and when he sat down on the edge of the bed the springs screeched and the frame thumped metallically against the head- board. She let herself down next to him, smoothing the black skirt so that it reached lower over her knees. His arm encircled her waist. Lightly he kissed the warm pliant cheek. "Come," he said.

Moving around her, he stretched out on his side. He patted the brown chenille spread. "Let me hold you."

She gazed steadily at him, as if to assess the danger. Still holding his eyes, she carefully lay down on her side, facing him. The skirt and blouse pulled taut against a surprisingly trim body. He thought how easy it had been, after all—candy from a baby. "No, turn around," he said. "I want to put my arms around you."

When she complied he slid tight against her, cradling them into spoons. Her hair, the color of grain, held a new-mown fragrance. He put his left arm around her waist. Beneath the softness he could feel her rigid as a board, almost to quivering. He wondered at the thoughts and emotions that persuaded her into a situation she feared so much. Still, she was now his for the plucking. He watched the blood surge pinkly through an artery in her throat. The beat seemed unusually rapid, until he measured it against the pounding in his own throat and discovered them apace.

He contemplated delicious choices, decided on the lower half as gate- way to other delights. Gently, almost imperceptibly, he slid his hand down. Startled by naked skin, his quick glance discovered the skirt half way up her thigh. Even while struggling to account for his action, he drew the hem down to a more demure length. She turned her head part way toward him with a little smile, and he felt her relax.

He lifted the hair off the nape of her neck. Softly he kissed the milky smoothness. Of a sudden, it all—the defenseless neck, the inches of naked thigh, her beating heart—struck him with a sense of her vulnerability. He saw them alone in a cold world, clutching each other for a bit of warmth.

"I love you," he said huskily, knowing he didn't mean it, only maybe he did, weren't there different kinds and levels of love, and if you wanted the best for someone, wanted only to shield her, wasn't that a kind of love too?

He disengaged, then shifting upright set a knee between her legs. He leaned down to press his lips against hers. She bit his playfully. Sliding one arm beneath her shoulder, the other settling on her breast, he kissed back hard, wanting to meld them together. Again he breathed, "I love you."

Her voice filtered through his lips, "It's just that I'm helping you feel less lonely. If you spent time with the waitress or the room maid, you'd love them instead."

"Think you're so wise, don't you?" But then the corners of his mouth turned south. He was startled by the small sob working its way up from his chest through his tightening throat. He got off her and fell back onto his side. Again he held her from behind, but this time as supplicant. He leaned his forehead against the nape of her neck.

"Tell me what it is," she said presently.

He recalled the image of breasts dropping into his hands like ripe pears. Not, he thought sheepishly, not serving as a pillow for a crybaby.

He shook his head. "It's not your problem."

"If it hurts you, then it's my problem too."

How curious that this girl, almost a stranger, should be willing to share his burden.

"Please tell me," she persisted softly.

But then, weren't farm girls more mature, responsible as they were for all those lives?

"My mom," he said, "is going to die."

She gasped. "Is she sick?"

"Not yet."

Her voice was caught between an indulgent chuckle and disbelief. "Not yet?"

"They operated nineteen months ago." He told her how they'd had to leave in a tiny bit, it would have been too dangerous to do more, she might have died right there on the table. After, the surgeon referred the case over to God. "If God is good to her," he'd said, "the cancer won't come back."

"But hon," she said, "if your mom's still okay…."

"God?" Arthur shook his head. "There are too many disasters. Too many children dying."

"Things will work out. You'll see."

"The doctor wanted to talk to someone from the family. My mom thought it was just about a prescription, and my father was away at work, so I was the one she sent. The doctor said he had something to tell me. From his face I knew, I knew. 'No,' I said, 'I don't want to hear it.' He slammed his desk drawer. 'Then why did they send you? I needed someone strong.' So I sat down. He told me about the bit he'd had to leave in. He said there was hope. But I know, from his face I knew right away."

Ellie pulled a hankie out of her sleeve. She tried to pat his eyes dry but he shook his head impatiently. "I couldn't tell my father that his wife is going to die. And how could I tell my sister about our mother? But I can't carry it around anymore, it's just too much."

"Hon, don't they have a right to know?"

"How can I tell them now, so late? Maybe nothing'll happen, maybe I'm wrong."

She shifted around to face him. She moved closer and her hands coaxed him forward until his head cradled against her chest. She said, "You need someone to share it, that's all. And now I also know, so me, I'll be the one."

He twisted his head around so he could see her face. "You here and me there? Share, what's to share?"

"Ah, don't get mad, hon. It don't matter where we are, as long as you know that somebody else cares. That's what counts, isn't it?"

He straightened his head against her chest. In the print on the opposite wall a dozen adolescents laughed on a hay wagon under a round moon. "Why?" he said. "Why should you care?"

"Didn't we say we're special to each other? You didn't mean it?"

"Sure I meant it."

"And you're coming back for me, aren't you?"

When he said nothing, she playfully rocked his head from side to side. "You promised," she insisted softly.

"Am I too heavy on you?" he asked.

"No, hon," she said. "You're light as a feather on me."

How did it get to this? he wondered. Trapped by an inept try at seduction.

Her torso pressured the top of his head as she leaned forward. She surprised him with a gentle kiss on the mouth. "You don't deserve such pain."

He smiled ruefully. "I tried to take advantage of you."

"You talked to me. You listened to me."

Her tenderness, softness, the fresh smell of her, stirred his desire. Fortified by sadness, it overwhelmed him. He lifted his head from her chest and twisted around to face her. Gently he pushed her by the shoulders. She fell back easily, arms extended. He slipped his hand under her blouse and deftly slid it up almost to her neck. He inserted a finger under the edge of her bra and lifted it enough to free her breasts. Pears dropped, opalescent as pearls. He fondled one then caught the other nipple in his mouth. His upward glance found her smiling down at him.

Presently she uncovered all her warm softnesses.

The cab came for him at nine-thirty the next morning to make the ten-fifteen train.

She was tearful. "I'll be waiting for you. Don't forget me."

Another declaration of love sprang to his lips, but just at the last he substituted, "No, I won't forget you."

Arthur left on the compartment light, like the lamp he always kept on at night in his room. In the bluish glow above his berth, clacking of ties, he recounted his experience of Ellie, like turning the pages of a favorite illustrated book. With relish and a bit of smugness he saw again her luminous flesh, felt it spring beneath his fingers, smelled her fragrance; gratefully, he recollected her generosity; indulgently, the child-like innocence.

He recalled his blurted declarations of love, told himself it was just part of the game, but then had to admit to some persistence of feeling. Still, in his limited experience these things didn't last, and he was confident it would soon enough evaporate. He wondered if he'd ever again meet the girl. It occurred to him that there'd often be someone from Weisbrod & Becker traveling to Ajax, and he might be able to send along a note for her. But just before sleep he decided that would look suspiciously unprofessional.

He set down his suitcase just inside the door. He walked past the faded yellow walls of the kitchen, which seemed much smaller now, and the table and chairs badly needing another repainting. The light filtering through to the tiny living room disclosed his mother on the warm tapestry sofa.

"Arthur!" her pleasure showed even in the weak light. "I wasn't expecting you so early. Did you have a good trip?"

"Fine, ma," he said, "everything went very well. How are you feeling?"

"Me? How should I feel? I'm feeling fine. Let me make you something to eat."

"No, don't bother," he said. "I'm really not hungry."

But of course she insisted. She stood up and they walked back into the kitchen. In the stronger light he saw her eyes.

"Why are your eyes are so red?"

"It's nothing."

"How could it be nothing? If your eyes are so red it must be something."

"It's just a cold. I caught a little cold, that's all."

"You sure?"

She drew a handkerchief out of her sleeve and held it to her nose. "Of course I'm sure."

Fear kept him from asking about the pallor, the gray suddenly eating away at the temples, the new lines deep around her eyes. But it sprang out at him anyway, that it was him she was concerned about, that now *he* was the one being protected from an awful secret. He sank onto a chair. After, he never forgot the terrible clarity of the cracks gouging its withering paint.

The Dream Traders

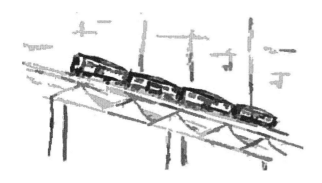

It is a bright hot Saturday in June, a sparkling clean innocent day not meant for breaking up friendships.

We are on our way back from Highland Park, all the way over to the Queens border. It's been a long hike for twelve year olds, eight or ten miles from home, and we've walked hours and miles through the park as well. But still, people and houses streaming past, I move swiftly as a marathon walker, automatically and without effort, disembodied except for the touch of breeze I myself push into motion.

Pennsylvania Avenue, its six lane width extravagant in those days of sparser traffic, slopes down before us broad and endless. From that high point, the single family homes lining both sides of the street, each fronted by its tiny lawn, seem barely to rise above the earth; instead, it is the gilded sky and its solitary clouds that are the principal subjects of the numberless snapshots my eyes register as I bob up and down. I imagine I can lift my arms high above my head and dip my hands into the inverted sea of ozone and then rub them dry on a passing cloud. But the sweetness of this day is edged with wistfulness. In minutes we will be leaving this clean, open, quiet street. We will too soon be back in our own neighborhood, where the sky is shut out by the tenements leaning forward above the narrow street, rooftops almost touching, like drunks supporting each other by grasping shoulders, foreheads joined.

In the afternoon stillness I can hear Kenny breathing hard as he struggles to keep up. My small and skinny friend is forever drenched in the sweat of some battle within his body or mind, so that the blond hair plastered to his skull appears already thinning, its color bleeding onto his complexion.

From somewhere behind me he puffs, "When we hit Livonia Avenue...let's stop off at Wheeler's poolroom."

I don't break stride or turn my head. "What for?"

"I got a buck down...on the Cubs game." He gulps air. "For cryin' out loud...slow it down, will ya?"

"You can't find out the score when you get home?"

"The radio's busted. It'll take Fleegle...a year to save up...enough to get it fixed."

I speed up, enjoying the sound of his wheezing. "So get the Daily News tonight."

"But I gotta know now. If I won...we can go right to...my cousin Albie...and collect."

"They won't let us up. They don't let kids up in the poolroom."

"Somebody'll take us up.... Somebody'll be looking...out of the window."

I stride on, listening to him suck air. When I have made him wait long enough, I give in. "Allright. You want, we'll stop off at the poolroom."

In the end, I always agree.

Our relationship is as complex and weird as any between adults. We have been best friends since suffering Miss Wadsworth together in the second grade. We do not really like each other very much.

It annoys me that Kenny leans on me so much. I help him with his homework; protect him from the schoolyard bullies; even, to please him, pretend interest in things I care nothing about. So that, for example, when he asked me to feel his calf muscle to see how hard it was getting since he took to riding his new bike, I obliged and faked amazement at his progress.

I am also annoyed by the symptoms of his poor health. Like his notorious sinus condition. His nose is always filling up, so that no matter where we are or what we are doing, Mrs Fleegle is chasing him down, handkerchief in outstretched hand, like a beggar with a tin cup. Her, "Kenny, blow your nose," is as much a part of the regular sounds of my life as the roar of the trains grinding along the elevated tracks down the block, or the indigestive moaning of the garbage truck swallowing a pickup at two in the morning. Sometimes, in the middle of eating, I suddenly recall the sound and sight of Kenny making a generous deposit into the handkerchief clutched in his mother's pleading hand.

But most of all, I am annoyed that I need Kenny to be my friend. Still, we hang together in spite of irritations and annoyances and, sometimes, outright hostility. The tie that binds is our mutual ability to provide what the other needs.

That's why I always agree, in the end.

Like that morning. After a chunk of pumpernickel with a glass of coffee, I threw myself back into bed to finish the latest Amazing Detective I'd been up with half the night. My window was shadowed by the gray backside of another tenement, admitting only a stingy light. This drabness, on top of the loss of sleep, tired my eyes, and I soon dozed off. I woke to find Kenny seated at the foot of the cot, watching me.

"What the hell're you doing here?"

"Your old man said it was okay to wait."

"Where is he? Is he all right?"

"He went out with the wagon."

"How long're you sitting here already?"

"I didn't keep track. You want to go to Highland Park?"

"Dammit, you have to sit there watching me?"

"Didja know you snore? With your eyes half open. C'mon, you goin'?"

I flung the magazine against the wall. Then I sat without moving, as if trying to decide. It fooled neither one of us. Slowly, I got out of bed. Quietly I said, "I gotta put on my sneakers."

We are illusionists bartering dreams. We are each other's customers as well as suppliers, dealers in fantasy. I offer the nose-blower a bit of self respect, an illusion of superiority. I get from him my ticket to adventure, mystery, romance. I agree with Kenny, always, because that's my part of the bargain, my coin of the realm.

It's really quite simple, just a matter of fathers: Kenny has two, I have less than one.

We live on Fourth Street, on this side of the tracks; Kenny also lives on Fourth, but on the next block, the first one past the el. On ours, the flats are cold water and some of the buildings are boarded up, abandoned with metal shields covering their dead eyes. On his, the apartment buildings are newer

and well kept, even mingling with a few neat single family homes, trees sprout from the sidewalks, and the faucets spill water as hot as you want. My dad was gassed in the First World War. My mom skipped out when I was three. I sometimes think her leaving had nothing to do with our being so poor, but that it was because she couldn't bear anymore to listen. My dad breathes with difficulty. Always, day and night, I am aware of his breathing—a half dozen quick shallow drafts, one deep gasp—as I would be of the ticking of a clock in a quiet room. Always, some part of me is coiled with dread of the instant when the spring will run down and the ticking stop.

Those days when my old man is able to drag himself out of bed he pushes a wagon through the streets, made out of a packing crate and skate wheels. He piles into it old newspapers and broken furniture pulled from the rubbish dumped in front of the tenements. The furniture is fed to the kitchen stove, providing us with some heat and a fire for cooking the food we buy with government disability checks. The paper is saved for the toilet.

Kenny Fleegle, on the other hand, lives with his mother and Mr. Fleegle. In school he is known as Kenneth Chase, this being the name of his natural father, Mrs. Fleegle's first husband. Fleegle provides for Kenny's worldly needs; Chase fulfills the spiritual.

Once every month Kenny disappears for a whole weekend. Late Sunday he seeks me out and drags me up to the Fleegle apartment. In the bedroom he makes a show out of displaying the spoils of his two day expedition. To open the production, he pulls from his pocket a five or ten dollar bill, unfolds it, then grasping the ends snaps it crisply before my eyes. Then the bill vanishes into a pocket and is replaced with a silver dollar, which he tosses, glittering toward the ceiling, catches, then tosses again. When the coin is spirited away a bank pass book materializes. Opening the book with a flourish, he points to an entry dated the previous day, evidencing a deposit, usually twenty-five dollars, then taps an index finger against the swelling balance in the account of Kenneth Chase.

And then, for the star turn, he kneels down before his bureau. Slowly, ever so slowly, he pulls out its bottom drawer, and my heart accelerates, and the slower the drawer the more rapid the palpitation. Until finally the contents is revealed, like the treasure in an unearthed sea chest: his latest haul of pulp magazines. At a princely wave of Kenny's hand I too sink to my knees. Like a miser counting his gold, I bury my soul and glittering eyes in the hungrily riffled hoard of adventure, detection, sports, fumbling impatiently when the cheap rough-papered leaves cling stubbornly together. Then, fingertips having memorized the gloss of the covers, nostrils sniffed the aroma of ink and new paper, pages all but tasted, I reverently lower them back into the drawer, knowing it's only a temporary banking, that when my turn finally comes the delay will have made it even sweeter.

And then comes the travelogue. "And you know where we went? We went to the Met. Were you ever in the Metropolitan Museum? And Saturday night Chase took me to the Stage Deli. We had pastrami on rye with celery tonic. And this morning we went downtown in Chase's Buick. To Orchard Street. And he bought me five ties. And a new pair of shoes. With arch supports. Eighteen dollars!"

I can do without the new shoes, the shiny bike, even the bank account. But forced to choose between the pulps and a limb, I would without hesitation place my arm on the chopping block.

I just can't get enough of reading. In my gluttony I devour every word in our branch of the public library, in old newspapers, on cereal boxes. But nothing gives me the fierce pleasure of the pulps. They put me into the seat of a Spad, guns blazing at the top of an Immelman turn. Or the shoes of an aging pitcher rushed in from the bullpen and, just one more time, saving the day and showing the rookies that the old man still has something left. It's the stuff of dreams for twelve year olds. And sure, the public library is a great place, but its offerings don't really come up to Kenny's, don't have the immediacy, the energy, that hard boiled edge. So I am hooked. To assure a steady supply of pulps I would willingly enter into a Faustian bargain. But the devil not being immediately at hand, I make my bargain with Kenny.

And I take, wherever possible, without acknowledging the charity.

Waiting until sure Kenny wasn't home, I would grab an armful of his pulps and scoot across to his block and up the two flights to the Fleegle apartment. Breathless, I put my ear to the door. In the absence of Kenny's shrill voice, I knock. When Mrs. Fleegle opens the door I ask innocently, "Is Kenny home?"

She tells me he is not. I express regret at not being able to return the magazines directly to their lender.

"Oh, you can give them to me," she says, "and I'll tell Kenny you brought them back." Then, seeing my great disappointment at missing him, she asks, "Want to take some more?"

"No," I shake my head judiciously, my voice a careful blend of diffidence and yearning, "I better not. Maybe he ain't read them yet."

"It don't matter. Come on, don't be bashful. You know where they are."

I follow her through the door, a tall, graceful woman, pleasant of face and disposition, but always disheveled, as if taking care of Kenny exhausts her. Always, Mr. Fleegle sits at the kitchen table, reading a newspaper. He wears a white shirt and a tie, as befits a professional man. (He works in a dental laboratory, sculpting false teeth. I suspect that the shirt and tie are intended as proof that the former Mrs. Chase did not lower her status when he succeeded the dry goods merchant.) Torturously shy, he never looks straight at you, but stares down at the floor with a faint grin, as though recollecting the smiling rows of false teeth he has worked on that day.

He says, grinning at the peeling linoleum, "You come for magazines?"

"No," Mrs. Fleegle says, "he's bringing them back. But I want he should take some more."

"Why not?" Mr. Fleegle asks the floor. "After all, he's Kenny's best friend. And friends like him ain't easy to find."

Suspecting sarcasm behind the downcast smile, I feel unclean, caught in an act of perversion. Still, it's less humbling than taking the charity directly from my friend's hand.

Alone in the bedroom, I drop to my knees, wrench open the bureau drawer, then shuffle feverishly through the stacks of smooth brilliant covers. Making a quick judgment as to the most I can take without appearing greedy, I reluctantly toss back one or two, then lug my haul to the kitchen.

222 An Impostor in Eden

"Is it okay if I take these? I don't want to take them if Kenny ain't read them yet."

"Take, take. Believe me, you deserve them. After all, how many friends does he have? I wish he was more like you instead of that bum Chase. He gambles, he throws his money away. Maybe if he didn't get so much from his father he'd be better off. He'd be more like you."

Passing by Mr. Fleegle enjoying the humorous floor, I would head for the door as slowly as haste permitted, and close it softly behind me. Then I would bound down the stairs, biting off huge chunks with each leap. Once outside, I gulped the euphoria of a daring mission success-fully accomplished—and tasted the bitterness of a victory that was somehow too costly.

Now we're getting close to home. We turn off the wide, open street and into Livonia Avenue. Elevated tracks run overhead, screening out the sun. Kenny catches up and double-times abreast of me.

"Who'd you bet on?" I ask him.

"The Cubs."

"I thought your team is the Dodgers."

"They already took three in a row. I figure Chicago's due. Besides, my cousin Albie gave me three to one."

"So you bet against your own team?"

"Odds like that, I'd bet against my own grandmother."

We cover the remaining distance quickly, crossing the street to stop before the loft building that houses Wheeler's Billiard Academy. The poolroom is a flight up, its windows on a level with, and just a few feet from, the elevated tracks. No one leans out of the open windows.

We stand there awhile, necks craned, gazing up hopefully into the huge opaque eyes. Soon I grow bored. "Let's go. C'mon, what's the use hangin' around?"

"Wait," Kenny says, "somebody's gotta come pretty soon."

"My old man'll be lookin' for me. I have to help him drag up some of the stuff."

"Just five minutes, will ya?"

Shrugging irritation, I of course agree.

Livonia Avenue is a market street. Each of its small shops specializes: groceries, fish, meat and poultry, fruits and vegetables, dry goods, appetizers. Stores cramped, much of the contents in open barrels on the worn, splintery floors, the shopkeepers extend selling space by setting up racks and stands outside, restricting the already narrow sidewalks still further. Shoppers, arms or carts loaded down with paper bags stuffed with hard-bargained victories, jostle each other as they navigate from store to store, stop to finger goods, express outrage at the prices, then sail back into the tide. Milling bodies, arguments and imaginative curses, aroma of food and odors of garbage, all under the crazy-quilt shadows cast by the el, flood the senses, overwhelming the bystander like a swimmer sucked under by a whirlpool.

As we wait, leaning against the brick wall, one on either side of the poolroom's doorway, a heavy-shouldered young man swivels his way through the mob. Carrying an equipment bag, he is headed upstairs for the ring in the rear of the poolroom.

"Hey," Kenny says, "take us up? We just need the Cubs score."

The boxer pulls open the door. "I look like a chaperone?" The door slams shut behind him.

We take up new stations, leaning against the el's black steel supports growing out of the macadam. Kenny stares up at the high unseeing windows, I keep an eye on the traffic; we could easily be mashed against the pillars on this dark and narrow street.

Impatience rears up again. "Nobody's here and nobody's coming. Let's go."

"Wait," he pleads. "Just a couple more minutes."

"See you later," I tell him.

His eyes leave the window and fix on mine. His head shake is adamant. "No," he says. "No. You go now, you don't see me later."

Overhead a train thunders by like an army of pneumatic drills. We stare at each other through this outrageous noise of battle. The sound begins to recede. Dropping my eyes, I sink back against the column.

"Listen," Kenny says. "Why don't we just get the hell up there? C'mon, what can they do? Shoot us?"

Reluctantly, I follow him across the sidewalk. He pulls open the metal poolroom door. It is heavy and the springs are loose, so when the door clangs against the brick wall it stays open. We climb the steep flight of creaking wooden stairs and enter the long, cool, shaded room. At the far end a couple of 8-ball players, cigarettes dangling, smoke drifting up to the green muted lamp over the table, ignore us. But Wheeler himself stands behind a stack of soda cases. Before we can grab a peek at the scores chalked off the radio play-by-plays, he yells, "Hey! Outta here, you lousy kids, get outta here!" and the short fat man waddles toward us whipping around a cue stick. We turn tail and run.

On the sidewalk, collapsed against a wall, Kenny stands with head lowered, shallow chest heaving. "Happy now?" I ask him. "Ready to go?"

He shrugs his thin shoulders. We turn to set off. But just then the shout comes from above us, "Hey! You kids! You wanna come up?"

Kenny yells back, "We just need the Dodger score."

"Wait there," the man yells, "I'm comin' down."

"Are you crazy?" I ask Kenny nervously. "Don't you know who that is?"

"So? Jimmy's okay, he takes kids up all the time."

I have heard whispers about Jimmy the Con. And I've seen that people are too anxious to please him. "Why're you bothering him with this stuff? Can't you just wait for the lousy score until later?"

But the door bangs open and he is there with us and it is too late. "Jimmy," Kenny addresses him respectfully, "Jimmy, what'd the Cubs do?"

Jimmy the Con looks us over, in no hurry to respond. He is perhaps forty, squat and powerfully built, and the impression of strength is reinforced by the thickness of his clipped dark hair. His clean-cut, handsome face is pierced by blue eyes that seem to smile until you notice they show as much feeling as two marbles. Leaning against the wall, he grins lazily. "You guys want me to take you up?"

"Could you please?"

"Just one. I'm afraid to get Wheeler mad at me." He smiles craftily at this pretense of concern.

But he makes no move, just stands there, hands in pockets, deliberating. A train overhead blocks out even more of the mutilated sunlight; stray beams, shooting between cars, are shredded by the ties, spraying the street with lightning. Within the numbing noise and darting light Jimmy appraises us, each in turn, a judge assigning points to the contestants in a pageant. Presently, squaring his shoulders, he pushes off the wall and saunters over. His left hand clamps onto Kenny's shoulder.

He steers Kenny towards the door. With his right hand Jimmy pulls on the knob. The door shoots open, slams against the wall, and stays there as if embedded. I watch them climb the stairs side by side. I hear the creak of the wooden steps. Half way up, Jimmy's hand slips from Kenny's shoulder and slides down his back. Jimmy grasps a buttock. He squeezes and fondles it as they climb to the top.

Waiting for Kenny, I puzzle over the weird, disconcerting incident. I finally decide, uncertainly, that Jimmy's behavior must have something to do with his years in jail. Pitiful, what Kenny'll do for a ball score. I consider what I would have done, was I picked instead. No question, even afraid of him I'd have shoved Jimmy down the stairs.

This heroic conclusion does not satisfy me.

Kenny comes clattering down. "Cubs won," he yells, taking the last three steps in a single leap. "C'mon, old buddy, let's go collect."

I hang back. I try to see Kenny as if for the first time. He is small and skinny and pasty-faced. His sinuses are always overflowing and clog his breathing. He's terrible at handball and stickball, and can't fight to save his life. He's a rotten speller; he stinks in arithmetic.

"I can't go," I tell him. "My old man's waiting for me."

"Five minutes," he whines, sidling off crabwise but still facing me. "You can't give me five minutes?"

I hold my ground only momentarily; habit, like a heavy hand, shoves me forward. "Why'd you let him do that to you?"

"Do what?" Kenny shrugs. "It don't mean anything."

"Just to get a baseball score? You know why he picked you? Because me, he tried that on me, I would've shoved him down the stairs. And he knew it."

Kenny's contemptuous stare impales me. "You? He had something you wanted? A magazine? A piece of candy, maybe? A nickel? You'd be up and down those stairs a dozen times. Begging for it. You? The Magazine Kid?"

We stop dead in our tracks. Gone are people, noise, smells. Only eyes are left, eyes boring into eyes. Searching for truth. Assessing damage.

I want to shove his words back down that scrawny throat. But my cords are frozen. The sky has tumbled, earth overhead hides the shredded sun, trains fly through the air salivating sparks, the rubbered wheels of shopping carts pulverize the air like pneumatic drills.

Kenny swivels around and walks off.

Struggling to stay upright I grab onto an oscillating strip of wall. From within the mob down the block Kenny leaps in and out of sight. Each time I catch him, my friend grows smaller.

The Venus of New Haven

Over breakfast in a booth at Friendly's, Nate Belkin and the Rabbi were once again arguing religion when this woman swept in, and I thought how if Belkin would just look up he'd be forced to accept the existence of God. This was a genius of a woman, the kind who immediately strikes a man as unattainable, yet persisting in memory spoils him for any others. In a softly tailored navy suit she stood tall and supple and assured, with a mass of jet hair piled above the dark eyes and finely boned face of a faintly dissolute Miss Alabama of 1980 or so. Her weight miraculously next to me rippled the red vinyl seat; I breathed in her scent.

"Still with the toasted english, Joshua?" With a sexy touch of mezzo.

A blushing Rabbi Joshua Epstein scanned for reactions, his face no more successful in guarding his delight than it would at the arrival of the Messiah. A silence overhung the table until he grudgingly offered,

"Ted Wolff, Nate Belkin, this is Julia Levy. Mrs. Levy Is Development Director at the rehab hospital."

Her glance barely troubled to alight on Belkin or me.

"And how's Mr. Levy?" the rabbi asked.

Blood-red nails gracefully arced in dismissal of a spouse. "Doing his thing. Out on the boat, shlepping to the Cape."

A waitress bent to accept her order for coffee.

Epstein explained to us his congregants, "I'm also chaplain at the rehab hospital."

Julia's white satiny blouse pressured her parted lapels. She tossed a doting smile the rabbi's way. "That's us," she nodded. "The sacred and the profane. I raise the funds to keep their bodies intact, and Joshua brings their souls to God."

My friend Belkin sectioned off some home fries. "But for such a cause, everything you do is sacred, isn't it?"

"And what is your sacred work, Mr. Belkin? Aside from breakfast with the rabbi."

"I force feed literature. At Sacred Heart College."

"Why, how nice. My own education didn't begin until after college. Roaming Europe with an oversexed Iranian."

She took a hurried sip of her coffee, clacked down the cup. "Sorry to eat and run, but I am after all a working girl. And Joshua, don't forget, meeting at three." And left us inhaling that libidinous scent, admiring that sinuous stride.

The rabbi toyed with his utensils. Having lined up knife and spoon he raised his eyes to Belkin's. "She does an exceptional job, that Julie." He saw me watching him. "Really committed to her work."

Already exhausted from the wars of a divorce, battling for visitations, I was yet called upon to watch my mother shrivel up with cancer.

Straight from the funeral I sought out the neighborhood synagogue to start the months of reciting the kaddish. Weekday mornings I'd stop off at Temple Beth-el on the way to my office nearby; evenings, on the way back to the apartment I'd taken short-term in my post-divorce indecision. The elderly congregants, rocking back and forth with eyes clenched in adoration, would converse with God in a rapid, slurred muttering like a verbal shorthand between old friends. In the Sabbath dusks of the basement sanctuary, awaiting star sightings, the old men would munch on pickled herring and sip schnapps. Their throats strained at sweet songs of devotion. God was in the words, but in their faraway eyes was lament: for the old country, lost love, youth. The timelessness of the ancient melodies was healing to me, as were the divulgences exchanged with Nate Belkin, my new-found comrade in mourning. Exploring each other's territories of despair, we discovered that our horrors had been simultaneous and symmetrical.

We owed God nothing if He didn't exist, and only ill will if He did. So side by side on a rear bench, mornings wrapped in prayer shawls and phylacteries, evenings in unadorned street clothes, we unheedingly shmoozed through the droning: baseball, the stock market, politics, whatever. Unlike the others, I'd not come to dialogue with Him, nor to beg His favors, nor express awe, but only to rise at the appropriate time to recite the prayer for our dead.

One Tuesday morning, unwinding the phylacteries from their impressions on our left arms, we watched the rabbi approach. Over the weeks he'd come to regard us as compatriots rather than congregants: we had in common our forties age and a more current world view than the retired shopkeepers and garment workers. Epstein looked an Everyman: average height, clean shaven, undistinguished features, gray felt hat, habitual suits of postman's gray. But he crackled with nervous energy, his clever eyes busy behind rimless glasses, and you got the impression he was always on one foot, anxious to get going on something.

"Gentlemen, you've earned breakfast. Meet me at the Friendly's?"

"I have to be in the office by eight," I told him.

"Not to worry, you'll make it in plenty of time."

Belkin admitted he didn't have a class until ten.

Separately we drove a mile up Main to rendezvous at the strip mall. Inside Friendly's the waitress hurried over to our booth. "The usual, Rabbi?" He nodded, and she tilted an inquiring brow my way. When I hesitated, trying to decide what would conform to the dietary laws, Epstein prompted, "I'm just having a toasted english with coffee."

"Sounds good," I told her.

Pencil over pad, she turned to Belkin. He ordered two scrambled with home fries.

Settling back, we bandied the stuff of blind dates or singles bars: What do you do, where're you from originally, what brought you to New Haven?

Over his coffee refill Belkin threw out waspishly, "How come the kaddish never mentions the dead, only the glory of God?"

"Because the rabbis were sure the mourners would blame God."

"Only if they can still believe someone's actually responsible for such an absurd world."

Which initiated their perpetual debate, and ended the inaugural meeting of the Tuesday breakfast club.

Belkin and I became each other's confessor and shrink, taking turns hosting the sessions. In late spring we were sprawled in his minimally furnished apartment in a town close to home for the convenience of the kid who never came to visit anyway.

We'd come to resemble forgetful elderly, repeating things ad nauseam, futile attempts to dislodge dark images stuck in the mind like splinters.

Belkin offered, "It was a rotten thing, abandoning the boy like that. But I had to walk out or risk murder or suicide, or both."

I traded him, "When I slammed the door behind me it was an animal chewing off its leg to escape a trap."

He bent to scoop a bottle from under the chair. He held up the offering, but I shook it off. "Tell me, my friend, which microorganism is it that can so suddenly turn love rancid?"

"If it's possible to fall in love on a dime," I said, "why not out of love too? Then you get pissed because you suspect you'd been sold a bill of goods way back when. So then you get divorced."

He lifted the beer to his mouth, took a sip, made a face at its warm bitterness.

"Last night was bad," I told him. "I dreamed my mother was alive. The bones of this lovely woman were sticking out of her flesh. She cried from the pain. I cried too, sponging the sweat off her. I woke up soaked and heartsick. Then I remembered she was no longer suffering. I thanked God she was dead. Imagine that, being glad that she was already dead."

"Me, I still scream," Belkin said. "I see her looking up at me, my maiden aunt, this little old lady. So damned trusting. 'Tell me, Nate, what I should do. Whatever you tell me, I'll do.' And me, I sent her off for that little bit of surgery they wanted and she didn't. To be murdered by malpractice. Whenever I'm alone I see that face looking up at me and trusting me. So I scrunch up my eyes and scream to drown out the face and the voice."

My fellow mourner was tall and thin and stoop-shouldered, the very model of the helpless academic. Below brown hair that rarely met a barber's shears, his brown eyes were as wistful as a puppy's. I could see where females with a need to be mothering might be attracted to him.

"Listen," I said, "maybe it's time for a change. Maybe we should go find us a couple of undiscriminating women."

He shook his head. "When you fall off a horse, get right back on again. Women? You're better off just laying where you fell."

The rabbi invited us to Friday night dinner. "It might do you good to spend an evening with a family." I imagined a meal tormented by restrictions and ceremonies and bratty kids. "I don't think so," I said. "I'm not yet fit company for anyone." But Nate, the rabbi's nemesis in their tortuous debate, surprisingly wouldn't have that. "Why not let the rabbi's family decide whether we're fit company?" So I gave in. The upshot was that the visitations became habitual. Friday night meals at the Epsteins' cast a warming light into my darkness.

After the service, the three of us stroll several blocks to the rabbi's home, a modest cape provided by the congregation. Once inside, Epstein removes his coat and replaces his felt hat with a skull cap. He stations himself at the center of the small tidy living room furnished with budget-grade furniture. The children, not brats but bright and engaging high schoolers and college students, four boys and a girl, take turns stepping forward to bow the head and receive his hand softly upon the crown in benediction.

In the dining room, white tablecloth glimmering under candlelight, the rabbi's wife—dumpy, scouring pad hair, but with a transforming smile—hastens in from the kitchen. "A good Shabbat," she greets us. Standing in place around the table, everybody joins in singing the Sholem Aleichem, which I luckily recall from childhood. Raising a pewter kiddush cup, Epstein cantorially renders the kiddush, sips, then doles out a bit of the wine to each. All line up at the kitchen sink for the ritual washing of hands, whispered thanks to the Creator for the water, then back to the table for the placid meal, chicken soup with dumplings, gefulte fish, boiled chicken, chulent, and other good things, all of it garnished with tranquil and respectful conversation. Seated at table, observing, I am the stranger gazing into the lighted window, imagining himself inside, belonging.

That first visit from Julie Levy expanded our Tuesday breakfast membership to four. We settled into a pattern. Julie would sweep into Friendly's late and rush out early. The rabbi was openly, blushfully adoring. Me, I had dreams in which I reached out for her yielding roundnesses and trim lengths, only to be lacerated by the barbed wire surrounding her like lovingly clinging vines. I had to acknowledge this warning from my unconscious, that with her beauty and vitality and sharp-tongued cleverness she'd be too much woman for me. As for Belkin, they were in a war of attrition. With a few words she could sever his head so cleanly that he'd just sit there waiting for it to topple into his lap. Like when he tried to one-up her and mentioned that the faculty had designated him a 'Distinguished Teacher.' She drawled astonishment that such an honor should be bestowed on a man whose I.Q. was lower than his body temperature.

Passing by one Thursday, I decide on a quick stopoff at Friendly's for a takeout of coffee and a muffin. Waiting at the counter I turn to survey the room. In a booth, Julia and the rabbi sit in animated conversation. I swivel around and bolt.

Some Tuesdays later, Julie seemed so intent on shredding Belkin that she hung around to the very end, slinging her barbs. Eventually we traded the cool of Friendly's for the heat of the parking lot. The sun ricocheted off the glass and chrome of the autos. Julie and Belkin ambled ahead of the rabbi and me. They maintained an impersonal pace apart, but I was half expecting them to erupt in another explosion. Next to me Epstein stuttered something about the rising cost of memorial plaques. I failed to catch it all, but nodded absently, absorbed in admiring twin marvels of architecture, silken calves smoothly curving into clever ankles. Suddenly Julie and Belkin halted. Simultaneously, each flung an

arm around the other's waist. They pulled each other close. Their smiling profiles, haloed in the sun, almost melded. In mid sentence the
rabbi gave a start, then speeded up. They separated at the sound of his
quickening footsteps.

After services that same evening Belkin insisted on coming up to my
apartment; he needed to talk. He hoarded his words until we sat back
with beers in the two easy chairs I'd rented, together with a floor lamp, a
TV, and a hi-rise bed that could pull apart to accommodate the little girl
I never got to bring. Belkin took a small impatient swig, as if afraid of
drowning the words lined up in his throat. He leaned forward. There was
less of the mourner about him now: the sad brown eyes were sparking.

"Our friend Joshua," he demanded. "Doesn't he puzzle you?"

I asked how so.

"He cuts corners."

Puzzled, I could only shrug. "He's a very nice, kind man. We owe him."

"A nice kind man who cuts corners. Orthodox rabbis don't eat breakfast in non kosher restaurants."

"What the hell, Nate? All those responsibilities to his congregation. A
wife and five kids. Toasted english at Friendly's is his wild night out with
the boys."

"What do you think of the rebbetzin?"

"A very sweet woman. Adores him."

"I agree," he said. "Absolutely. A sweet woman. Kind, bright, charming. Adores him. What more could he possibly want?"

"Sure," I said, "what more?" But friends have an obligation for frank-
ness. "Truth is, it must've taken a hell of a lot to knock her up. And five
times, yet."

Belkin jabbed an index finger at me, a hellfire preacher warning
against sinning. "He's not supposed to even look at a woman not his
wife. So that's another corner that so-called man of God is cutting."

"Nate," I said, "please tell me this ain't about Julie."

Belkin punched the chair arm. "It's a sin, what he's doing."

"That harmless little flirtation?" The puff of dust rising from the beaten upholstery was like an idea floating to the surface of my mind. It finally broke through. "Oh. Changed your mind, did you? About lying where you fell? Nate, that's a hell of a wild horse to get back up on."

"I had no intentions. You saw us, how we were walking apart? I was just trying to think of something clever to cut her up with. It was like we were separate candles, plenty of space between us, but still it got too hot and we melted in each other's heat."

I set down the bottle. "You're getting ready to stab a good man in the back. So what you do is, you blame the victim. Keeps your conscience bright and shiny."

Belkin stared at me as if this was a truth he could obliterate with the intensity of his gaze.

I stared back until his shoulders drooped. "I need this one, Teddy. I want my life back."

"You mean Mrs. Levy, wife to Mr. Samuel Levy and great friend to Rabbi Epstein? That Julie Levy?"

"I'll take whatever I can get."

"I suppose scruples and morality don't enter this at all?"

"You're trying to argue away a thunderstorm. Listen: When I was young there was a girl I loved to pieces. I had a check book but nothing in the account. Wanting to give her something, I wrote a check for a million dollars and marked it 'void'. She clutched that silly piece of paper like it was the real thing. Because she recognized it was an IOU for all I'd ever have." Belkin's cheeks flamed. "After all these years I'm wanting to give an IOU again."

It was really none of my damned business, but he was a friend and fellow mourner, and I had a duty to waste my breath. "An arm around the waist, that's the whole deal? Maybe it's just that her old man gave her such a good night that she loved the whole world, even you."

"She looked right in my eyes and smiled like we were saying hello for the first time. When her waist moved under my hand I knew I was holding on to everything I'd ever want in this world. Who knows what might've happened if Epstein wasn't right there in back of us?"

"Dreams of glory don't really give you much to go on."

"So suck on this: she already phoned me this afternoon. There's a fund raiser in a couple of weeks. The governor, a senator, all kinds of fat cats. And me, she wants little old me to be her escort."

"And that makes you the queen's consort? The rabbi's stuck with the rebbetzin and her husband's away on the yacht, so you got the job by default."

"Still, it's me she asked. I mean, she didn't ask you, did she?"

"And you're going?"

"Even if the party was in hell."

The rebbetzin, moving nimbly within a shapeless garment, supervised her offspring in clearing the table of everything except a pie and our teacups. Budding jowls just above her collar made me wonder why she'd wear something that drew imagination to the bulk within. Until I recalled that the Friday evening service welcomes the Sabbath bride, and recalled too that it is a mitzvah to make love on the day of rest. The robe simply meant that Chava Epstein was ready for action. I glanced across the table at the rabbi. That usually effervescent man was lining up challah crumbs on the white tablecloth. My heart went out to him.

The youngsters, done with the cleanup, abandoned the dining room to their supposedly more mature elders.

Belkin said, "It's late already, we should be going."

"What's your rush?" Chava Epstein wheedled.

"We don't want to overstay your very gracious welcome."

"Stay a while yet. We'll have some dessert, drink a glezeleh tea, talk."

I didn't mind at all, but I could tell Belkin settled back with reluctance.

"Some more tea?" Chava asked. "That pie is a masterpiece. No credit to me, it's from Blattner's kosher bakery."

We begged off, pleading overindulgence.

"Anyway, where else would you go now?" she asked. "What is there to do on the Sabbath, except read and talk with friends?"

The rabbi got up from his place and reseated himself near the center of the table, next to his Chava. I'd never seen him so subdued, his endless supply of energy short circuited. "You too," she said to us, "why don't you move closer so we can talk."

We moved up to sit opposite them.

She said, "When I mentioned 'a glezeleh tea' before, it reminded me that my parents, off the boat from Russia, drank their tea out of a glass, holding a sugar cube between the front teeth. As a kid I drank it that way too."

"I never tried it," I said, "but I do remember my grandmother slurping tea through a sugar cube."

Which seemed to exhaust the subject. "Joshua," she prompted, "you are uncharacteristically quiet." By her side he merely shrugged. Silence returned. Like a hostess abhorring a dead spot, she threw out, "By the way, how is Julie Levy?"

I flinched, the body reacting to an explosion before the mind registers it. But the rabbi just answered matter-of-factly, "Julie's out of town. A seminar down in Boca."

"On what?" Belkin sneered. "How to separate people from their money? I thought she was already an expert at that." I was surprised at such asperity, then decided it was intended as a bit of cover.

Epstein smiled. "Yes, she's already very good at that. God willing, she'll be back safely on Thursday."

Trying to comprehend such amiability, I glanced away from the couple across the table. On a wall off to the side hung the portrait of a bearded man in a skull cap, chin in hand over a book. I saw the amateur daubings as a work of cliched reverence for the old time virtues. How had it came to decorate the wall of a man whose humanity ranged well beyond the narrow piety of mere study? Was it meant to underscore how far the rules had since evolved?

Chava broke into my reverie. "Talk about drinking tea from a glass…. It brings back my childhood, and now I'm remembering things. When I was eight, maybe younger, my brother Shmuel, may he rest in peace, would take me along to the public library two or three times a week. He'd hold my hand crossing the bridge over the railroad tracks. In those days I was free in the afternoons, because girls weren't supposed to become learned in the holy books. So between afternoon and bed I'd swallow two books every day. More on the Sabbath. I still remember the smell of the library, dust and old paper. And discovering Dr. Doolittle. How I loved Dr. Doolittle, with those drawings of the animals. Just a few simple lines, but the hippo looked so solid and heavy, and at the same time so funny." Chava shuttered her eyes. "What was his name, that fellow who did the drawings, it's right at the tip of my tongue?"

Belkin said, "Hugh Lofting."

"Oh yes. How clever of you. So then," Chava went on, "came 'Little Women.' Actually, I wasn't that choosy, I'd read anything on the shelves. Until one day. Oh, the day that I found Hemingway! I don't recall how old I was by then, but those no-nonsense sentences about life and death and courage…." Shamefaced, she clapped her hand to her forehead. "I'm talking too much."

Epstein's indulgent smile seemed to rise out of a sad yet proud place. "But after all, how often is a rabbi privileged to hear the rebbetzin deliver a sermon?"

"You're recalling my childhood too," Belkin said.

Chava glowed with the passion of her subject. In the candlelight her eyes sparkled; the candles breathed shadows that erased the blemishes and redefined the planes of her face. It came to me that this, this rather than all those other moments, was the truth of her.

"And then," she said, "my initiation into sex." She broke off with a smile, confident that we were now her prisoners. She pointed to the apple pie. Belkin shook his head impatiently. She raised a brow at me and I too shook my head. She took a breath. "I discovered Maupassant. Guy de Maupassant! Those stingy peasants, the girls in business selling themselves, the illegitimate children. 'Madame Tellier's Excursion.' 'Boule de Soif.'

"Listen. Assuming Nate isn't in such a hurry to leave, I'll tell you a story. Okay? A story out of de Maupassant."

Belkin's hand motioned an invitation.

"'The Venus of Braniza.' It's about this Talmudist, celebrated for his learning and for his beautiful wife. Maupassant writes that she was referred to as a Venus because her great beauty was especially startling, since the wives of Jewish philosophers are as a rule ugly or defective.

"He explains it this way: Marriages are made in heaven, and just as a good father takes his best merchandise to market and keeps the damaged goods for his children, so God saves for the Talmudists those women whom other men wouldn't care to have." Chava extended her hand to Epstein's shirt-sleeved arm. "Which, Joshua, since you are one of God's beloved children, I guess explains me." Her gaze at him was like a kiss. She turned back to us. "Well, one day this Venus asks her husband when the Messiah will come. He responds that the Talmud says it will be when the Jews are either all bad or all virtuous. Eventually he comes to learn that she's betrayed him with a hussar, one of the Hungarian cavalry stationed in town. He confronts her. It's true, she admits, but she was only doing her duty to bring the Messiah faster. End of story.

"Tea anyone?" There was no response. "Be right back." I watched her jounce out of the room, no longer seeing her as a defective creature saved by God for one of his own. She returned bearing a cup and saucer.

Cooking being forbidden on the Sabbath, no steam rose from the luke-warm cup.

She picked up the thread. "My sympathies ran the wrong way. I was supposed to rejoice at how the learned man was made a fool of, but I couldn't. Someone who'd spent his life in study and good deeds didn't deserve to be mocked. Did deMaupassant mean that such a man must be deprived of any beauty except what's in the holy books? Never to watch a pretty woman smile at his humor or admire his cleverness? Never feel that delicious tweak in the belly imagining she'd run away with him if he just snapped his fingers? Yes, I know very well how it is, the pleasure of those little games of the imagination. "And where's the harm, I ask you?" She waited two beats. "Even if her name is Julie Levy," she demanded, "where's the harm?"

The echo challenged us across the table. Belkin stared back, expressions flitting across his face. He stammered something about the holy books forbidding a pious man…, but she cut him off. "Because he might be tempted. But if he's a good man just getting kicks out of a little flirtation, who will be hurt? So I repeat, Where's the harm?"

The rabbi, head bent, stared down at his deployment of challah crumbs.

Like a debater buying time, Chava took a sip of her cold tea. She said, "Please understand, this is for me too." She set down the cup with a ching. "If I am what God saved for Joshua, he deserves more. I want him to not miss out on the joy of God's more saleable merchandise."

In the stilled room the shimmering of the candlelight felt like another sort of sound. I sat assimilating her plea, her declaration of love. Epstein removed his glasses and rubbed his eyes vigorously. Carefully setting the glasses on the white tablecloth, he lifted tired eyes to us. "When the candles burn low, my Chava's romantic soul some-times leads her into little imaginings.' He smiled fondly at his wife. "Must be all those novels."

Belkin pushed his chair away from the table. "When the candles burn low," he said, rising, "it means the guests have stayed too long."

Belkin failed to show up at services the following day, Saturday, and Sunday as well, so we didn't catch up with each other until Monday morning. Side by side, we for once didn't schmooze, because Belkin sat hunched into his prayer shawl like a scrupulously attentive old world patriarch. Only near the end did he turn to me. "How'd the Mets do last night?"

It took me a moment to adjust to such a query from an old world patriarch. "Lost again," I told him. "Middle inning relief is killing them."

Somebody's tap on my shoulder prompted me. I tapped Belkin in turn, and we stood up to recite yet another of our thousand repetitions of the kaddish. Even our inflectionless mutterings could not disguise the majesty of those syllables that always left you feeling noble. We sat down again.

"How's your love life?" I asked. "Julie Levy back yet?"

"Still down in Boca, I guess. I left a message on her answering machine."

I couldn't help a sneer. "'Hurry home, dearest darling, I miss you?'"

"'Sorry, have to beg off, don't own a dark suit.'"

He outwaited my vacant expression. Then he said, "He took me in. He fed me. I refuse to be the hussar to our corner-cutting Talmudist."

"Crisis of conscience," I said smugly.

"It is not our nature to be hussars. Besides, there's the rebbetzin."

"That easy?" I said. "The rebbetzin asks you to keep hands off and that's enough?"

"She remembers the smell of the library. Doolittle's hippo. Discovering Hemingway and deMaupassant."

"Ah," I said, "a kindred spirit."

"It's not just a voided check she's giving away. Out of modesty she surrenders what's rightfully hers. Out of love she gives of herself."

And out of sorrow, I thought, comes finer men.

After, crossing the sidewalk, I said, "Being so virtuous, you're not helping to bring the Messiah any sooner."

"Who knows, maybe we'll all turn virtuous. Besides," my friend Belkin shrugged, "we've waited this long, what's another millennium or two?"

The breakfast club was disbanded. Some mornings, though, for old times' sake and a whiff of her scent, I'd stop in at Friendly's for a toasted english and coffee. I'd listen to Julie complain about the dearth of charitable giving; the rabbi bemoan the venality of synagogue politics. They would argue, I was convinced, just for the joy of it.

"Dear Lord," she might interject, shaking her head in despair, "why dost Thou keep our poor Joshua so long in the dark?"

Each such barb would glint in her fine dark clever eyes. Each would raise a flush of pleasure in the rabbi's enraptured face.

A Man and His Dog

Shortly after dawn, Jess slips out of the bedroom and down the stairs. The pointer opens an eye and rises up on the family room sofa. Unsteady on the cushions, she lowers her front paws to the carpet, then with a little leap drops down on her slim hind legs. She dances expectantly while he fastens her leash.

When Jess warily opens the front door of the sleeping house, Margie, tail slashing, drags him jogging down the long graveled driveway, then along the asphalt road still cratered from last winter's frosts. In the chill of the waking sun, steam rises from the lake on their right, obscuring it. A squirrel rooted quivering in the road scoots into secret foliage, leaving the world to them alone.

Their route is the same as on any other morning: twice around the lake plus one more half circuit to the Munson's mail box makes up their five miles. The third time they reach the crest at the Munson's, Jess, sweat down his back and pulse in his temple, halts and raises his face skyward. In a neutral tone he tells a passing cloud, "Okay, time to start back." To his unfailing wonder, Margie instantly faces around and vigorously leads him home.

After showering he shaves. In the mirror he concentrates on each successive patch of skin, deliberately avoiding eye contact. But after, inspecting his work, he is drawn to stare at a tight-skinned dour face, the face of a 'thirties dust bowl Okie.

He spends more time than usual at the closet. He finally pulls out the summerweight blue with muted checks, and puts this on with a white shirt and figured blue tie.

Downstairs in the kitchen, Cindy sits at the golden oak table, eyes in the Times. Her forehead is drawn tight by the white plastic curlers torturing her honey hair, the kind that always remind him of the round latticed cooling units atop antique refrigerators. At the level of her high cheekbones and improbably perfect profile, the smoke from her first cigarette twines around the steam from her first coffee.

"Debbie's sniffles any better?" Jess asks.

"She's well enough to go to school. Want your coffee now?"

"No time for it."

The little stiffening of her shoulders tautens the newspaper. He quickly adds, "Finance committee meeting. And anyway, they'll be serving breakfast."

He opens the connecting door to the garage. Margie is of course through it in an eye blink. Glancing back over his shoulder, he verifies that Cindy's attention is still on the newspaper. He opens the car door. Margie leaps inside, and he shuts her in.

At the bottom of the driveway Jess hits the brake pedal. He bows his head over the wheel. After a moment he straightens up. For the first time in a thousand weekday mornings he turns the wheel left instead of right. Two miles down the road, at the stop sign, he slips off his tie, tosses it into the back seat, then unbuttons his shirt collar. A quarter of a mile further on they enter the highway ramp marked, "West."

When he gets it up to sixty he takes one hand off the steering wheel to shrug himself out of the suit jacket. He tosses that, too, into the back seat. Grasping the wheel with alternating hands, he rolls up his shirt sleeves. Margie lies curved into the contour of the bucket seat, paired legs crossed in the fetal position. Within her immobility the eyes dart around, searching for the meaning of this departure from pattern.

From his breast pocket Jess extracts a cigarette, sneaked earlier out of Cindy's pack. He sets it aglow with the dashboard lighter, assuring himself he has good and ample reason for abandoning a hard-won abstinence. After a deep drag he coughs wrackingly. He kills the cigarette.

For an instant unfastening his eyes from the road, Jess reaches over to pat Margie's silken head. Closing her eyes, she pushes up, pressuring his hand to encourage the caress. How is it, he asks silently, that your life and mine have intersected? How is it, he asks, still rubbing her head, that we have gotten so entangled in each other?

He sets his mind to recall, hardly a difficult feat; the images crowd around, awaiting their cues. But stronger than any image is that bitter feeling. He can still taste the crushing sense of futility, humiliation, outrage. Eight years of failure, of misfirings, of Cindy's phantom pregnancies, tubal pregnancies, miscarriages. Of seeking out yet dreading the derision, or at least pity, even in the eyes of friends.

How about, she hit him with it out of the blue one fine day, how about a dog, we could sure use a watchdog? He was shaken by this overture to surrender. He'd never had a pet, he told her, wouldn't know how to care for one; needed time to consider it. He lay awake nights brooding about being the last of his line, until in one of those dark hours a traitorous thought crept in. Maybe, it went, instead of settling for a pet he'd do better to find someone else to try for kids with. But then in the honest light of day he saw how her every word for him, each little deed, was wrapped in caring like gift candies in gilt foil. And then one afternoon, on his way home recalling some grocery need, he popped into the Grand Union, and down an aisle glimpsed a young woman, and My what a pretty girl! flashed through his mind before he realized with a little catch it was his own Cindy. His heart almost burst with pride and humility and love. It came to him, then, that it wasn't just her prettiness, it was the whole package: mutual interests and experiences, and all the clichés of sharing and togetherness. They were no longer divisible. There was no choice but love over propagation.

In the pound they moved haltingly between the rows of cages, potential rescuers among yelping suppliants. Through the clamor and stench they finally settled on a regally aloof collie. The bottle blonde behind the counter, told their selection, caucused with the cop in charge. The cop stepped forward to bluster unlikely objections. "He's too dangerous, he bites," and, " We can't release this dog to someone who lives in an apartment," etcetera. Jess suspected the cop had a way to make money out of such a valuable animal, and there was no chance they'd win an argument with a badge in reach of easy bucks.

So they went back inside to try again. Within the din Cindy spotted this lively little one, only just weaned but struggling to emit grownup barks, black patches on a pepper and salt background—pewter instead of run-of-the-mill solid—and she stuck her finger through the wire cage and the puppy licked it. This time the cop and the blonde greeted them with smiles of approval. In the car on the way home they christened the puppy after the bottle blonde.

Eyes on the road, Jess reaches out and rubs the dog's coat. "You okay, Margie?"

At sound of her name the pointer lifts her head. Rising unsteadily, she balances herself against the car's roll. She presses her nose to the window, then repeatedly swivels her head towards Jess and back to the window again. He pushes a button and the glass slides down. She lifts her front paws to the arm rest, then sticks her head out. He slows the car a bit, down to sixty, and Margie narrows her eyes into the wind, teetering on her perch.

"You get something in your eyes, don't go blaming me," he warns.

His glance touches the dog, then back to the road again. For the hundredth time he wonders about rules of classification that relegate her to a lower order. The vet had explained how she was less than pure: ears too small, tail too long. Did their slide rules replace eyes and heart then, those so-called experts? Tight arcing symmetry from barrel chest to thin small stomach; slender racing legs out of muscled shoulders and narrow flanks; curving tail powerful as a club, its milk-white tip delicate as thistle; narrow long-nosed nobility; amber eyes mulling over difficult equations in a higher realm. Didn't such throat-tightening grace and beauty, speed and power, trump any idiosyncracy of ear or tail?

Jess pats the passenger seat. "Come, girl," he coaxes. "C'mon, sit down."

But her head stays out the window, eyes narrowed in the wind. He flicks at her tail. She twitches it but otherwise ignores him.

"Still insist on your own way, don't you? I suppose we can expect you to be a pain in the butt right up to the end. But what the hell, why stop now? You were untrainable, a sneak and a coward and a thief. My God, you've given me so many embarrassing and awful moments! The next house down the road. Mrs. Bowles, the old widow lady, with her cocker spaniel. Snuck in there one day and ripped that cocker's throat from ear to ear. After the poor woman's sad outraged letter I paid the vet's bill for sewing up her dog. And she sold the house and moved away."

Someone was always after him to have Margie killed. They would refer to it as 'putting down,' as if renaming poison renders it harmless. And if he had any brains he'd have done it a long time ago, whatever they called it.

"No, Margie old girl, it ain't exactly been all beer and skittles between us."

A twist of highway brings them face to face with the sun. Jess flips down the visor. Margie pulls in her head and he slides her window back up. She carefully circles the seat, each revolution a little lower, screwing herself into it, and finally settles into the chosen spot.

Two years out of the pound she came down with the mange. Coat dry and torn, bleeding where she scratched. Vet called it incurable. Advised them to have Margie 'put down'.

Seemed like everybody had her marked for death, for one reason or another, by one name or another. But the two of them weren't experienced enough dog lovers to be able to do that. Instead, Cindy ran out and grabbed up every kind of soap and shampoo she could lay her hands on. Bathed, she bathed that dog half a dozen times a day. And in a few weeks she'd worked a miracle. She'd done it for Margie, sure, but it was for him too, she knew how much it meant to him. Holding Cindy tight, he promised never to forget. Maybe, he shakes his head now, maybe what came after was because I didn't keep my promise.

An hour from home a blue sign with white lettering announces food gas lodging. Jess turns off at the exit and a little way down the road spots a golden arch. He calls his order to the menu board, then drives up to the window to collect three burgers and a large Coke. Parked in back, he pulls the burgers from the paper bag, lifts the lid off two, and sets these on a napkin placed in Margie's seat. Then he delves back into the bag and draws out a couple of ketchup packets. He tears these open and spreads the contents over her burgers.

"Here, this ought to satisfy your gourmet tastes. We know you'll slobber it all over the seat, don't we, but what's the difference now?"

Chewing, he recalls that high point, the memory of which invariably causes his heart to lurch happily. After nine barren years a pregnancy actually brought to term. A little girl like a pink rose. He'd walked around smiling, couldn't wipe the smirk off his face, once even caught himself waltzing around the room. It just doesn't get any better than this, he'd remind himself incessantly, like chanting an insightful mantra, a goad to joy. Although looking back later on, he wondered if he hadn't really been warning himself that things not getting better stand a fine chance of getting worse.

And then the awakening. An old story, the kind of thing that only happens to some other poor misguided bastard, never to you. But with the baby's arrival it is suddenly your turn, now it happens to you too. Those little gifts of love now get slipped instead to the new kid on the block. And you, you're obsolete, to be devoured after fertilizing the egg. In those old dark hours, while he debated abandonment, Cindy too must have had her traitorous thoughts. Only she'd never cast hers off, she'd hung on to them and nursed them. And now, like removing a mask, her naked face showed only as mother, no longer as wife. Cindy's indifference to him was edged with hostility; little Debbie was the weapon.

If love's combustion can be spontaneous, can't its expiration be so too? A hundred times he'd asked himself that favorite question of the jilted. The lie we pose only to fool ourselves, because deep down we always do know the answer, don't we? "Talk to me," she would whine," why don't you ever talk to me?" But he, impatient, never bothered to understand she was begging to share more than just their roof. So he'd put it down as the bleatings of a bored housewife, the kind of thing they cure with a shopping binge. Then he'd go back to whatever he was busy with that she had no part in.

Jess thinks how much it was like that old joke about the guy in the button business. Forty years made a good living, kept his records in his hat. His son, new MBA, talks him into hiring an accountant. "More businesslike." Accountant finds the business is bankrupt. "Dummy," the old man screams at his son, "if I didn't know, I could've kept on making a living." Which is how it had been with Jess. If only his partner hadn't called his attention to the firm's bankruptcy.

Somewhere along the line it became understood that Margie was his alone. Suddenly, little Debbie, pink and fragrant and dearer than his life, was Cindy's responsibility, the dog his. Every one of Margie's miserable little tricks was ruled a felony committed by him against home and all decent society. She stole meat thawing on the counter, shed on the furniture, grabbed the baby's cracker, whatever. All his fault, all a reason for upset and coldness.

Jess opens the paper bag and draws out the cup. He takes a long pull on the straw, then notices Margie's eyes fixed on him as she sucks air onto her tongue. He removes the straw and sets the cup on the floor. Margie, front paws lowered, laps greedily. When the level sinks out of reach, he tilts the cup for her. Thirst slaked, she climbs back up and screws herself into the seat. Jess squashes the rubbish into a lump, bags it, and tosses it into the back seat.

"Ready?" He twists the ignition. On the highway the draft is a breath of hell; he raises the window and tunes the air conditioning to maximum.

Lonely weekend afternoons the two of them, man and dog, would go for long sad drives in the country. Evenings, while he sat reading away time, the dog lay at his feet. Probably, Jess smiles faintly, dreaming up ways to get us into trouble. Or if he was under the weather, Margie'd shamble alongside, matching his sluggish gait, sharing his infirmity. In between, she absconded periodically, just long enough to nip a jogger or two, and he was paying for tetanus shots and suffering cries of outrage from the victims and lectures from the town police.

Jess shoves the accelerator to the floor and they shoot across the broken line and around the eighteen wheeler struggling up the grade. He eases up on the pedal and gets it back down to sixty-five.

Glancing at the mirror to gauge their distance from the truck, he recalls the day he came home from work and the dog was gone. Returned to the pound, Cindy told him, shrugging.

"How could you do that?" he'd begged, curdling inside. "Don't you know they'll kill her? They're going to kill Margie."

She said, "There's only so much nonsense and aggravation I can take from your stupid dog."

"Maybe," he told her, calming his voice, tuning in to her wave length, "maybe we could've found someone to take her. We could've put an ad in the paper."

"And what would the ad say?" she wanted to know, hands on hips. "Would it say the dog is untrainable, and bites and steals and is useless? Don't worry," she said, "they hold them two weeks before putting them down, so I'll go back after a week plus six days. If no fool's taken her by then I'll bring her home."

He knew he must have looked a gutless character, not standing up to her. But that's how it is in a marriage. It's too easy to get angry and throw your weight around, but there's the little girl to think of; you don't want to do anything that might break up her unit. So sometimes you have to keep your mouth shut and just take it. Besides, he couldn't believe she would go through with it.

Sure enough, a week later he came home from the office and when he opened the door there was the dog, her dumb tail wagging, slobbering all over his shoes. Conscience had made Cindy go pick her up early. Turned out the enthusiastic putter-downers at the pound already had Margie penciled in. One day later and she'd have bought the farm.

The rescue was Cindy's declaration of truce. Since then, they'd lived a frigid armistice.

Jess reaches across to pat Margie. "See that sign? Ten miles to exit 103."

He remembers what it's like to have someone bang on the door ten at night, and when you open it a cop is standing there, rainwater pouring off his wide-brimmed boy scout hat and yellow slicker, and with him a dedicated jogger, fit and indignant, sleeveing off his face and screaming your dog chewed up his backside. And how come, the cop wants to know, such a dangerous animal is running around loose?

He apologized to the jogger and explained that he'd had to let her out, he'd been sick and couldn't walk her that day; the dog is a hunter, doesn't bite, just playfully chases. And anyway, how should he expect anyone in his right mind to be out jogging at ten of a dark night in the middle of a rain storm? And he'd be more than willing to pay for the tetanus shot.

"Sorry, sir, but this will have to be reported."

When they'd gone he'd rolled up a newspaper and wacked Margie good, this time really meaning to kill her. He was raging mad at her and at that idiot who was out at such a ridiculous time, making him look uncaring and a fool. The dog stood with head bowed, flinching each time he raised his arm, quivering with each blow, just taking the punishment. Until suddenly he saw them both as if from outside: Margie, finely made, naked and defenseless; him, hulking over her, beating her just for being a dog and doing dog things. Beating her, maybe, for the way his own life was going. He wanted to rip out his heart. He dropped to his knees. He rubbed her chest and neck and scratched between her eyes, putting healing and a plea for forgiveness into his touch. And she, she reached up and licked his murderous hand. Which is when he swore he would never ever again touch her in anger. Or let anyone else.

When Jess came home the next day, a white panel truck with 'police' markings blocked the driveway. In the kitchen a broad-beamed Valkyrie in cop uniform held one end of a rope, the other in a noose around Margie's neck. The pointer's head hung down. Jess could see her trembling.

Cindy and the cop stood at the door opened onto the deck, exchanging pleasantries in a civilized little chat. Empty tea cups on the table. Ladies politely resolving the small matter of taking a dog out to be killed. "Put down."

He jumped between them and shoved the door shut. "Get that rope off her," he yelled at the fat-assed cop.

Why, Cindy screamed, was he making a fuss over such a miserable dog?

"What's the law?" he demanded. "Must I give her up?"

"It's your choice," the cop said evenly, "but I wouldn't envy you. Mister, she bites even a flea, you go straight to jail."

"Fair enough. Now get out of my house."

The cop pointed a finger between his eyes. "It's your funeral." She stamped out, dragging her rope behind her.

Now, for almost a year, there is no more of blame, no recrimination. There is only silence.

The green sign with white lettering marks exit 103, and Jess takes its curving ramp off the highway. At the bottom he turns left, then follows the twisting road for three miles. Slowing for the sharp curve at the girls' camp, pre-teeners leaping about, shouting, tumbling on the grass, Jess follows the right fork. From there, the graveled road climbs at forty-five degrees for almost a mile.

At the topmost point, just before the downslope again, he veers off the road. The car jounces across a hundred yards of meadow before he brakes, cuts the engine. Margie stands up on the seat. Through the windshield they can see, past the falling curve of meadow, the valley far below. A haze rises from the valley floor, dusting with pastels its white doll houses amid broccoli trees.

Jess droops over the steering wheel. Presently, straightening up, he reaches across to shove open the passenger door. Margie spurts out. She races a hundred yards down the meadow, then abruptly reverses direction in a tangle of grass, galloping in a wide arc back toward the car. Slowly he climbs out. He stands watching her bound through the tall growth in narrowing circles. Then he kneels and she comes to him, pewter in the grass, her tongue sipping the tart air. She beds down next to him.

He says, "It's for the sake of the little girl."

"It's all gone wrong," he says, kneading her coat, "all gone wrong." He says, "It was your sad fate, my friend, to fall into the hands of a cowardly and inept fool."

He strokes from the crown of her head down between the eyes, and Margie's lids shut with the pleasure of it. "You know, don't you, that sooner or later you'd sneak through a door and take a nip at somebody? And they'd throw me in jail and put you down anyway. It's not a question of whether, only when."

Jess turns the dog over onto her back. He rubs the ash-gray belly. Her eyes stay open, staring at him.

"They've never watched you like I have. Never seen you go flat out, eating up ground, ears back, muscles sliding under the skin. It's like you're taking flight, as beautiful and graceful as anything in God's creation. My heart blooms, and I think how it must please Him that He made you.

"I know it would be more humane to let them put you down. But I just can't do that. I refuse to let the bastards get either one of us."

Jess stands up. Through the tall grass he wades towards the car. The dog follows. By the side of the car he stoops down, and with one hand grips the slack skin under her jaw. He kisses the black silk top of her head. "Goodbye," he says.

He opens the door. Margie bends her forelegs, tensing for the leap inside. He shakes his head. "No, old girl," he says softly, "you're not coming."

He climbs inside and shuts the door. She stands quietly, tail twitching, amber eyes locked on his past the window. At the cough of the engine she leaps expectantly, then prances in tight little circles.

The car bumps slowly through the meadow. When he gets it back on the road Jess can see Margie in the rear view mirror, racing after him, running easy.

He speeds up. Still she comes. At thirty she keeps pace with him, right behind the car. At forty she begins to fade. On the downslope she grows smaller. Then the road curves away.

All the Little Fishes

Way back when I was so new to the world that I saw it as an enormous pond stocked full with exciting possibilities, especially all sorts of girl possibilities, there came along a special girl I couldn't marry because of one of those reasons I was a genius at inventing, so she ran off in a huff to put at least one ocean between us, and I, much relieved, already looking forward to the next possibility, found instead that my soft brain and quivering heart refused to let go of this one, and after four suicidal months I gave in and chased over to her continent.

In Paris I hung around a couple of weeks with the unforgettable girl, but she'd discovered quickly enough that it wasn't to propose an eternal arrangement that I'd come, but only for the nefarious and wholly inadequate reason that I couldn't live without her, so she wouldn't even give me the time of day.

"Out of all the billions in this world, all the trillions of possibilities, it is you and I who have connected up in love," I told her. "Is it only a signed contract that will validate this miracle?"

The once generous lips were tightly compressed, like a bridge drawn up over its moat. "The miracle we need to validate is your commitment. Finally taking a stand in this life."

What we also need in this life is to know when to cut our losses. "All right," I told her with much regret, "all right. I am taking a stand."

With one week still remaining of my vacation three, and seeing Paris in August abandoned to caretakers and tourists, everyone else and especially those wonderfully chic girls migrating south, I decided to go with the flow. What stays with me most clearly is our parting embrace at

Orly, tight enough for an exchange of body prints, as if to experience in
the space of a dozen heart beats all our might-have-beens. Then I tore
myself away and boarded Air France to go see what the Riviera was like,
hoping in this way to forget.

In Nice I took the bus in from the airport, then wandered around lost
before stumbling on the visitors bureau, clogged with lines of travelers
seeking accommodations. The buzz reaching the end of my line was
that rooms were scarce and expensive, and the bureau was awash with
the despair of tired travelers with no place to rest. Visions of me bedded
down in a doorway or on a park bench danced about my head, until I
noticed a middle-aged couple a bit apart from everyone else clandes-
tinely motioning to someone, and it took a moment to realize their target was me.

Dressed in the worn but neat clothes of the impecunious
respectable, they politely explained that they had this so *jolie chambre*
they might rent for a *petite* sum to some nice person, and should I care
to accompany them a so short way I should be pleased with what they
had to show me. Smiling secretly at having beaten out the poor slobs
still moldering on line, I trudged gratefully beside my rescuers the half
dozen blocks and then up two flights. In the back of their apartment
they showed me the room: threadbare, stifling in fetid air that
whispered of careless habits and immoral practices. Never able to say
no, a trait which had once driven my old man to sneer that had I been
a girl I would be forever pregnant, I nevertheless managed an escape by
deploring the tattered financial condition that put far beyond my poor
means the so reasonable twenty-eight francs they asked for the so
lovely room.

Dragging back to the visitors bureau, I got on the end of the line
again, and finally by late evening reached the front, only to be informed
that regrettably the only room available in all the town was in a forbid-
dingly expensive four star hotel. But when I for the hell of it asked the
price was told forty francs the night, working out to eight bucks, which

even the slave wages of a newly minted liberal arts grad could handle. So I wound up in the marbled magnificence of the Ruhl, one of the grand old dames of the Riviera, with the floor's maid and butler just itching to respond to the buzzer attached to my headboard.

For a couple of blue-gold days and sultry nights I wandered lonely as a cloud, mostly along the Promenade des Anglais, the wide boulevard lined with palm trees and chic shops running between the cream-colored art nouveau hotels and the Mediterranean beach, and from there studied the bikini'd creatures rising from the sea, soon convinced that some playful god had tipped over the earth and poured its most glorious creations onto that narrow strip of sand in the south of France. But I had little money and even less of the language, and in the course of my observations concluded that each lovely's knowledge of english was in inverse proportion to the degree of her desirability. There was no way I could beat the system.

To stretch my capital, as well as to know what it was I was ordering, this habitué of a four star hotel took his meals in an english tearoom up one of the side streets. Seated in the little room with its chintz curtains and tiny tables hiding under checkered cloths, I would while awaiting the tasteless but mercifully skimpy meal brood about life and love, astonished at how easy it is to slide from feast to famine, like spending nights in a luxurious hotel but the days in cheap tearooms, like loving and being loved by a girl with amethyst eyes and cherry lips but foolishly casting her adrift, and now so badly wanting her again but having neither her nor anyone at all.

At lunch the third day, having ordered the usual *sandwiche frommage* and pea salad, and just beginning to fall into the usual mournful meditation, I glimpsed out of the corner of my eye someone stand up suddenly on the other side of the room and then hurry across. The young man came to a halt before my table.

His pronunciation so nonchalant that not all of his vowels and consonants bothered showing up, I just barely made out, "Say, after nothing but frog all week, it's great to hear the king's english again."

Taking the hand he held out across the table I almost lost the use of mine, crushed in his enthusiasm, and invited to join me he scampered back to his place and then returned balancing a plate bearing a half eaten *sandwiche frommage.* He was about my own age, medium height, standard shape and quantity of features, nondescript except for the nose that was sharp and curved like a scimitar blade. He was dressed as if not quite caught up with the time and place, his shirt a button-down white oxford, perfect for the office, which he'd modified for the southern sun by rolling its sleeves to the elbow, his baggy trousers of some thick black material, and his shoes executively wing tipped. But you got the feeling that it wasn't exteriors that counted with this Cockney; there was a brashness in his approach, a self-confidence in his attitude, that made you think of nondescript young men who grow up to become Prime Minister. In any case, it wasn't a fashion plate I needed, just someone to maybe go places with, pal around with.

"Ted," he announced, sitting down and holding out his hand again, and taking it gingerly I said, "Arthur," and we ate while he recited autobiography, how back in London he was a clerk in the office of a large film company, due for quite a big promotion any moment now, and how he'd been down here a week on holiday with one more yet to go, and was bored silly.

Finished munching our *sandwiches frommage,* we strolled the Promenade among Maseratis, Lamborghinis, Rolls Royces, horse-drawn carriages, sleek ladies, becalmed palm trees, and shop windows displaying price tags resembling ransom demands.

After a couple of hours of wandering back and forth under the mad dog sun, tempted by a hundred unattainables, Ted mumbled something which after several repetitions I deciphered as, "What's on the agenda for tonight?"

I shrugged, irritated at being anointed tour guide. He said, "How about Monte Carlo? The casino," and pointed to the road we could see running from the Promenade up the coastline to a city atop a hill.

"How far?" I asked.

"We can lease an auto and be there in no time at all."

In a rental agency down a side street we contracted for a Beetle, the most affordable car available. Inspecting the bill, I told him, "Your half of the deposit comes to a hundred francs."

He smiled, savoring the joke he was about to lay on me: "Sorry, chum, I seem to be caught short at the moment." He said this a bit too airily, implying we both understood that he had no money, didn't intend to pay, and I could damn well go ahead with our plan or drop it, it was all the same to him. Considering the car rental idea was his to begin with, I thought this declaration of insolvency badly timed, but then told myself I might never come this way again, so I paid his share too, feeling like a love-starved older woman picking up the tab for her gigolo.

We rendezvoused at eight in front of the Ruhl. It was no trouble at all to locate our road to adventure, easy to believe it such because by then it was well into the blue hour, and with traffic under their rules restricted to parking lamps we were not night-blinded, could watch the lights magically popping like fireflies along the arcing coastline and in the villas nesting in the hills, while the fading purple of the Mediterranean dropped away beneath us.

Merging our Volkswagen with a herd of exotic autos already grazing on a sidewalk, we set off on foot, fighting our way up along Monte Carlo's inclines through the mobs cluttering the narrow streets or sprawled at outside tables ogling the strollers. At the top of the hill the casino's weakly lighted, landscaped grounds seemed deserted, apparently abandoned to the crickets. Uneasy in the soft dark, I followed a confident Ted to the doors of the casino, sure we'd come at the wrong time to a place we didn't belong in, he in his electric blue polyester creation with cockney dialect, and I the well known Dumont Avenue stickball player and perpetrator of as yet unusable ad copy. But we made it past the front door without being arrested, and after shelling out the admission for myself and my indigent friend, I led our adventurous little duo into the vaulted, hushed, and holy elegance of mahogany, polished brass, and red velvet.

Tourists stood around open-mouthed, too frozen in awe to make the leap from observer to participant, and some of the tables were closed down for lack of action. Discreet notices set forth the rules of play, and to my relief declared the minimum allowable bet to be an affordable ten francs—probably, I supposed, as inducement to the tourist trade.

At one of the barred cashier windows I bought a hundred francs' worth of chips, openhanded with my twenty bucks, then stepped aside to make way for Ted. With a grin and shrug as if performing a magic trick he pulled out an empty pocket. Not wanting an albatross around my neck, I slipped him a few of my chips and we headed for separate tables.

The wheel started its spin and a bored croupier intoned, *"Rien ne va plus,"* and the few players seemed hypnotized by the whirling wheel, and when the little ball dropped exhausted into twenty-nine black and the tuxedoed croupier swept away their contributions, they watched fatalistically, as if resigned to the foolhardiness of betting on one number out of thirty-eight possibilities and expecting to come out winning. But then one player positioned his chips on a corner between four numbers, and when the wheel stopped spinning he was rewarded by the croupier for the one number out of his four that matched the winning slot, and I understood how to play this game: bet on a corner and cover four numbers and, yes, the odds are reduced and the payoff is smaller but the chances of winning are quadrupled.

"Onze," the croupier announced, and slipped eight chips alongside the single one I had placed on a corner that included number eleven.

"*Huit*," he said not long after, when the little ball dropped into the eight slot, and he shoveled another eight chips to my place. The old ticker looped into cartwheels, because I'd just uncovered another of life's marvelous possibilities, the ultimate one: getting rich without effort. All it took, I saw, was the right system. And sure enough, at the end of half an hour I'd won about every fourth bet at odds of eight to one, putting me nicely ahead of the house, But then I got caught up in the sure thing and suddenly it was all too tame, so I doubled up on my bets, and the system kept right on ticking. Every quarter hour or so there was a grumbling at my elbow and it was Ted, broke again and terminally ill from boredom, whining about wanting to leave. Each time I tossed him some chips from my growing hoard, ransoming a few minutes of peace.

And then and then I began to feel that heaven's cinematographer was taking a hand in all this, directing me in a romantic opus to open soon in 987 theatres simultaneously across the country, because I had accreted a following, systems players carefully jotting my play in their notebooks, and others just mimicking a winner, and every time I placed a bet ten or fifteen hopefuls cast their chips prayerfully on the same numbers, bread upon the waters, burdening me with a responsibility similar to what I imagined the leader of a cult must lug around. Sweating, I took off my jacket and rolled up my sleeves and loosened my collar and went back to winning, but by then I craved even more action so I quadrupled my bets and, as I had seen them do in the movies, periodically tossed several chips to the croupier, presumably for working so hard on my behalf. Except for quarter-hourly ransom payments to Ted, the pile kept on building until, the mound becoming unwieldy, the round chips were gradually replaced by the croupier with larger rectangles, each equivalent to several of the round chips, and then I was tossing Ted and the croupier rectangles instead of circles, and then, without knowing why, maybe out of tension, or exhilaration, or just to test the allegiance of my groupies, I

stood up and marched myself off to another table, seeing myself in
my mind's eye as I would appear in the movie, a clever, brash, steely-
eyed interloper in this playground of the rich and famous, strolling
nonchalantly from one table to another, seersucker jacket slung over
my shoulder, placing extravagant and unerringly successful wagers,
like the Pied Piper shadowed by an adoring mob, including several
business types and some attractive and wide-eyed young ladies. This
change of tables left my system unaffected, the pile of chips still growing even while I continued tithing my friend and the croupier, and the
mob swelled, as if word of my cleverness and daring had swept through
the cafes.

It was then, just when the right side of my brain began to broach the
notion to its companion left about breaking the bank—breaking the
bank at Monte Carlo!—that I heard this voice at my elbow, and I automatically grabbed some chips for tossing to Ted before realizing that this
time it was not a complaining grumble or anguished cry of boredom but
the whisper of a cool stream, the tinkle of a temple bell, and when drawn
by its musicality and invitation I turned toward it discovered it the voice
of a young lady with hair of gold and model's cheekbones framing green
almond eyes, a black sheath dress disclosing lines better engineered than
even those of the Maseratis and Lamborghinis perched outside. She said
breathily, "Thank you," and my hand with the chips froze, suspended
over the table, and flustered I asked, "For what?" and the bets of a dozen
groupies were also suspended awaiting my decision, and she replied in a
charmingly slavic accent, "For showing me how to do it," and when I
brilliantly responded with, "Do it?" she said, "I've been following you
and winning. Quite a lot, actually."

"Really?" I said, amazed not to have noticed her before, and so
delighted to have been of service to the bewitching creature that I even
disregarded the croupier's warning cry.

She said prettily, "I would love to show my gratitude."

Well, then, let's go, I wanted to say, and toss my chips in the air, but then saw the couple of dozen eyes fastened on me, reminders of the obligations incurred by success, to the prayerful gamblers depending on me for a religious experience, to gigolo Ted, to the croupier, and to my loyal groupies, to say nothing of my ambition to break the bank at Monte Carlo.

"Regretfully," I told her, "I must remain at the table."

"I understand," she smiled sweet reassurance. "Perhaps we can meet after."

"I look forward to it," I said.

"My name is Tatiana," she said. "I will wait here for you and observe." Pursing her lips, she prettily blew me a kiss. "Bonne chance,"she breathed, and I felt myself melting down to a wet blob. Tatiana, I thought, Tatiana, Tatiana, thinking it sounded like the heroine of a Shakespearian romantic mixup, All's Well that Ends Well or A Midsummer Night's Dream, or maybe a Tchaikowsky opera, possibly even something I might myself create, positive she could easily inspire men of little talent to create masterpieces.

I immediately doubled my bets, feeling lucky, wanting to impress the girl with my gutsiness and smarts, wanting to get the thing done with, wanting to get back to Tatiana. And it went so well that soon I was sure that either Providence or casino management was doing tricks with the wheel, Providence to make up for all the bad times over the years, management so that my example might lure the tourist trade. Maybe it was this sense of invincibility, and my impatience, that led to a certain carelessness, because I began to blanket the table with rectangles, tossing them at corners, and on black or red and odd or even, and just for the hell of it on individual numbers too, and pretty soon the winnings turned less generous than the bets, and friend Ted was still coming around for handouts, and the croupier looked at me balefully because he wasn't earning any gratuities, and the little man with thick glasses who'd been meticulously recording my every move in his notebook left to search for another hero, as did the two bet-sharing elderly ladies, noses wrinkled in disgust. The sweat down my back now a running stream, I glanced around and saw the girl, and smiling she winked an almond eye at me and held up her hand in a gesture that meant, Take it easy, *mon ami*, go slow. So seeing this, that she cared enough to still be there, patiently waiting, I obeyed her signal and slowed down and went back to my system, and things got back on an even keel, and the pile in front of me swelled up again, and the little man with his notebook came hurrying back, and for the first time since Paris I felt the familiar sick weak sweet feeling of love.

"*Rien ne va plus*," cautioned the croupier in his sepulchral tones, and the wheel spun, and just when the ball popped out of orbit to rattle around the base of the wheel, Ted's whine came from behind my right shoulder, "Ain't you 'ad enough yet?"

The ball chose a wrong slot to bed down in. "Damn!" tore out of me, but not having intended to be so abrupt, I said more temperately, "You're losing more of this money than I am. Can't you please find another way to amuse yourself? For just a little while longer?"

I pulled out the car keys and tossed it to him. "Why don't you go take in the sights? Pick me up in, say, an hour?

His smile was half gratitude, half triumph. A glance at his watch. A mock salute. "Sir! See you at ten-thirty. Sir!" He twirled the keys and sailed away on a cloud of electric blue. I turned back to the table and smothered my lucky corner in a fistful of chips. The wheel spun. "*Rien ne va plus.*"

No more, my mind echoed. 'Nevermore, quoth the Raven.' The wheel whirled itself into a frenzy trying to decide where to ditch the little ball, and watching it I suddenly found myself not caring, the ball would either drop into the right slot or it wouldn't, and I would as a result be a bit richer or a bit poorer, but either way would no longer make much difference; the film was in the can, the thrill was gone, and I was a damned fool to be standing there trying to win another few meaningless francs, keeping a beautiful and willing girl waiting, the patience of beautiful girls being notoriously limited.

The wheel made its decision, and since I no longer cared it of course slipped the ball into huit, and the croupier shoved a stack of chips onto my corner of the board. I looked around for my girl, my Tatiana, heart sinking when I couldn't immediately locate her, but then did spot her down the room, temporarily monitoring another table. She caught my wave out of the corner of her eye and ducked her head in delight at my summons, and I open-mouthed watched the approach of a Boticelli of blood and breath. True beauty sometimes brings tears, but the sight of this one was beyond that, just made me want to laugh and dance.

"Forgive me," I told her, shaking my head abjectly. "Only a fool and insensitive clod would keep you waiting like this," and with a little smile she nodded to acknowledge my small inept attempt at chivalry.

And then slowly, slowly, so as to provide the maximum impact, ever so slowly I place my arms around the entire pile of hard-won chips, heaven alone knowing how many thousands of francs, and shove them all, all, onto my favorite corner, flooding it, holding out only a single hundred franc rectangular, and a gasp rends the air, and I can see the croupier fighting to remain blasé but he is unable to keep a startled brow from shooting up, and me knowing that a win breaks the bank at Monte Carlo but a loss, ah, that's the glory of it! a loss is not a loss, a loss still leaves me with a hundred francs and the world's most beautiful girl, and the wheel begins its whirl, and no one breathes, "*Rien ne va plus*," her arm soft against mine, her fragrance seeping through my lungs into my heart, the world frozen in place while the wheel spins and spins, and then it begins to slow and presently slows enough for the little ball to climb off, and exhausted it drops into zero, and the collective exhale is a keening of disappointment and sorrow, and the croupier timidly extends his little rake and regretfully sweeps in my bet, all my chips, but me, I merely shrug indifferently while the beautiful girl shakes her head as if to say, What a pity! but there is admiration in it too.

Only I'm not through yet, but scoop up the remaining chip, the lone remaining rectangle, and toss it to the croupier; not expecting this, but reflexively he catches it and smiles hugely and, holding out his arms as if to embrace a hero, comes marching around the table and places his hands on my shoulders and kisses me on both cheeks—the croupier, on both cheeks—and I think, Wow! What a hell of a great way to end the movie!

Triumphant, exalted, ecstatic, even if deep down just a dollop regretful, I turned back to my girl, my prize on this night of wonders, my Tatiana, but as I'm sure you've already guessed, she was gone.

But of course abandonment never occurred to me, I thought she'd slipped off to powder her nose, grieve my loss, pawn her jewels to provide us with another stake, and so that she could more easily find me I remained right there, next to the table, close by the sounds of spinning wheel and clacking ball and "*Rien ne va plus*," and the oooh's and aaah's of my successor glory seekers. After the many minutes there was still no waning of confidence that she would return, it was only that I began to suspect something might have happened, that my Tatiana was the victim of some unforeseen occurrence, anything from a run in her stocking to an accident to foul play. Hesitantly, but driven by a sense of foreboding, I moved slowly away from the table, searching the salon for some sign of the girl, some clue to her whereabouts, dragging along guilt, the need to make up for muffing my responsibility to take care of her.

Intent on small signs, finding her was so unexpected that I failed at first to realize the discovery, and it wasn't until a moment passed that I recognized Tatiana. She was standing by one of those barred cashier's windows, with Ted—my friend, my gigolo, my charity, Ted—just then shoving a mass of chips across the counter. Her arm rested on his electric blue shoulder. The cashier counted out a thick sheaf of notes and passed them across the counter. Ted picked up the money, bowing playfully toward Tatiana, at the same time listening intently to the song of the notes he riffled next to his ear. She smiled admiringly at him, her golden head inclining toward the riffling bundle as if to share his appreciation of the expensive music. When they turned to go, her arm around his waist, my Tatiana glanced up and saw me. Saw me as a pane of glass, something to look through.

"Hello, Tatiana," I said. Her gaze at him held, her face frozen in adoration.

"Arthur!" he said, as if pleased to see me. "Here, chum," sliding a note off the top of the bundle, "my share of the auto deposit. I know how you must need it."

"What about the car keys?" I said, wanting to get back a bit of my own.

"Oh, sorry," he said, and freed another couple of bills. "Here, why don't you grab a taxi? Tatiana and I can return the auto in the morning."

My mind puzzled at its sudden facility in comprehending his accent-smothered speech; I had the premonition I was about to comprehend other things as well. With scant success I tried a smile. "You must have done very well at the tables," I told him, feigning admiration, inwardly wincing with the hurt of it. "Making up all your losses in such a short time."

"Tables?" he grinned. "What tables? Losses? What losses?"

So that was the first thing I comprehended. That it was me the shrewd little guy had all along been playing; me, the sure thing, not the silly capricious wheel.

And I saw then that my view of the world was correct, that it truly was stocked full with all sorts of exciting possibilities. Only I'd neglected to recognize that to others we are ourselves possibilities. Out of the whole enormous pond, those two had selected me as their possibility, had angled for me. And I, I had gone for the bait. Leapt at it, taken it, and swallowed it. Hook, line and sinker.

Now, dangling at the end of his line, I meekly accepted Ted's handout of my own money. I turned on my heels and made my foolish way out, thinking how I was doomed to be a runner-up in this life, always to be bested by those more clever and audacious.

But then the door opened to reveal the starlit world. As if seeing it for the first time, I suddenly realized things. I stood contemplating in wonder its pure beauty, remarkable architecture, perfect symmetry: for every action there is a reaction, a yin for every yang, no light without dark, no sweet without sour.

Walking out into the fragrant beckoning night I calculated how many vacation days were still left to me. If there was time enough to add some sweet to the sour. Time enough to go back and see the girl I'd loved before this one.

About the Author

Irving Werner, a graduate of City College of New York, has been chief financial officer of New York's Plaza Hotel, Princeton Hospital, and St. Vincent's Medical Center in Bridgeport, Connecticut. For the past decade he has devoted himself to writing plays and short fiction. His play, Kickbacks, adapted from a story in this collection, has been produced off-Broadway. His stories have appeared in various publications and in a Doubleday anthology.

Made in the USA
Middletown, DE
29 June 2020